HOUSE

on the

FORGOTTEN

COAST

To Tracie —
It was fun
having you read
my book & answering
and asking questions.

Ruth Coe Chambers

HOUSE

on the

FORGOTTEN

COAST

By

RUTH COE CHAMBERS

SHE WRITES PRESS

Published 2017
Printed in the United States of America
ISBN: 978-1-63152-300-7 pbk
ISBN: 978-1-63152-301-4 ebk
Library of Congress Control Number: 2017937975

Book design by Stacey Aaronson

For information, address:
She Writes Press
1563 Solano Ave #546
Berkeley, CA 94707

She Writes Press is a division of SparkPoint Studio, LLC.

This is a work of fiction. Names, characters, all incidents, and the houses and business establishments in Apalachicola are products of the author's imagination and are used fictionally. Any resemblance to persons living or dead or to events are by coincidence.

To my husband, Jack,
without whom this book would never have left my computer

This book began with a dream. I still remember it vividly,
but I owe thanks to many people who encouraged me along the way.
Ray Bradbury believed in the book and in the muse who wrote most
of it. He was an inspiration and cheerleader always.

PROLOGUE

APALACHICOLA, FLORIDA
(May 1879)

*A*nnelise woke with a start and remembered it was her wedding day. She bit her quivering lower lip and looked around at the familiar room, but when she saw the door-knob turn she feigned sleep. It didn't work. Ruby walked noisily into the room and dropped an orange tabby cat onto Annelise's chest.

"Ruby, how could you!"

"You know better than to try foolin' Ruby. You wasn't sleeping, Annelise Lovett, not today you wasn't."

"But it's my last morning . . ."

"It is, and you better be 'bout your business. Your poor mama been up since dawn. She got Asberry and Joe putting candles in all the sconces in the ballroom, and then they be putting up tables in the hall to hold the food. Hattie and Corrine been working on that food since before day."

"Maybe I'll tiptoe down the hall and have a peek in the door. Everybody's being so secretive."

"You're not doing no peeking in that ballroom, not 'til Mr. Coulton brings you back here as his wife. Miss Agnes wants it to be a surprise."

"Did Mrs. Bell make the wedding cake?"

"Didn't I just tell you your mama wants you to be surprised? You know how busy Mrs. Bell is, running a bakery and a hotel to support her family. Poor soul."

"But she made my friend Sora's wedding cake and . . ."

"I don't know nothing about Sora's wedding. I will tell you Mrs. Bell will be bringing some food from her bakery. She makes all those beautiful things, and her poor blind husband can't see a single bit of it."

"He wasn't always blind, was he?"

"No, not always. Happened in the war. Breaks your heart for him and her both. But come on now. We got rain water warming and your mama want you to get that mass of hair washed so you can dry it in the early sun. You know it take forever to dry."

"I need my coffee. I'm no good without my coffee."

"Miss Agnes says you gon' have your coffee downstairs today."

"Oh, Ruby, I wish you were coming with me to my new house."

"You know Ruby can't leave your mama. Miss Agnes ain't never recovered from having a second baby when she was old as she was. What I'm wondering though is if you ain't seen that house your papa had built for you, missy. You sure you ain't sneaked out some dark night and taken a peek at it with that murdering scoundrel that built it?"

"Ruby! You just imagine things. And nobody's proved Seth is a murderer."

"Where there's smoke, there's fire, and if he'd murder, he'd show you that house."

"I don't know what you're talking about."

"Humph! I'm talking 'bout where you sneak out to after

dark, about what you done with the picture that scoundrel painted of you in your mama's weddin' dress."

"How dare you snoop into my private business!"

"You go to the stable after dark, I want to know why."

"Don't you go telling anybody about the painting, you hear?"

"I thought maybe it'd be Mr. Coulton's weddin' gift."

"Just mind your own business. Oh, Ruby, I hope I'm doing the right thing."

"Your papa wouldn't have you do it if it weren't."

"I still can't believe Seth . . . Ruby, do you think it's possible to love two people, two men, at the same time?"

"What a thing to be asking on your weddin' day."

"Sometimes my heart says one thing and my head another. Papa never gave Seth a chance. I didn't have a lot of say."

"Your papa the one with the say."

"I adore Coulton, but he's older, and sometimes he treats me like a child."

"You is a child."

"Were you ever in love, Ruby?"

"I may been colored all my life, but I ain't always been old. I was seventeen once myself. I know what love feels like. Course a black seventeen's older than a white seventeen."

"Now what's that supposed to mean?"

"You know what it means, missy. Don't go playing innocent with me. You younger today than I ever was."

"I'm an adult. I'll be eighteen next month, and I'm getting married, remember?"

"You ain't if you don't climb out of that bed and get that hair washed."

"ANNELISE! PUT FLYNNIE DOWN BEFORE he snags your dress. Next you'll have that cat following you down the aisle. And do you really plan to wear a baby necklace on your wedding day?"

"No, Mother, I just forgot. I've worn it as a bracelet since I was six years old when it got too tight for my neck."

"Hand it to Ruby. We need to go."

"No, just a minute." She took the necklace from her arm, pulled Flynnie to her and slipped the chain around his neck. "My forever gift, Flynnie," she said and kissed the star on top of his head.

Her mother knelt and adjusted the folds of the skirt. "You were right. My dress is perfect. It looks better on you than it did on me."

"Of course it doesn't, Mother. You were a beautiful bride. We have the painting to prove it."

"We'll have your picture painted in it too, one day soon."

Ruby smiled, and Annelise cast her a withering look, daring her to say anything.

Agnes Lovett blinked back tears and kissed her daughter's cheek. "Oh, darling, how I'll miss you."

"I'm not leaving Apalachicola, Mother. I'll just be a few miles away. That much I know about my new house."

"It won't be the same though. But come on, it's time to leave for the church. Your father is waiting in the buggy out front now."

Annelise looked back at the servants and saw Ruby crying.

"Be happy for me, Ruby, don't cry."

"These be happy tears, missy. Happy tears."

"Well, they'd better be." Annelise swallowed hard and walked down the front steps, pausing to gaze at the sunlight reflected on the river. She fought the urge to run back to her room and get in bed. Where had the day gone?

Then she was standing at the door of the Trinity Episcopal Church where she'd been christened and had no memory of getting there. She took a deep breath and looked up at the stenciled ceiling, realizing she was scared. *Am I doing the right thing? Why, I hardly know Coulton! Maybe I'm not an adult after all.*

Her father tilted her chin with his forefinger. "You okay, sweetheart?"

She shivered. "Somebody just walked across my grave, Papa."

"You have a case of wedding jitters. Here we go now."

The organist began the wedding march, engulfing the sanctuary in a giant wave of music that carried Annelise down the aisle on the arm of her father. Coulton was so handsome in his white suit, but when he turned and looked at her, she shivered again. The minister's voice seemed far away, and then she was a wife. They ran down the church steps to Coulton's buggy where he kissed her passionately.

Annelise detected a hint of whiskey and stammered, "Why, Coulton, I never . . ."

"Come, my love, no more chaperoning. You're mine now. Didn't your father just give you to me?"

Annelise felt uneasy. She'd never known Coulton to be so bold, so different from the gentlemanly suitor she'd known.

It was a short drive back to Annelise's home, and when Coulton ushered her into the ballroom for the reception, her indrawn breath was testament to the remarkable job her mother had done. The wide double doors were usually kept locked, but tonight the floors gleamed, and garlands of ribbons and greenery were draped between the sconces and around the gilt-framed mirrors that lined the walls. Baskets of pink and white roses formed a backdrop for the musicians. Annelise kissed her mother and whispered, "Thank you," before Coulton pressed her hand to his lips, and they glided onto the floor for the first dance. Others joined them and soon the room was filled with a kaleidoscope of dancing couples reflected in the oval mirrors.

Mrs. Bell had indeed made the wedding cake. No one else could have created such a work of art. Annelise felt a pang of guilt when she and Coulton cut the first slice. Everyone seemed so happy. Why did her happiness seem more pretense than real?

It grew dark, and Annelise watched as Asberry lit the candles in the sconces. "This has to be the shortest day of the year," she confided to a friend just as Coulton walked up, snatched the glass of wine from her hand and began to drink from it.

"Coulton, you made me spill wine on my dress."

"Sorry, darling. I had an uncontrollable urge to share what your lips had touched, and . . ."

"It's just that this was my mother's dress . . ."

"Coulton, over here," Mr. Lovett called. "There's someone I'd like you to meet."

"I won't be long, darling," Coulton said, but he was. When she tired of waiting, Annelise walked toward her room where she saw Flynnie rubbing against the door. "Now how did you get out of there?" She scooped him into her arms and walked into the moonlit room. She gasped when a voice whispered, "Annelise, it's Seth. Close the door quick."

"But how . . .?"

"I can't explain except to tell you I'm not a murderer."

"What was I supposed to think, no good-bye, nothing!"

"They were looking for me. I didn't dare come here. I'm sorry. I've been in Alabama trying to unravel the riddle of a murder people believe involves me. When I saw an announcement in an old Alabama newspaper saying you were to marry Coulton Morgan, I started back right then but not soon enough to stop the wedding. We don't have time to talk though. I'll come for you later tonight at the riverboat house. It's the best plan I could work out. Everybody will be there waiting for your reaction to seeing the house for the first time. I figure in all the confusion . . . but, Annelise, you must get away from Coulton. You're in danger. Don't go to your marriage bed. Plead illness, anything, and go to the hidden stairway. You remember, don't you?"

"Of course. I know that house like the back of my hand."

"I'll come for you there, and we'll leave together."

"But, Seth, I can't. Papa . . ."

"He'll thank me when he finds out what I learned about Coulton. Go to the ballroom. Act like nothing has happened. I can't save you if they catch me before I clear myself. Go!"

Annelise started back to the reception, trying to still her trembling hands when she saw her mother at the top of the stairs.

"Find Coulton, darling. This is the orchestra's final number."

Numb with terror, Seth's words rang in her head. *Act like nothing has happened.* Annelise rushed downstairs to her father's study, thinking he and Coulton might still be talking. She paused just inside and saw Coulton with a woman near the moonlit window, her back to his chest, his hands cupping her breasts. She tried to stifle a gasp and ran back to the ballroom. Annelise hesitated at the door and saw Asberry trying to straighten a candle in one of the sconces. Asberry had been getting her out of trouble most of her life, and she rushed toward him as she heard Coulton calling her name. She looked back as she grabbed Asberry's arm, jarring the burning candle from his hand. It bounced from his grasp, igniting her blue black hair.

She screamed and raced for the door. The horror of the scene registered on Coulton's face as he dropped the handkerchief he'd just touched to his lips and ran after her calling,

"ANNELISE! ANNELISE!" The guests froze, certain she was heading for the river, never realizing she was running from her husband who continued calling, *"ANNELISE! ANNELISE!"*

I

❧

APALACHICOLA, FLORIDA

(May 1987)

*E*choing the balconies and curves of an old paddle wheeler, Annelise's house reigned for more than a hundred years as the showplace of a small fishing village called Apalachicola. No matter who lived there, it would always belong to Annelise, but the realtor declined to share that knowledge with the new owners, Margaret and Edwin Foster. Not knowing themselves, the Fosters couldn't tell their daughter, eighteen-year-old Elise, for who would have imagined the house was about to become a portal whereby two young women from different centuries would meet? Surely not Peyton Roberts, who passed the house every morning on his way to work. He never questioned why he always slowed the truck and tipped his hat to the memory of the lovely Annelise. Later he might have cause to wonder.

But now, all over town people were stirring, getting ready for a new day. Peyton stood on the sidewalk in front of his shoe store and stretched, fingers laced high above his head. He was no longer young, but he was still a handsome man and just cocky enough to realize it. In the dim light he squinted at the newly refurbished store next to his and spit.

In another part of town, Nadine Fletcher peered through the screen door at the padded rocker on her front porch. Gnarled hands, palms flat against the dirty screen, framed her face. Already the heat, as only Florida can brew it, seeped through each tiny square.

A few miles away Dallas Anderson remained in bed, reluctant to start the day, her silver-streaked hair smooth as a cap on her eyelet pillowcase. She'd open one eye soon and remember she was a widow, but in the meantime, she'd draw a deep breath and think of something cheerful—like the welcome jolt of a cup of strong coffee.

Peyton rolled his shoulders and twisted slightly to the right, looking toward the town's one traffic light changing colors in the mist and the emptiness of a pre-dawn morning. Turning back to the left, he dropped his arms and sprinted down the street toward the Gorrie Bridge, eager to watch day break over the water, never tiring of seeing his day unfold like a shimmering net cast over the morning-still surface of the river.

He stretched once more and then, hands on his hips, stood motionless, waiting for his day to begin.

That he was alone remained an ever-present wound. He had no one to share the beauty of shrimp boats beginning their journey to the Gulf, no one by his side as sparkling stars of sunlight went skimming across the surface of the water. He hadn't planned it this way, never imagined himself the town's lonely bachelor. He thought of Nadine Fletcher spending most of the last fifty years sitting in a rocker on her front porch. Had she grown accustomed to growing old alone, living all these years without her high school sweetheart beside her? Maybe he should ask her. He laughed to himself. *Not a chance, old buddy. Hide your sorrow in your gut where it belongs.*

There were a lot of new people in town, but he didn't look

to any of them to ease his loneliness, not even the saucy divor-
cée who'd opened a jewelry store across the street and lined the
sidewalk in front of the store with flower-laden wine barrels.

"If one of them wine barrels comes through my window,"
he'd warned her, "you're paying every dime, not me."

"Why in the world would one of my wine barrels go crash-
ing through your window?" she'd asked.

"Y'all never heard of hurricanes up north? Ever see what
wind at a hundred miles an hour or more can do to a house or
tree, much less a wine barrel?"

"In the first place, I'm not from 'up north' as you call it.
And anyway, how often do you have hurricanes like that?"

"Oh, it's been a long time. A whole two years, I'd say. In '85
we had a couple of bad ones. I call 'em the holiday hurricanes.
Elena paid us a visit near Labor Day. We thought that was bad
enough, but then around Thanksgiving here comes Kate.
Looked like she was hell-bent on destroying us. Those storms
travel up and down this coast like it's a major highway. Ask the
people in Port St. Joe, 'bout thirty miles down the road, what
happens when a hurricane gives birth to a tidal wave. Get 'em to
show you old St. Joseph—what's left of it—that's underneath
the bay. September through November, keep your rosary handy."

Nobody had to tell her Peyton was among the residents who
resented the recent changes that threatened to alter what was
old, familiar, and comfortable into something trendy. Bright
awnings, siding, and gallons of paint had transformed withered
derelicts into jewels that sparkled among faded neighbors like
Peyton's Shoe Store.

Peyton sighed and looked away from the water. He bent
over and touched his hands to the ground a few times before
beginning his jog back to town.

2

*I*n their own dusty time, the residents of Apalachicola waited for the arrival of the newcomers, accustomed, if not always pleased, to strangers sharing their space, their heat on a summer day, their salt breeze, and the quiet that inhabited the town like a benevolent spirit. Even newcomers couldn't dispel the quiet or the stillness that were sure and lasting residents of the small fishing village.

When the Fosters arrived from Atlanta, their year-old 1986 silver Jaguar nosed down Highway 98 going east into town. In no way grand, the entrance retained the humble origins of its first settlers, certainly not Jaguar *haute.*

It was dark when the Fosters' journey ended and the headlights illuminated the raw simplicity of their surroundings. Margaret Foster closed her eyes and thought back to her life in Atlanta, remembered the joy she derived from telling people about this move. "Fishing village" still lay on her tongue like fine caviar. How she'd loved saying it. Loved even more seeing people's reactions when they learned it wasn't just a rumor—Edwin and Margaret Foster really were retiring, leaving the sophistication of Atlanta for a fishing village on the Gulf Coast of Florida. The stunned disbelief of friends and acquaintances made the pain of their decision more bearable.

The Fosters neglected to dwell on these details. They romanticized the idea of carving out a new life with primitive tools, of actually sweating over a day's work. Sharing these tidbits was surprisingly cleansing, rejuvenating. It was the struggle that intrigued them. That's what they told their friends anyway. Apalachicola would be their fountain of youth. They would be young, starting all over again. They dined on envy and felt renewed.

◦⟋◦

ALL THROUGH THE PLANNING STAGES, all the time spent trying to decide where they wanted to live, right down to looking at housing in Apalachicola, they never once considered their daughter, Elise, in their plans.

"It'd be a fight, Edwin. It's our decision, and Elise can just live with it. I for one am tired of arguing. With Elise everything is an argument."

Elise had heard her parents talking about the move, but she was tired of arguing too. And anyway, she never won. They held all the cards. She built a brittle veneer to protect herself, to disagree without feeling the pain of rejection. This time, though, her veneer had hairline cracks by the time her mother finally broached the subject of the move. She felt the heat of her anger all the way to the roots of her hair. She was nearly eighteen years old, and they still held the map to her life. They plotted her course, and her consent was taken for granted.

Margaret held a pencil and yellow legal pad. She tapped the eraser nervously on the paper as she stared at her daughter, still lanky at seventeen, still something of a tomboy. "Elise, we'd like you to postpone going to college for a year."

Elise's eyes hardened to hold back the tears, and with deliberate nonchalance, she plucked a piece of lint from her casual but expensive shirt. She held her breath, afraid to breathe. *Not my hard-earned freedom. Please, not that.*

"Did you say something?"

Elise shook her head. "I'm speechless. This is the one thing I never expected."

"It's only a year and then you can go anyplace you like. We should have said something sooner, I guess, but you know how busy we've been."

Oh, I know how busy you've been all right. To Margaret she merely shrugged and said, "Yeah, I know."

"*Yes, ma'am*', Elise. Just because you'll be eighteen soon doesn't give you the right to be rude."

"Mom, this is the '80s. I'm not some Southern belle."

"Elise, you need never worry about anyone mistaking you for a Southern belle."

"I assume that's a compliment?"

"No, it isn't. Not in my book anyway."

"Mom, why don't I get a job? That'll help with the money, won't it?"

"No, you don't have to take a job. You can help us get settled in our new location. As for the money for college, we have it, of course, but it's tied up just now."

Time and again Elise had overheard her mother telling people about this fishing village, and she couldn't imagine how such a move could be financially devastating.

"Isn't that all the more reason for me to take a job? I could stay here in Atlanta and go to Georgia State part time."

"No, you can't stay here in Atlanta. Didn't you hear what I said? We need your help getting settled."

"You've never had a problem hiring help before."

Margaret's nostrils flared slightly. "I told you we have our money tied up just now. Elise, we didn't plan this. We just believe it's the best solution to Edwin's problems. I'd think you could be more considerate. This hasn't been pleasant for any of us. And surely you realize that your father and I are a little anxious about this move ourselves."

Elise wasn't sure how to respond, but anxious wasn't the word she'd have chosen to describe her parents' reaction to this upheaval in their lives. She continued to stare at her mother, quite occupied with her interior monologue.

Margaret slammed the legal pad on the table. "I knew we should have taken you with us when we flew down to scout things out and look at housing, but Edwin felt that since you were just starting your senior year, it wouldn't be fair to have you miss several weeks of school."

"Mom, you don't really think he cares about what's fair to me, do you? He just didn't want me along."

"Don't be ridiculous. Of course he cares about you, about being fair." This wasn't going well, not at all the way Margaret had envisioned. "I know you won't believe this, but Edwin has your best interests at heart. It's just that we feel that for the family, for all of us, this move is necessary. A total change of scene."

Move to a fishing village? That'll be a change of scene all right. She probably thinks it'll be an easy transition.

It wasn't as though Elise would be giving up a wide circle of friends. She'd heard her mother remark often enough that Elise didn't have close friends. Margaret, on the other hand, had always been popular. She had the yearbooks and trophies to prove it. In high school she'd been a cheerleader, and in college, Sweetheart of Sigma Chi! It was apparent to Elise that her mother was quite at a loss in trying to deal with a daughter who was anything but popular—a loner, tomboy, introvert.

"If you'd only invite people over, Elise." How many times had she heard that! "You can't get to know people if you don't spend time with them. Smile more. Don't be so caustic."

It all centered on her mouth—the sharp tongue, the elusive smile. A real Mona Lisa. Help me then. Help me understand why we don't like each other, why I don't even look like you. I've heard you say so!

Her only consolation was that she'd never look like portly old Edwin. Her real father had been blessed with good looks. If only he'd lived . . .

Stop! I can't go there. It's like the pain I used to get looking in the mirror. If I hadn't been crying that day, Daddy would still be alive. It was my fault. Try smiling with that on your conscience, Mom.

But she knew it was more than her looks, more than blame. Elise knew that. She'd overheard girls at school talking about her often enough. "Elise? Oh, she's a nice girl, but . . ." There was always a but. "But she's odd." Elise knew her take on the world was off-center and different from theirs, but it didn't keep her from wanting to be happy, to have friends. She'd truly tried, but she could never keep up the pretense of being sweet or giddy. Regret always trumped sweet.

Even when Elise was too young to understand why, her mother was forever urging her to smile. She'd kneel on the floor and pinch Elise's cheeks ever so gently and say, "Don't look so sad, precious." As though Elise was not only sad but deaf as well, Margaret would tilt her head back and look up at Edwin. "Why doesn't she laugh? Why does she look so sad?"

"She doesn't look sad, Margaret. She looks serious."

"Yes, well, I hope that's all it is."

But Elise learned that it was more than a serious expression that bothered her mother. One day she heard the words that would form her view of herself.

"Oh, Edwin, why can't she be pretty?"

"Don't be ridiculous, Margaret. Do you really think you could have had an ugly child? She'll be beautiful some day. High cheekbones make a woman. And I don't want to hear any more about her carrying the burden of your guilt. She was too young to realize what was happening anyway."

"Do you think so, Edwin? I wonder. Sometimes I really wonder."

As Elise grew older and attempted to confide her unhappiness to her mother, she could see Margaret's eyes glaze over with incomprehension.

Elise knew what her mother was thinking. She was wondering, "*Where does she get that boyish figure? No curves whatsoever. It's not unbecoming; it's just not like our family.*"

Mother and daughter were alike in some ways. Both preferred interior dialogue to communicating with one another.

When Elise was in the fifth grade, her mother said, "Oh, just wait until you're in junior high. You'll see a big change then, Elise. Junior high will be the making of you." And then, "Well, it's only junior high, after all. High school will be different. Believe me, you'll find your place then." Here she was, Class of '87, about to graduate, and she was still caught between floors, still searching for happiness and settling for resentment.

She knew something lurked in the back of her mind, but she could never quite grasp the fogged memory that seemed overlaid with her fear of mirrors, a fear so terrifying she could take only hurried glimpses of her own reflection.

It began when she was small, that painful flash of bright light in her brain when she faced a mirror. She always thought that if she could only remember what prompted the fear maybe it would go away. She'd tried to talk to her mother about it, but Margaret seemed almost frightened by her questions. Elise finally quit trying. Over time the flashes subsided somewhat, but not the shortcomings she saw reflected. The good features she'd inherited from her parents—large blue-gray eyes, long, wheat-colored hair and slender build—sounded beautiful, but she was convinced that on her they were arranged in all the wrong ways.

Could her mother be right after all? Was it because she'd never conformed that she grew comfortable being different? She remembered a day when she was twelve. The school children were at recess when it began snowing. She stood with a group of girls, laughing as they held their mouths open catching snowflakes.

"They're so cold," one remarked.

"Not for long," another laughed.

"They taste pink." Immediately every mouth closed. They looked at Elise and then at each other.

"You're weird, Elise. You always say such weird things. You can't taste colors."

"I can."

"No, you can't," and in one synchronized movement they returned to the school building and left Elise alone in the snow. She heard someone say, "She always spoils things."

"You're just jealous," she called after them. "You're jealous because you never tasted pink." She stood her ground, her navy tights emphasizing the frailty of her long, thin legs. Hoping the girls were watching her, in an exaggerated move, she threw her head back, opened her mouth wide and caught snowflake after snowflake, each one a flavorful, delicate pink. She held back the tears and walked into the classroom licking her lips.

Things didn't improve as she grew older. You had to be silly or giddy to be fun, and if you weren't fun, you didn't have friends. The few she'd had never understood her. Her closest friend wasn't even a girl, but the son of one of her dad's business partners. And he wasn't really a close friend, just someone who stopped by fairly often. Elise never understood why Ronnie wanted to be with her, but he seemed as much of a misfit as she was, so how could she turn him away?

Ronnie was two years younger than Elise and unbearably shy. He was also incredibly bright. Tall and thin, he had huge hands and feet and was at ease with his body only when he smoked pot. Elise hated pot. It made her slightly nauseous and dizzy, but Ronnie said it wasn't fun if you smoked alone, so they'd light up behind the hedge in her backyard.

It gave Elise a measure of satisfaction to learn her mother didn't approve of their friendship. She'd gone to the kitchen for Cokes when she heard Margaret laugh and say to Edwin, "Real soulmates, those two."

"Good lord, Margaret, at least he's human. Remember her make-believe playmate, that, that . . . Damn! What was his name? I remember it was such an odd choice for a kid's name. We thought she'd never give him up. Remember trying to convince her he wasn't there? Surely Ronnie's better than somebody who never existed."

"Yes, I guess so. Oh, of course he is, Edwin. It's just that Elise isn't like anyone I've ever known. If she and I were class-mates, we wouldn't even be friends! I feel like such a failure. Everything always came easy for me. Why is it so hard being a mother?"

Before Edwin could answer, they saw Elise standing in the door. She took Cokes from the refrigerator, and stared hard at her parents as she bumped the door shut with her hip. She left the room with no one saying a word.

"I suppose she heard that," Margaret said.

"Yes, I imagine she did." Edwin poured two glasses of wine before Margaret answered.

"She could have heard worse."

"Margaret, don't . . ."

"I'm sorry. It just slipped out."

Her mother didn't have a clue! *You forced me to give up my real soulmate years ago. Ronnie and I are just a couple of misfits.* She handed him a Coke. "Let's go outside. It's stifling in here."

They leaned back in lounge chairs behind the hedge, facing the pool. The air grew sweet with the scent of pot. Elise leaned over and took a short, shallow drag from Ronnie's joint. He inhaled deeply and relaxed but could see Elise was upset. She turned to him quite suddenly and asked, "Ronnie, are you a virgin?"

He turned beet red, swallowed smoke, and nearly fell out of his chair coughing.

"Lord, Ronnie, I didn't mean to upset you."

"I'm not upset. Why would you ask me that?"

"Why won't you answer?"

"For one thing, we've never talked about anything like that before."

"Well, are you?"

He sighed. "Yes. Are you?"

"Yes, but I don't want to be."

"Elise, I'm not going to . . ."

She burst out laughing. "Oh, Ronnie, I'm not asking you to. I'm just so frustrated with life, with everything. It's like having an itch I can't scratch. This would be my decision, something under my control that would have nothing to do with my mother."

"I'm not sure losing your virginity would solve anything. Despite your differences, there's no reason to resent your mother's looks. You're beautiful too, even if you don't look like her. I'd think it would make you proud to have a beautiful mother." His Southern accent always grew heavy when he had a buzz on.

"That's because you never had one." Elise put her hand over her mouth. "Oh, Ronnie, I'm sorry. I really like your mother."

"Mom's cool. I never said she was beautiful. But look, Elise, it's no piece of cake having a dad who wants you to be a jock."

"But you're so smart. Surely that counts for something."

"It embarrasses him. He was this big athlete in school. I

have to watch what I say, or he thinks I'm putting him down. We got in a big argument the other night because I introduced pheromones into the conversation."

"Pheromones?" Elise drew her legs up akimbo.

"You know, the scent animals give off to their own species. It's a way of communicating."

"Really?"

"Yeah, really."

"Wish I could communicate with my mom that way and not have to talk to her." Elise turned her head from side to side pretending to sniff something. "She thinks I'm a dork."

"Well, you're not."

Elise leaned over for another drag and then stood up and did a cartwheel.

Ronnie gave an appreciative whistle. "Mom says you're the most mature young girl she's ever known and that you have a sense of fashion beyond your years."

Elise laughed and shook her head. "Yeah. Mature girls do cartwheels."

"I'm serious. She says you have a gift and that maybe you should consider a career in fashion design."

"Your mother said that?"

"Yep. You have a look, Elise, that sets you apart from other people."

"Apart from my mother, you mean."

"Your mother has nothing to do with it. You're a lovely anachronism."

"Sure I am. But tell me that word again."

"Anachronism."

"No, silly. The other one."

"Pheromones?"

"Yeah. I like that. What it implies."

"Just don't forget who introduced you to it." He popped some Tic Tacs in his mouth.

"I promise." She pursed her lips. "Pheromones," she said, letting it roll over her tongue like smoke. "Pheromones."

Elise knew it bothered her mother that she seldom dated, yet was friends with Ronnie. On the rare occasion she had a date, Margaret was ecstatic, but Elise felt diminished as soon as a guy laid eyes on her mother. Slender with long shapely legs, Margaret Foster still had the fluid movements of a model, and Elise always resented her for it.

3

"*H*ear the news, Dallas?"

"Well hello to you too, Peyton. This must be some news. I can't remember the last time you honored me with a phone call."

"That's cause I'd rather look at your pretty face than talk to you on the phone. In fact, why don't you meet me at the drugstore for coffee? That way I can see the surprise on your face when you hear my news."

"Why not, Peyton? It's not as though my dance card is filled these days. My keys are about to jingle, and if you'll start for the drugstore, I'll be right there, but, Peyton . . ."

"Yes?"

"You'd better have some real news, not just complaining about the millionaire Yankees moving to St. George Island."

"Now would I kid you? You know me better than that. Dallas? Dallas?" *Damn. She's left already.* "Hey, Bobby, mind the store, will you? A beautiful woman is waiting for me at the drugstore."

"Sure, Peyton. You and Dallas have fun."

Peyton waved as Dallas parked her car and rushed over to open the door for her. "Nothing like a cup of Joe to get the cobwebs out, Dallas."

"Speak for yourself. This won't be my first cup, and my cobwebs are history. I'm primed for news."

"Sit down, sweetheart, here it is. Sarah has sold the house!"

"Annelise's house?"

"The very one."

"That is news. I never thought she'd let go of it. Even after she moved to Tallahassee I thought she'd just rent it, that maybe she'd move back home. Bet you hoped she would, you who were so crazy about Sarah all those years. No wonder this is such big news to you."

"I didn't hope for anything, Dallas. And just for the record, Sarah is ancient history."

Dallas laughed. "Well the next time Sarah honors Apalachicola with a visit, I dare you to tell her that. If anybody is ancient history it's Annelise. She's never left us or we wouldn't still be calling the riverboat house hers."

"I guess not, but Sarah should have kept the house in the family, so to speak, and not sold it to some strangers from Atlanta."

"You're a hard man to please, Peyton. At least she didn't sell to one of those millionaire Yankees you hate so much."

"You don't hate them? We never had bed and breakfast places or four-star restaurants until all those millionaires moved to St. George Island."

"Peyton, Apalach is on the brink of a metamorphosis, and who knows where it'll take us."

"I'll tell you one place it won't take us."

"And where's that, Mr. Smarty?"

"To the real estate office cause we're not selling what they're coming here to buy."

"Is that so?"

"It's so, all right. They are after a way of life, and that's not for sale."

"You're right there, Peyton, it isn't. Thank God some things are still sacred."

SACRED OR NOT, MOST OF Apalach's residents were just simple people who didn't live in houses built in the shape of boats. Many were unaware that their town was fast outpacing them. For years Apalach had been little more than a bump in the road on Highway 98 that ran east and west straight through the heart of town. But of late, the fishing village had become a destination. Cars arriving from the west traveled through a tunnel of pines and water. Houses, many high on stilts, rose above the road on the bay side. Across the narrow highway from the water, there were breaks in the pines that supported humble dwellings and pitiful stores. This was Peyton's favorite part of Highway 98. When Dallas had asked him why, he said it was because it had character. He could live without the eastbound highway that boasted a school, a cemetery, a Methodist church, the Coca-Cola bottling plant, several eating places, and simple wooden homes—little more to his mind than tokens on a Monopoly board. Closer to town, there were a few large, showy places, but these were recent converts to bed and breakfast establishments. "Bed and breakfast" stuck in Peyton's throat like a serving of cold grits.

There were plenty of people who, like Peyton, resented change, had been happy with things the way they were, but Peyton knew that most of the women who bought their shoes from him could talk of little else. For years the only thing that had changed in their lives had been the weather, and they felt helpless and a little excited in the wake of a metamorphosis, even when they didn't like it. Oh, he heard them every day.

"It's just not fair that they should come in here and act like they own the place."

Another woman laughed. "But they do."

"I know they do, but I'll never get used to it. Never! My own great-great-grandfather helped settle Apalachicola. They have no right to change things. It's our heritage, not theirs."

"Yep, bunch of damn Yankees. Never did envy them towns filled with tourists, and now we're getting some of the overflow."

"Oh, they're not tourists. They live here!"

Peyton listened and kept his own counsel, knowing they were totally unaware that for years people in neighboring towns had been looking down their noses at them. In the 1940s and '50s, people would have said you were crazy if you'd predicted such a change in a place so backward. There'd be no renaissance for Apalachicola! Not again! Not in a million years.

Theirs was a mixed population of Italians and Greeks, human succulents drawn to the water, and merchants who were mainly English. They'd blended over the years. They got along. The Greek men who had come there in the 1800s to harvest sponges, those golden-bodied fishermen, were something to behold. More than one woman said you could gaze on such men all day, and your eyes would never grow tired.

While the men were hauling in nets of shrimp and harvesting oysters, their wives stayed home and cared for the babies. And then it seemed Howard and Weston wrote a song just for them. *Shrimp Boats.* They claimed it, and it was part of the air they breathed, a whispered prayer at bedtime, a reason to get up in the morning. They transformed bad days by singing that song and believing it. And because there were lots of bad days, they sang and sang. They would continue to sing the shrimp boat song as long as a shrimp boat existed. That song made them feel famous. Boosted their spirits. Made their un-air-conditioned houses less oppressive in the summer heat. Even tired wives noticed once more what handsome husbands they'd married.

This was the way life had been for more years than anyone

cared to remember. Change was a bitter pill to swallow, more permanent than a summer storm. Many of their favorite restaurants closed or changed hands, their owners happy to be bought out for more than they'd ever dreamed the places were worth.

"You won't believe what that sap-sucker paid me for this café. Why, the plumbing is bad and the electric downright scary, but who am I to turn him down if he's in such a hurry to be parted from his money? Never thought I'd live to see the day . . ."

Locals had known the name of every proprietor in town. Waitresses knew what a customer would order before he picked up a menu. Knew who liked grits and who didn't. Knew who'd empty the pot of coffee before he left the café on Saturday morning. Barely a handful of the old timers were left any more. Who could say where the metamorphis would take them?

4

The nearer the time came for their move, the more Elise retreated to her room, trying to imagine life in a fishing village. *Wouldn't it be ironic if I like it there? What if I'm actually happy? What's it like, though—being happy?*

All Elise had known of happiness had been as a young child, when she retreated to the secret, unseen world of her playmate. His world was quiet as a dream, a place where she felt safe. He was older than Elise and protected her, but her parents brought his visits to an end.

Edwin had shamed her for thinking only of herself. Shaking his finger in her face, he told her that each time her playmate visited, the boy became weaker and would soon die if she didn't quit seeing him. She cried herself to sleep every night, afraid to even think of him for fear of the harm she might do. All those years ago, and she missed him still.

Unlike their daughter, Margaret and Edwin Foster had no trouble defining happiness. Happiness was a comfortable income, yearly vacations, a home in the right neighborhood, a successful law practice for him, a career in interior decorating for her, expensive bourbon, imported wine . . . They might have been lifted from the pages of *Southern Living*, a family portrait waiting to happen. Yet, in the boldest move of their entire lives, they were moving to a fishing village, to seclusion.

If they enjoyed their new locale half as much as they enjoyed the cocktail party attention their plans sparked, it would be yet another good decision in a long line of highly successful ventures. Business associates and friends alike couldn't seem to get enough of them. The Fosters complained that they were nearly exhausted from so many farewell parties, knowing all the while they coveted the attention. They couldn't help it. They loved being envied.

Only occasionally did doubt nudge the edge of Margaret's consciousness. "They do envy us, don't they, Edwin?"

"They sure as hell do. They wish they had the guts to strike out like this. Why, all these parties. They just hope to catch a whiff of the stuff we're made of."

At her mother's insistence, Elise agreed to accompany them to a party hosted by Edwin's business partners. "Maybe Ronnie will be there," Margaret encouraged.

Elise nearly laughed. *A lot I care if Ronnie's there. Oh, why must I hate my life? Of course, I wish Ronnie would be there.*

"Elise, quit staring at me like that. It won't kill you to do something for us for a change. I expect you to be ready at seven Saturday night."

Elise shrugged and turned to walk away.

"And for God's sake, Elise, don't shrug when people talk to you."

RONNIE WASN'T AT THE PARTY, and Elise didn't know if she was relieved or disappointed. People smiled and a few attempted to talk to her, but as the evening wore on and more drinks were consumed, she found herself alone. She was a voyeur, drunk on overheard conversations.

"A regular Stepford family," someone remarked and Elise nearly laughed.

Smug with things she'd heard people saying about her family, she wandered to another room and heard someone else ask, "Haven't the Fosters always led charmed lives?"

"Except for Elise," a man replied.

"Shhh."

Elise turned her back, hoping to be unnoticed in the dimly lit room.

"Well, it's true," the man continued. "Margaret is a stunning woman, a bit of a bitch, but stunning. Edwin's no dog either, but Elise, she's strange. Nothing like them. Nothing."

A woman with a throaty voice said, "My niece says she doesn't have a wide circle of friends, and her sarcasm is legend. Surely that comes from Margaret."

The man looked at her. "No doubt. Edwin has the personality of stale crackers."

There was a ringing in Elise's head, but she couldn't move, couldn't stop listening.

"I don't think Edwin's her father. I heard Margaret was married before."

"Well, that figures." The spiteful man again. "Elise is the only chink in their ideal existence."

"Do I detect a green-eyed monster? I thought you liked the Fosters."

"I do. In a way. It's just that everything is always so perfect for them."

"Do you really believe Margaret and Edwin are perfect?"

The woman hesitated briefly and lowered her voice. "Do you think leaving a major city for a fishing village is normal? Makes me wonder if life is as grand as they've made it out to be. Maybe it's all an act. It's bizarre if you ask me. Downright bizarre. I can't imagine it."

The man cleared his throat. "There was that business with

Edwin a year or so ago. Remember when he was sick? Emory wasn't good enough for him. Went to a hospital out of state for some tests, Mayo or some place."

"I'd forgotten that. It all seemed so casual, nobody thought much of it."

"That was just a bump in the road for them, I guess, but yeah, I know that nobody's life is perfect, not really. I don't care who they are. There has to be a skeleton in the closet someplace."

The woman laughed. "You hope, but maybe, maybe not. At any rate, they'll be gone soon, and we'll be none the wiser."

"Oh, my God," someone said, and they moved away. Elise supposed they'd seen her standing beside the potted palm.

5

"*I*t's a combination graduation/eighteenth-birthday gift, Elise," Margaret said and handed her a small square package.

Hesitantly Elise opened the burgundy velvet box. She was stunned by the beauty of the long strand of creamy pearls set off by a half dozen emerald and diamond roundels. The color drained from her face as she spread the necklace over her lap and looked up quizzically. *Pearls but not college?* Her eyes were bright with unshed tears.

"Why, Elise," her dad began, "we thought . . . we hoped you'd like them."

"Oh, they're lovely." She hesitated only briefly, trying to steady her voice and conceal her disappointment. "I just never expected anything so expensive, not with the move and all."

"They aren't new, *darling*," Margaret said soberly but with a hint of vinegar on the darling.

Puzzled, Elise looked at her mother.

"These pearls belonged to your paternal grandmother. She willed them to you before she died."

"My real father's mother?"

"Edwin is your real father, Elise, the only father you've ever known, really." *Must I explain this to you now!* "Gene was your biological father. You were just a baby when his parents died. These were Ingrid's, Gene's mother's pearls. We had them restrung. It was Edwin's idea to add the roundels."

Elise looked at Edwin with surprise, snippets of unkind conversation from the cocktail party drifting like confetti about her head. *As sarcastic as you are, you still have to kiss him. He's done something very nice.* It felt awkward, but she leaned forward and kissed him on the cheek. "Thanks," she swallowed hard, "for such a beautiful gift." *I'm sure emeralds and pearls will be all the rage in a fishing village.*

"I hoped you'd be pleased. You really are my daughter, you know." He hesitated only a second, but it was enough for Elise to notice. *Stale crackers indeed.* "And I love you. It's important that you know that. I chose emeralds because they're the color of your eyes, and . . ."

Margaret's laughter interrupted his fine speech. "Why, Edwin, Elise has blue eyes! But be glad of the mistake, darling. Emeralds are very expensive." Margaret continued to laugh quietly for several minutes.

Elise stood holding the elegant necklace, not knowing quite what to do.

Edwin was beet-red and clearly flustered. "Well, they always seemed green to me. Maybe I'm colorblind. Or maybe your eyes are blue-green."

Margaret couldn't let it drop. "In that case, Elise, hold out for aquamarines next time."

Edwin was clearly annoyed now. "As I was about to say, Elise, the emeralds complement the diamonds. I just wanted to do something really special for you," he looked defiantly at Margaret, "to give you a gift from Gene and me both."

It was Margaret's turn to blush. "Edwin!"

"It's only fair, Margaret. He was her father, and now that I think of it, Gene's eyes were green."

"Hazel," Margaret said, "not green."

Edwin ignored her and turned to Elise. "We don't often say it, but we do love you," he looked back at Margaret, "regardless of the color of your eyes."

It was quite a speech coming from her stern, taciturn father, and she felt worse for what it said about their relationship than for him not knowing the color of her eyes. For the first time in her life, she actually felt sorry for him. It was never pleasant being on the receiving end of Margaret's wit.

Elise stood on tiptoe and gave him another quick kiss before turning to hug her mother, careful that she didn't disturb her hair. "I'll always treasure them." Her voice was choked with emotion that had nothing to do with the pearls. Edwin had actually mentioned her father. His name was seldom uttered, was deliberately avoided. She was surprised when it surfaced again a few weeks later.

THINKING OF THE UNCERTAINTY AND hope for happiness that their move might bring, Elise was shocked that she was overcome with sadness when Edwin locked the front door of their home for the last time. The only memories she had of her real father were behind that door. Would the house hold her memories, the echoes of her past? She longed to run back inside and clutch something of him to her. How could they just drive away and leave him like this? Surely her mother had memories too, but Margaret walked to the car without a backward glance. Elise stood motionless, her head tilted back, looking at the window of her parents' second-floor bedroom. She imagined she saw her dad looking down at her. *You can't come with us, can you?*

"Blow the horn, Edwin. We should have left hours ago. We

need to get started if we're going to make that stop in Tallahas-see. Now why do you suppose Elise is staring at the house like that?"

"This is the only home she's ever known, Margaret. It has to be hard." He blew the horn anyway.

Elise jumped and her heart pounded, but she turned and started toward the car. *Why am I afraid to mention him? Why has he always been a forbidden subject?* She didn't know how old she was when she realized that, but she lived with the fear that she might forget and say her dad's name.

The wheels turned on hard blacktop; the speedometer inched higher and higher, taking them closer to the fishing village, to their new home.

The drone of her parents' voices reached Elise in the back seat, but their words were muted and lost.

Margaret lowered the visor and looked at Elise through the makeup mirror. "Aren't you at all interested in the scenery?"

Elise looked up from her book and caught a brief glimpse of Margaret's face in the mirror. There was a bright flash, and she quickly closed her eyes and turned away. The old, familiar headache returned and she spoke to the window. "The scenery gets boring."

"Well, you won't have too much longer to be bored," Edwin said. "We'll be there tonight in spite of our late start."

Margaret stared straight ahead. "It really isn't that far, not in terms of miles anyway."

Still, it was later than they'd expected when the Fosters continued down the eastbound highway into town. It was black as pitch out, threatening rain. "Being off the interstate really slows you down," Edwin commented hopefully, but Margaret wasn't to be deterred.

"Drive by the house, Edwin. I want to see it tonight."

"Really, Margaret, it's too dark to see anything. Can't it wait until morning?"

She didn't answer and Edwin guided the car down side roads until he thought he was at the right place. He'd barely cut the engine when Margaret opened the door and stepped out of the car. Elise pressed her face to the window, but she couldn't see too much. It was dark and hot, and the air weighed on them heavy as guilt.

The car door stood open and provided a feeble light as Margaret walked toward the glimmer of white, illuminated by bursts of lightning. Thunder ripped the silence like a drum roll of anticipation, but Margaret didn't flinch.

Edwin opened his door and stood just inside its embrace, facing the house. "Marking her territory," he grumbled under his breath before calling out, "Margaret, you can't see a thing. We didn't come here for you to be struck by lightning. Let's come by early in the morning. I'm tired and want a good night's sleep."

A loud clap of thunder sent Margaret scurrying for the car. Her foot hit something and she stumbled, catching hold of the car door to keep from falling.

"You okay?" Edwin asked.

"I think so. Felt like I hit a brick. I guess we'd better move on or we'll get drenched. It's been months since we saw the place. I'd hoped that real estate agent would have left some lights on."

"Maybe she hasn't had the electricity turned on yet."

"Oh, Edwin, surely you don't think she hasn't taken care of that. I can't believe . . ."

"Well, there's nothing to be done about it tonight. I have a feeling there'll be plenty facing us tomorrow so we'd better turn in soon." He looked over his shoulder to the back seat. "Still with us, Elise?"

"Yes, sir, I'm here." She continued to sit with her face pressed to the window, hungry for the sight of the house, troubled by its familiarity.

Edwin looked at her through the rearview mirror. "Oh, honey, don't cry. I know it's different than anything you've known, but it'll work out. You'll see."

Elise was surprised by his tenderness. Most of his exchanges with her were stern, brusque at times to the point of rudeness, but she couldn't answer. It took all her concentration to control her emotions. She didn't know why she was crying, why sadness enveloped her like a cloak.

He turned and backed the car around. "Our new life," he said, "a whole new life."

Under her breath Margaret muttered, like a prayer, "Please, let it be. I so need a new life." She looked over her shoulder at Elise. "We have reservations at a restored inn. Edwin and I stayed there when we came down to look for a house. It's nothing elaborate but clean and comfortable. They even have a small restaurant and bar!"

"And good food," Edwin added. "In fact, I don't think you can find anything but good food here. Apalachicola's famous for its oysters. If they had an Oscar for oysters, Apalach would win hands down."

"Your father should know. I think he ate oysters prepared every way possible."

"And I'm ready to start at the beginning of the menu again. There was a guy here, Ed somebody, selling some hot sauce he called an oyster's best friend. And it was. Makes my mouth water just to think about it. Hope you'll try 'em, Elise. A real delicacy. Never mealy. Just sweet and juicy."

Elise wiped her eyes. *Wouldn't you know if he's enthusiastic over something, it'd be food.*

They were hardly inside the inn when it began to rain. It came down in torrents, so loud it created thunder inside as well as out. Elise looked toward the ceiling, and the woman behind the desk smiled. "It's the tin roof. Creates a thunder all its own."

"I like it," Elise declared emphatically and jammed her hands into the back pockets of her jeans.

"You would. I just hope it doesn't keep me awake," Margaret said irritably and glared at Elise as though she could control the weather.

Settled in her room, Elise lay awake for hours listening to the storm, thrilling to its threat, and enjoying the safety of a tin roof to shield her.

At eight-thirty the next morning, Margaret sat up in bed wild-eyed, trying to recall where she was. Looking at Edwin's travel alarm, she couldn't believe it was so late. "Do you realize, Edwin, that we haven't slept past six o'clock in years?"

"This is our new life, Margaret. We don't have to get up if we don't want to."

"Well, I want to. I must call that real estate woman and be sure all the utilities have been turned on."

Edwin pulled the shade back and looked out the window. "Thank goodness the rain stopped. I'd better see if Elise is up. We have a busy day ahead of us." Edwin knocked on the door to Elise's room just as she was about to leave.

Elise opened the door and said, "I'm going down for coffee. Okay?"

"Coffee? I've never known you to drink a cup of coffee in your life."

At a loss to explain her sudden craving for coffee, Elise tried to force a smile. "It's my new life too."

"Well, sure it is. We'll join you as soon as we shower and dress."

Elise had walked a short distance down the hall when she saw an orange tabby cat sleeping on an antique table. As she approached, it raised its head and looked at her. It was nearly like a command to stop, and there was a brief standoff as they stared at each other. Elise felt the drowsiness of a sleepless night wrap her in a dark fog. She closed her eyes for a few seconds. When she opened them, the cat was nowhere in sight.

A FEW HOURS LATER MARGARET stood with her hands on her hips, giving their new home a critical appraisal. "Well, it's a bit more run-down than I'd remembered, but that's okay. We have all the time in the world."

"That we do, my dear. And don't forget you kept insisting you wanted to get dirty, to roll your sleeves up and work. I think you'll get your wish."

"It's a bit closer to the street than I'm used to, but that seems to be the norm here." Margaret turned to see Elise walking around like a sleepwalker and called to her. "We'll have the distinction, Elise, of living in a house that's listed as a historical site in the National Register. I don't know why that pleases me so much, but it does. Careful of that stone, Elise," she cautioned, "I'm told ladies used it when they stepped down from their horse-drawn carriages. I'll have it taken up right away."

"No way! Please. It belongs here. Besides, it's probably in the National Register too."

"That must be what I stumbled over last night. I just don't like to think of someone falling over the thing and suing me."

"But it's been here so long. Obviously it hasn't been a problem or it wouldn't still be here."

"We can't worry about it now anyway. The furniture will be

here in three days, and we need to be sure we're ready when it arrives." At the front door Margaret lifted the doormat. "Just where she told me it'd be." She held the key high for them to see.

Edwin started to follow her up the steps but turned to look for Elise. She stood in the middle of the yard with a stunned expression on her face. At that moment he realized what a pretty girl she'd become. The sun glinted off her blond hair, and her tank top and shorts flattered her boyish figure.

"It's okay, Elise," he said. "It'll look better soon. A bit of paint will do wonders. You'll see."

"It's a boat."

"What?"

"The house. It's a boat. See the shape? It's like an old riverboat."

Edwin came back down the steps and looked from one end to the other. "Maybe it is. Yes, I can see that. An old paddle wheeler."

"Look at all the porch railings, upstairs and down, all the way around the house. I wonder how someone came to build it in the shape of a boat?"

"Damned if I know, Elise, but you're right. For whatever reason, we're going to be living in a boat. Wait'll we tell Margaret," he said and laughed.

"Don't tell her! I want to see if she notices."

"Oh, I think she'll notice soon enough, but we'll wait and see. I'd like something to catch her off guard for once."

Elise tilted her head and looked up at him quizzically.

"I'm joking, but you know how she's always one step ahead of the rest of us. This is going to be even more fun than I'd imagined."

It was probably the biggest surprise of her life that Elise was totally captivated by the large two-storied structure. She wasn't unaware of the fine piece of real estate she'd called home for eighteen years, but it didn't have the character or history of this exquisite creation. Elise possessed an uncanny ability to sense emotions, but this was the first time she'd felt some knowledge of a building. She shaded her eyes with her hand and was looking at the second floor windows when Edwin called her to come inside. "Your mother's dying to have you see the place."

As she stepped over the threshold she felt like a bride. *Bride? How can that be? I've never even been in love.*

"Well, what do you think?" Margaret asked with unconcealed pride.

"Oh!" Elise gasped and held her palm to her chest.

"What in the world's the matter with you?" Margaret asked irritably.

"Just before I came in, I thought I saw you standing at the upstairs window."

"Hardly. I may be fast, but I can't take stairs that quickly."

"I guess not," Elise said, looking around.

"Yes or no, Elise. Do you like it?"

"Oh, yes, it's beautiful. I've never seen anything like it." She looked at Edwin, and he winked. It was more than beautiful. It seemed to possess her.

The wood floors looked recently polished, and while it was dusty and filled with cobwebs, the walls gleamed under new paint. Nearly every room boasted a fireplace, and the ceilings soared skyward, with ornately-carved crown molding highlighting their pale blue color. Several rooms had giant doors that could be pulled together to form walls. Opened, they slid quietly into the ancient recesses of the house. Row after row of French doors opened onto the decks—she couldn't think of them as porches—and the tall windows framed glass that was old and wavy, creating eerie images of the giant trees that shaded the house.

Her parents ambled slowly to other parts of the house, and though she could hear their voices, she couldn't tell what they were saying as she drifted aimlessly from room to room, as though swimming underwater, passing through pockets of cold air. Polished steps led down to the spacious living room, and on either side were graceful railings topped with glossy walnut. These were repeated on the winding staircase that led to the second floor. "Fishing village?" she whispered.

When her parents returned from the back of the house, Edwin asked, "Rather grand, isn't it?"

"Oh, it is. Not at all what I expected from a fishing village."

Margaret bristled. "Surely you didn't think I'd bought a shack."

"No, ma'am, but I didn't expect this either. It's awesome."

"Well, thank you. I don't recall your ever giving a compliment freely. I always felt I had to beg for your approval of my decorating."

"Your decorating?" Elise laughed, not unkindly. "Oh, Mom, I don't think so. But I do credit you with the very good taste to have bought it." She turned slowly, her arms outstretched. "It's just that this is so different, like a living, breathing thing."

"Oh, God, Elise, don't start that," her dad said.

She felt the chill of his words, the tenderness gone, replaced by the old, familiar fear.

"No nonsense now. None of those strange ideas you get at times. Let's help your mother get this place in shape."

Elise had seldom seen her mother with a broom in her hands and wondered how the manicure would survive. She was accustomed to seeing Margaret in business suits, dealing with legal pads and telephones, but true to her word, Margaret Foster was getting dirty.

One morning Elise saw Margaret standing at the edge of

the yard, shading her eyes with her hand. She was looking back at the house. When she came inside she said to no one in particular, "This house is built in the shape of a boat."

Edwin walked up and laid a hand on Elise's shoulder. "We wondered when you'd notice."

Margaret shot them a dirty look. "Well I'm sure I would have noticed a lot sooner if I hadn't been so busy trying to clean the place."

Edwin tried to find help, but the three of them ended up doing most of the cleaning themselves. They hired someone to clean the outside windows and do some yard work, but the inside was all theirs. By the time the moving van arrived, Margaret had gotten dirty, sweated, and discovered that she felt older, not younger, from the effort. She kept that bit of information to herself, though.

Their fountain of youth, Edwin confided to Elise, was proving to be more like a bucket of sweat, but the day finally came when they could move out of the inn and take up residence in their new home. Walking down the now-familiar hall with her suitcase, Elise looked for the cat one last time. She stopped in a room that was being cleaned and asked the maid if she'd seen an orange tabby cat any place.

"Cat? I haven't seen a cat. I've only worked here a month, but I've never seen no cat."

It wasn't until they left the inn and moved into the house that the nightmares began. The first night Elise woke up with her heart pounding, her skin cold and clammy. She sat bolt upright in bed looking around her, gasping with fright. *What am I afraid of? How can a place this beautiful bring so much terror?* When morning came and she looked over the balcony to the yard below, it didn't seem possible she'd been so frightened just a short time before.

It took far longer than they had ever imagined to unpack the belongings from their Atlanta life and have everything arranged. Elise was too busy during the day to worry about her night frights. And she joined Edwin in trying to keep Margaret content. It was more and more of an irritation to Margaret that they couldn't find domestic help. But, after all, they were retired and could do the work if they had to. Hot and exhausted by nightfall, Margaret recalled with longing their carefree farewell parties. She wondered what happened to their fountain of youth. She admitted only to herself that she would be too weary to drink from it.

Edwin sensed her weariness, and even though the move had been her idea, he was determined to prove they hadn't made a mistake. This was too big a step. They had too much invested, not just in terms of money but in their reputations as well.

When it seemed the work would never end, one day they realized they were unpacked, drapes were hung, the bathrooms sparkled, and the modern kitchen was equipped with every accessory Margaret could think of. They were done. Had they known any people, they would have had a party. As it was they made drinks and retired to Edwin's leather swathed, bookbound study. This would become their ritual, having drinks there each evening. The dark walls provided a shaded haven from the bright Florida sun, and the massive desk Edwin brought from his law firm fit perfectly.

Margaret leaned back in her chair and closed her eyes. "What will you do, Edwin?"

"Do?"

"With this room. That desk. I've never seen it free of papers before."

"Oh, I don't know. I've been too busy and tired to think about it. What will you do?" he asked.

Margaret winked at him. "Oh, I don't know. I've been too busy and too tired to think about it."

Elise could hear them laughing as she came to the door.

"Hi, come join us," her dad said. "We're just relaxing and delighting in being retired."

She still hadn't adjusted to this gentle demeanor that seemed more and more his style, to his wanting her to join them. She tried to get a sense of his true feelings, but nothing came to her. They seemed genuine.

"Thanks, but I think I'll walk around outside a bit."

Margaret sat forward and looked around at her daughter. "I swear, Elise, you remind me of those women in novels who stand on the widow's walk searching for some sight of their sea-faring husbands. You'll walk the paint off the porch floors."

"Oh, leave her alone, Margaret."

"You know I don't mean anything, Elise. Enjoy yourself. Call us if you see a ship."

She could hear them laughing again as she walked toward the front door.

Margaret plucked an olive from her martini. "Have you noticed, Edwin, that Elise is different somehow? Since we moved here, I mean. I can't put my finger on it, but she seems changed, maybe more feminine."

"I haven't noticed any difference. I wish I had." He took a sip of his drink and sat the glass down hard.

Margaret raised her eyebrows, and Edwin gave a weak smile.

"I'm sorry, but you know as well as I do that even though we love her, she isn't the easiest person to be around."

Margaret sighed. "I know. Maybe we're changing too. Edwin?"

"Yeah?"

"We are enjoying being retired, aren't we?"

"Well, of course. Sure we are, but, Margaret, there's something I should tell you."

A look of alarm crossed her face. "Oh, Edwin, you are happy, aren't you? I thought a total change of scene was what we needed, would lift that burden you've carried all these years and make things okay again."

"I'm sure that with time it will make things easier. The doctors thought the move was a good idea too. God, you don't know how awful I feel about what's happened. After so many years that this would catch up with me and send me into that damned depression. I've let you down—twice."

"Don't be ridiculous. I'm the one who should have gotten sick, not you. I'm the guilty party."

"Now who's being ridiculous? You were just a pawn, nothing but a pawn. But I don't want to discuss it. I'm glad we moved, that we left all that behind. I'm happy here. Aren't you?"

"Yes. No. Oh, Edwin, we're much too young to be retired, really we are."

"I can't say that I'm totally disappointed that you've come to that conclusion. See, this is our fountain of youth after all."

"I've thought about it a lot. Unpacking gives one hours of time to think, and, Edwin, I think we should open a stationery and bath shop."

Edwin nearly strangled on his drink. When his coughing subsided he said, "You really have done a lot of thinking, haven't you?"

"Well, yes I have. After being an interior decorator for so long, I have too many contacts to just let those years of work go to waste."

"Actually, I'm glad you feel that way because I was about to tell you that I didn't totally sever my partnership with the firm. Not totally. I still have my hand in."

"But you never said a word!"

"I was afraid you'd be upset after giving up your career. I wasn't sure how to approach it, but now that you have this other interest, well, you won't mind if I do some consulting from time to time."

"No, I won't mind if you're certain that's what you want. I'm convinced I can make a success of this venture. I'm really pleased about the idea, and we'll both have our careers again. Why, Edwin, just think of it, bath products and stationery. We'd be meeting two basic needs of newcomers and locals alike. It'll double the business," she assured him. They smiled, pleased with their keen sense of business acumen.

But "fishing village" was in some ways still an apt description of Apalach, one the Fosters didn't fully understand. They might fill a local need with soap, perhaps with soap, but lined tablet paper, the main writing vehicle of the locals, was not part of Margaret and Edwin Foster's vocabulary.

6

Sunshine streamed through the windows of the sun porch where Margaret poured coffee into heavy pottery mugs. Edwin sipped his brew appreciatively. "Margaret, this is your idea, and I'll support it, but I don't want to run all over the place looking for a building to house your shop. Why don't you and Elise do that?"

Margaret leaned over and kissed him. "That was just what I was hoping you'd say. Oh, Edwin, I'm really excited about this. I guess I never admitted my misgivings, but I really think this will work out."

"God, I sure hope so, Margaret. If it doesn't, we're up Shit Creek."

She laughed and took another sip of coffee.

Margaret spent a great deal of time poring over catalogs and sending letters to people in Atlanta and New York. The more she considered the idea, the more adrenalin pumped through her slender, well-toned body.

She was like a thoroughbred straining for the race to begin. When she had her business plan in order, she was ready to act. She walked into Elise's room one morning and slapped her backside, jumping back when Elise screamed and rolled off the bed to the floor. "What in the world is the matter? I didn't mean to frighten you. Get dressed. We're going shopping." She walked around the room opening shutters and humming.

"Shopping for what?" Elise asked sleepily.

"A building! We need a building for my bath and stationery store."

The frightening dreams that disturbed Elise's sleep left her with a headache, but there was no getting out of this trip. They began their search by walking, appraising their surroundings. Some buildings seemed to have been deserted with no further thought to their usefulness, cast off like unwanted pets. They leaned and sagged like ancient crones.

"That's disgusting," Margaret complained. "Those places should be condemned and torn down. They're eyesores."

"Apalach's homeless people," Elise said softly. "They make me sad."

"Well, it doesn't make me sad," Margaret snapped. "It's just plain slovenly, that's what it is."

These were Elise's first tentative steps in exploring her new surroundings. Apalach was different from anything she'd ever known, yet she felt an instant kinship with it. She was glad her mother forced her out of the house where she had begun to feel captive to her dreams. She could never recall them fully, except to know they were disturbing. In the beginning they were nothing more than mists and dark jumbled voices that left her uneasy.

While Elise rubbed shoulders with a town she found familiar and inviting, Margaret Foster sniffed change in the air. She saw only its promise, chose to ignore its history, and scorned a present that didn't include her. They pressed their noses to dusty windows and tried the handles of dented doorknobs. If those doors were closed to her, Margaret never hesitated to march right into a store open to business and ask if the owner would consider selling or leasing to her.

Apalach had begun tempering Elise's forward manner, and

she hung back with embarrassment, not realizing the locals were past being surprised by such offers.

Margaret Foster and Peyton Roberts were cut from opposite ends of the same cloth. The only difference was that Peyton was cut against the grain. They rubbed each other the wrong way the minute Margaret stepped inside his shoe store.

She had learned to dress comfortably for her excursions and wore a striped v-neck blouse with an expensive golf skirt, top-siders, and a stylish straw hat. No one would have taken her for a local.

"Mr. Roberts?" Margaret walked forward and extended her hand. He might have been a suit-clad man from Atlanta, a successful Peachtree Street executive.

"Peyton," he answered, rubbing his palm on the side of his khakis before grasping her soft, slender hand.

"Mr. Roberts, I'm new to town and . . ."

"You don't need to tell me that," he interrupted and several men who'd been talking to him laughed.

"I beg your pardon?"

"You don't look like you belong here, ma'am. I do look like I belong here." He winked at her. "That's how I know you're new in town."

Margaret's nostrils flared slightly, and she forced a smile. "Well, Mr. Roberts . . ."

"Peyton," he interrupted again.

"Oh yes, Peyton. Well, Peyton, I may not look like I belong here, but I assure you that I do. I own a home and furthermore, I intend to open a business here."

"That right?"

"That's right."

"Well, if you don't mind my asking, what's that got to do with me?"

"I might be a customer wanting to buy something, for all you know. I hope you don't give all your customers the third degree."

"Is that a fact?"

"Yes, that's a fact, and I do want to buy something. I'd like to buy your store, Mr. Roberts."

"Peyton."

"Damn! Excuse me. I'm sorry. Peyton." She heaved a sigh of exasperation.

"Is there a for sale sign out there, Miss, Mrs. . . .?"

"Foster. Margaret Foster."

"You see, I don't recall putting my place up for sale, but being a local and all maybe it slipped my mind."

"There isn't a sign. I just thought that perhaps you might consider it."

"You just thought. Just because I don't have a barrel of posies out front, you thought it was time for me to move on. Well, I'm not moving on, not yet, lady."

"Foster," she countered. "Margaret Foster."

The men laughed again, and Peyton made an elaborate bow. "Margaret Foster, of course."

"I won't waste any more of your time or mine. It was nice meeting you, Mr. Roberts."

"A beautiful woman is always welcome," he called after her.

Elise couldn't help herself. She looked back and winked.

"Can you believe that guy?" Margaret asked Elise when they were outside.

Elise thought that perhaps she'd just had her first sip of happiness. "We're off to a great start, aren't we?"

"Hush. Don't you start, Elise. I've had enough for one day. Elise? Elise, what are you staring at? Come on."

Elise tried to quit staring at the wavy glass of a vacant store, but she was sure she heard voices inside. It sounded as though a black woman and a young girl were arguing and the glass appeared to cast moving shadows. One of her waking dreams maybe? She leaned closer to see if she could hear, but Margaret grabbed her arm and pulled her away.

"A true flower of the South," Peyton said when Margaret was out of earshot. "Walks around like she's as delicate as a gardenia in a hail storm, but, gentlemen, let me tell you, her backbone is pure steel. Nothing less. Bet she's got one pussy-whipped husband too."

"Now, Peyton. You got customers."

"Yeah, well let 'em listen. Give 'em something to talk about besides the weather. She sails in here with that blouse half-buttoned and her tight little ass bound up in that expensive skirt. You'd have thought she owned the place already."

"Don't tell me you're thinking of selling to her?"

"I didn't say one way or the other now did I, Bobby? I'd hate to think of her in here, in my space. But if she wants to sweeten the pot with enough money, who knows? I'd never set foot in here again though, I tell you that."

"Well, it'd sure save you money redoing all that electrical you're so worried about."

"Yep, and don't go broadcasting it. If I sell to the likes of her, she'll be buying more than she reckoned for, and I won't feel a bit bad about it. Coming in here so high and mighty. You catch the way the girl winked at me? Saucy. I like that in a girl. She knew her mother had no business coming in here like that."

"She sure was a looker though, Peyton."

"The girl?"

"Oh, the girl's striking all right. There's no denying that, but I was talking about the mother. She's a piece of work. I guess she was the mother, but she didn't hardly look old enough."

"Yeah, I've known women like her. She's the quintessential sorority type, boys, out to improve the world."

"She sure must have got under your skin, Peyton. You never use big words unless you get good and mad."

"I'm just tired of people fooling with Apalach. Apalach is like a good woman that's paid her dues, and these new people want to trade her in for some shallow, flashy broad. It turns my stomach."

❧

PEYTON ROBERTS DISTURBED MARGARET IN ways she didn't care to admit. With her background she'd felt like a sighted person among the blind, and she was quite beside herself at the thought of some uneducated yokel getting the best of her.

"I'm not about to be taken advantage of," she told Edwin that evening. "This may take awhile, but I have the time. I'll wait." Elise was in the next room and didn't hear the figure she named but knew it was considerable when she heard Edwin whistle.

"That's a lot of paper and soap, Margaret."

"You've always acknowledged that I have a good head for business. You've never questioned my judgment before."

"But we're in different circumstances now. These people aren't like us."

"Of course they aren't. If they were, we wouldn't be here buying them out."

The more she was frustrated by her attempts to open a new business, the more attention she focused on Elise. "Now, Elise," she began one morning at breakfast, "just because I'm having a little trouble finding a vacant building is no reason for you to be complacent."

"Complacent?" Elise stared at her feet stretched on the chair in front of her and took a sip of coffee. "We just got here."

"A year will pass before you know it. You were accepted at several colleges. Think about what you want to do. Get letters in the mail. Keep your applications active."

Elise swung her feet off the chair and stood up. "You're sure we'll have the money a year from now, that it won't be tied up in stationery and soap?"

Margaret wanted to slap her, slap her silly, but she forced a weak smile and said, "Of course I'm sure."

"Then I'll be ready," she replied, not at all sure she wanted to be.

"See that you are!" Margaret snapped and left the room.

I will be ready, won't I? She'd counted on college for such a long time. College was going to wash her insecurities away. She'd find herself then, feel at home in her own body. Wouldn't she? Or was she doomed to be a misfit?

She knew it was more than her avoidance of mirrors that set her apart. All through high school while other girls preened and primped, more often than not, Elise passed mirrors with quick sidelong glances.

But she'd already sensed that Apalachicola didn't need mirrors. It was its own bright reflection, and Elise had fallen in love with it. The last thing she wanted to do was leave. Let her mother use the money on her new shop. She hoped she would. Apalach touched a wellspring of emotion she hadn't known existed, and like her, it was a place of conflict.

Day after day Elise explored, unaccountably drawn to the river where she stood mesmerized, staring at the water. Sometimes it took a dead fish or bird washing up at her feet to break the spell. She wandered lonely streets, looked at lovely old homes scattered among neighborhoods of neglect and wondered at their history. Her favorite, of course, was her beloved river-boat house. There was something otherworldly about it, as though it was caught in another dimension. Even the nightmares that continued to plague her didn't diminish her love or respect for its unique design.

Elise felt the tension Apalach shouldered, and it made her skin tingle. Discontent was a breeze that ruffled her hair. Margaret said she was being foolish, imagining things. All her life her mother had been telling her she was imagining things. Only Elise knew better.

7

*N*ight after night Elise heard her parents discuss their business prospects. It made her so unbearably sad she finally spoke out against the idea. "I wish y'all wouldn't open a business here. Can't you see we don't belong? Let these people be."

A stern expression, reminiscent of the Atlanta Edwin, washed over her dad's face, and her mother gave a disgusted sigh. "Elise, it isn't like you to interfere in our business. We belong here as much as they do. Maybe more. We can afford to be here. It's not like we're tearing down a home to put up a parking garage. It's more like a blood transfusion. These people should get down on their knees and thank the ones who are putting their money into fixing this place up."

Elise realized she was treading on dangerous ground, but she couldn't help sensing how the people felt and had developed a kinship with them she didn't have with her own family. Progress made the locals feel they didn't belong any more. She knew what it was like not to belong, but it was worse for them. She'd never belonged. They had, and they missed it.

Elise cleared her throat and tried once more. "But I hear them talking. It's like the Civil War all over again, neighbor pitted against neighbor. One person wants to keep things like they've always been and another doesn't."

"So now you're listening in on people's conversations! I've never known you to be so interested in the concerns of strangers."

"If we're going to live here, Mom, they won't always be strangers."

"Perhaps not. I surely don't want to offend a potential customer. But keep your distance. These people are nothing to you. Nothing."

But they did mean something to Elise, and her heart went out to them. All her life she'd felt like she was on the outside looking in. Many times now she really was on the outside looking in. There was a home several blocks from the Fosters that had a large screened porch on one end. Elise liked to slip out of the house at night and stare at the porch, lit by floor lamps and cooled by two large ceiling fans. Even in Atlanta she'd loved walking their neighborhood after dark, trying to see inside the pale yellow spaces lit from within. Rooms and people in them seemed transformed, softened and surreal. The few times she'd looked inside her own home, she strained to see herself transformed, softened by the yellow glow of lamplight. She couldn't control the urge, could never quit searching for a glimpse of herself.

The illumination of the screened porch, so much more than a window, was a gift Elise had never expected. She'd seen young people playing Monopoly and thrilled to their jokes and laughter. It was better than a movie. This was real, more real than her own life, which seemed possessed by dreams that somehow blended into her waking hours. Faintly, clear as though etched on glass, she could hear people talking, but that didn't seem as unusual as the familiarity of what they said.

Miss Annelise, Ruby knows you sneak out at night dressed like a boy. You best watch yourself, missy.

Don't you talk to me like that, Ruby. You're just imagining things.
Humph!

The conversation faded, and the voices came from the porch.

"Oh, no, she has Park Place now."

"She always goes for Park Place."

"I'm a railroad man myself." More laughter.

"I don't know why I like Park Place so much."

"I don't either. You never win."

Elise laughed with them. It was the small Italian girl called Jill who always wanted Park Place.

"Well, there's more to life than winning," Jill countered.

"Why didn't you tell your old man that before he sold your house to that big developer?"

Jill stood up, and her paper money fluttered to the floor. "I can't help what my dad did. Everybody hates me now, and I didn't have a thing to do with it."

"Aw, sit down, Jill. It's just a game."

"Not any more it isn't! I'm going home."

The screen door slammed, and Elise stepped farther back into the shadows, glad she'd worn pants that protected her legs from briars growing on the vacant lot.

Someone yelled from the porch, "Maybe you can afford Park Place for real now, Jill. Think about that."

She turned with one parting shot. "Maybe you can get on the train and leave town too!"

"John, that wasn't nice. Jill's right. It wasn't her fault."

"Well, my dad wanted to buy that property. Why wasn't his money good enough? No, he sells to a total stranger."

"The stranger's money wasn't any better. Maybe there was just more of it."

"Maybe so, but my dad sure was upset."

It wasn't long before Elise picked up on the scheduled activities hosted on the porch. Monopoly night was fun, but Tuesday night was her favorite when four women of varying ages gathered to play bridge. She moved closer to the porch, shielded from sight by a giant camellia bush and watched as they tapped cards on the table. Slippery sounds echoed from the hands they dealt for bridge.

The woman called Frances reminded Elise a bit of a high-class hooker. She wore a smart pants suit, and her red hair was expertly dyed and coiffed. She was the only woman at the table wearing spike heels and smoking. She blew smoke up over her head and ground her cigarette out in a beanbag ashtray she kept on the floor. "I still can't believe Sarah sold her house to those new people from Atlanta. That house gave her dignity she never deserved, but she always acted like it was her birthright, some special dispensation that had been passed down to her. That's why she always acted like she was a cut above the rest of us. It was that house."

Pulled by the conversation from the porch, Elise had difficulty turning away, but the voices in her own head, growing more familiar each day, came unbidden and gave her pause.

Seth! You've drawn plans for a house?

I've drawn plans for lots of houses, but this one is special, Annelise. You gave me the idea with your talk about your dad's love for boats, and paddle wheelers reminding you of women in long, flouncy dresses. You could make me famous, you know.

You're already famous with me.

She knew the women had to be talking about her house, its previous owner having been someone named Sarah, and there seemed to be some kind of argument about it.

"Now, Frances, don't be catty. Life wasn't always kind to Sarah, and anyway, you know there are other beautiful houses here, albeit some of the nicer ones are run down now."

"Don't you 'Now, Frances,' me, Sue. You always want to play the peacemaker, but you know it's true. Somehow I think just growing up in that house made Sarah like she is, made her think she was too good for Peyton too."

"Well, its history had to have an impact. But for what happened, her family might never have had that house in the first place." This from the woman they called Dallas.

"Impact, my arse."

Dallas laid her cards on the table. "Frances, don't be crude. It isn't becoming, any more than your smoking is. Smoking doesn't make you sophisticated any more these days."

"Do I care?"

Sue, tall and plain with short-cropped blond hair, held her cards against her bosom and drawled, "Of course you do. But you can't let go of that image or that silver cigarette case. And you've never cursed, Frances. Why should you start now?"

"Never?" Frances countered.

Sue smiled. "Well, hardly ever."

"Good lord," Dallas interrupted, "you two have never gotten over that high school production of *The H. M. S. Pinafore,* have you?"

"Is there a need to get over it, Dallas? That play was a high point for lots of us. But anyway, people can change, you know. Maybe I want to be someone else, someone who curses on a regular basis. Everything else is changing, why shouldn't I?"

Louise, owner of the porch, interrupted. "Okay, ladies, who wants their iced tea freshened?"

"Iced sugar, you mean," Frances muttered quietly.

"I heard that, Frances," Louise said, shaking her head. "I

don't know how Bob has put up with your barbs all these years."

"Bob has no complaints. He always said he wouldn't give *that*," she said, snapping her fingers, "for a girl without a little vinegar."

"He must be a mighty happy man then," Dallas drawled.

"Well, don't you know he is?" Frances smirked.

"This tea pitcher is getting heavy, Frances. Tea or not? I've never heard you complain about my tea before."

"You know I like your tea, Louise, but I hear all these Yankees complaining when they're served sweet tea in a restaurant. Anyway, I need to watch my weight."

"I don't know what's happening to us." Louise let out a deep sigh. "We can't play a decent game of bridge without being at each other's throats. Maybe you don't want to play bridge any more. Want to give Tuesday evenings over to something else?"

Dallas replied in her throaty, cigarette voice. "I vote to keep the bridge club going. I'm a tad older than the rest of you. It keeps my mind active and gives me some place to go at least once a week. It isn't easy being a widow, ladies."

"Frances?" Louise queried.

"Count me in, but I can't promise not to curse."

Louise laughed. "We're not asking for miracles, only a little consideration. And I don't guess I need to poll Sue. She was born with a deck of cards in her hand."

Sue stretched her arms over her head. "A long line of gamblers, I guess."

Frances leapt to the bait. "Too bad you weren't born in a riverboat house."

"Okay," Louise said, "we're playing cards and that's all. No more talk of real estate or I'll bring out the Monopoly board."

You're letting Papa have your house plans? Our house plans, Seth?

I need the money, darling, and I've never seen anyone so taken with a house. He said it was as though I'd read his mind.

But it's our house. I can't believe you're . . .

Please don't cry. Please. Annelise, if I tell you something, will you promise never to tell?

Never?

Never.

I promise.

Your daddy is having the house built for you. It's to be a surprise, a wedding gift when you get married.

Married?

You're sixteen. He figures it won't be long before, before . . .

I fall in love? I've already done that.

My hope is that it'll be our house some day. In a way it's already ours, our idea. No matter what, it'll always belong to us.

Oh, Seth!

Your daddy loved the stable I built, and now these plans even more. Maybe I'll earn his respect and can ask for your hand.

I'm already yours. Not just my hand, all of me, my very spirit. Always.

Sue's voice cut through the night air, and Elise blinked hard and shook her head.

"We can talk about neutral people, can't we, Louise?" Sue placed her cards face down on the table. "I keep wondering if Sarah or Doris or anyone told the new people about the history of the house they bought."

"I doubt Sarah would take the time, and Doris sure wouldn't. Ever know a real estate woman to give a bit of information she didn't have to, and why should they? It's not like a murder was committed there or anything."

Frances coughed. "We don't know that. Remember after the

house had been shut up all those years, and when it was finally sold, the workers sent in to clean and repair things found human bones."

"I'd nearly forgotten that," Louise said.

Sue slapped her hand on the table. "Only you could forget something like that, Louise. There was a hidden stairway, or would have been hidden, had the door not been slightly ajar. That's where they found them."

"It still wasn't murder," Louise insisted. "They figured some vagrant wandered in there and suffocated hiding in that small space."

"I never bought that for one minute."

"Oh, you wouldn't, Dallas."

"I wasn't the only one, Sue."

"Well, nobody wanted a scandal, and it was all history by then anyway."

"It had been deeded over to Coulton and Annelise. They never found Coulton. Poor man must have been crazy with grief to just walk off and leave, furniture and everything. The house finally went back to Mr. Lovett. Not that it did him any good. He couldn't bear the memory or the heartache, never set foot in the door after Annelise died. That house has had a life all its own." Dallas sighed. "If that isn't a tragedy, I don't know what is."

Frances smirked. "You're right, Dallas. Don't you suppose the new people have wondered why they couldn't hire anyone to help clean the place up? The poor, ignorant servant women are scared of that house. Don't think Sarah didn't have her hands full keeping help there and her mother before her, probably the grandparents too. They labored under a curse living there."

Dallas folded her cards. "Stop it, Frances. Such ridiculous rumors have grown up about the place. I feel sorry for the new people, I really do. But maybe they can change things. All the problems and unhappiness Sarah had there didn't do a thing to improve its image. Poor Sarah. Sometimes I think the only reason Chandler married her was to get her house. He'd always had this idea he wanted to be an architect. He doted on it as an architectural marvel."

"Why, Dallas, I'm surprised at you."

"Surprised how?"

Frances smiled. "Well, now, this is all water under the bridge, but since you think I have my mind set on high school, I'm reminded that a little bird told me you were kind of sweet on Chandler yourself at one time. Are you saying Sarah had the advantage over you by owning that house?"

Dallas sat up straighter. "Wipe that smile off your face, Frances. It doesn't change what you said one bit."

Sue turned her cards face down on the table, hard. "Leave it to you, Frances, to bring up ancient history."

"Well, if that doesn't beat all," Dallas said with obvious disgust. "I may not be a girl any more, Sue, but I surely don't consider myself ancient by any means. And Frances, yes, since you brought it up, at one time I was sweet on Chandler. Oh, ladies, are you so old that you've forgotten how easy it is to love a scoundrel? Oh my God, but it's easy to love a scoundrel. And Chandler was the classic scoundrel, so handsome and dashing, so full of himself. How could I, or anyone else for that matter, ever forget that dark hair and quick smile? When that boy smiled the whole world stopped spinning. And the way he walked like he had springs in his feet. Oh, he was a scoundrel all right."

"If I didn't know better, Dallas, I'd say you never got over him."

"Oh, I got over him all right, Frances. It's easy to love a scoundrel. It's just not easy to be married to one. Sarah could have told you that. He drank her money and womanized her into ill health. We all know he did. My Tom was worth ten Chandlers. No, a hundred Chandlers."

"Peyton Roberts was worth more than Chandler too," Louise added.

"Well, of course he was. He just never had the dash and dander Chandler had, and Sarah couldn't see beyond that no matter how much Peyton loved her. Furthermore, Peyton made the mistake of trying to ride on the coattails of all his illustrious ancestors. No, I would never have traded my life for Sarah's, not even for that grand riverboat house."

"Or a romp in the hay with Chandler?"

Louise gasped. "Frances! Honestly, I can't believe we're having this discussion."

Dallas raised her lovely arched eyebrows. "How do you know I didn't?"

"Dallas!"

"I didn't say I did, but then, I didn't say I didn't."

Rolling in soft and quiet as fog, Frances began singing, *"Things are seldom what they seem,"* and Sue followed with, *"Skim milk masquerades as cream . . ."*

Dallas interrupted, "Ladies, I've had enough *Pinafore* for one evening."

"Me too," Louise said, her voice so soft Elise had trouble hearing her. "Sometimes I feel like that house really was cursed. Built with such good intentions, it never brought anything but heartache to the people who lived there. Sarah's mother was an invalid most of her life."

Frances put the back of her hand to her forehead and sighed. "Here we go again."

Sue picked up her cards. "It could all be coincidence. If there's a curse on a house, I'd say it's the Lovett house on the river. That's where it all began."

"We'll never know if there's a curse on either house, not any more than you'll know if Chandler had his way with me. Oh, ladies, I was desirable, even without a riverboat house."

The three women stared open-mouthed at Dallas. She ignored them and studied her cards with downcast eyes.

Frances was the first to regain her composure. "Lord, y'all are giving me chills. Let's play cards or I'll start cursing again."

They laughed, and with the serenity that comes from the security of age and familiarity, they resumed their bridge game.

Only Elise was shaken by the experience. She rubbed her arms, chilled with goose flesh. *A curse? What curse?* She walked back to her beautiful home, determined to avoid the carriage stone. She stumbled over it just the same.

Careful. Don't trip. I had the carriage stone put in today.
Seth took Annelise's arm and guided her through the moonless night.

Elise stared downward, puzzled how she could have hit the carriage stone, but maybe the voices had distracted her. What did they have to do with her? Was she not afraid because they were like leftover dreams? She didn't dare talk to her mother about it. If Margaret thought her fear of mirrors was weird, Elise couldn't imagine what she'd think if she knew her daughter was hearing voices. She turned and sat on the hard surface, rubbing the toe of her scuffed shoe. It was cold as a tombstone, but she sat for some time with her chin on her hand, staring at the mysterious riverboat house.

8

*W*ithout realizing it, Margaret set in motion Elise's obsession with Apalachicola. As they looked into possibilities for Margaret's shop, Elise felt herself drawn deeper and deeper into the town's essence. She hungered for it, longed to know its history, its dreams, and disappointments. Every day she walked, retracing her steps, trying to be one with something she couldn't fully comprehend. She threw her shoulders back, quickened her pace, and sensed somehow she was meant to be there.

Meanwhile, the disturbing dreams were becoming more distinct and troubling, men shouting obscenities . . .

How did you get in here?
It was easy. I built this house, remember.
You bastard. I'll see you in hell.
Go ahead. Kill me. You've had practice.
Ahhhh!

Elise's scream was only a whisper, but enough to wake her. The dream didn't vary and was no less frightening than the night before. Many mornings her parents found her already in the kitchen with a cup of coffee clutched between her palms to still her trembling hands and fight the chill that clung to her.

"I can never get over your sudden taste for coffee." Margaret looked at Elise and shook her head.

"Neither can I, but some mornings it's the reason I get out of bed," she replied dully.

"You come by it honest, Elise. Gene loved his coffee." Edwin spoke defiantly, as though daring Margaret to say anything.

Elise froze, the cup midway to her lips. Why lately did Edwin persist in mentioning her father? For years his name wasn't uttered. Seeing her mother's stunned look, Elise jumped up and put her cup in the dishwasher. "Well, I'm off on my explorations."

"You're in the sun so much," her mother replied weakly, "The sun can do terrible things to your skin. Protect yourself."

"I will. I promise."

Elise was hardly out of the room when she heard her mother say, "Edwin, I don't know what's gotten into you lately. I know you've had problems, but . . ."

Elise didn't hear the rest as she continued upstairs to her room. She didn't want to hear more, afraid of what she might learn. Lost in thought and dream-groggy, she wandered into her parents' room by mistake. The antique cheval, left by the previous owner, faced Elise from the corner of the room. She started to turn away, but not quickly enough to stop the blinding flash, this time accompanied by voices, distant and muffled but definitely angry.

Seth! What are you doing here?

I might ask you the same thing.

This is my father's stable. You only built it.

Yes, but at this late hour I thought all debutantes were in bed.

I repeat. What are you doing here? The stable is finished.

There were a few finishing touches I wanted to make here in the office. Mr. Lovett was so taken with the idea of an office in his stable, I want it to be perfect.

We thought it was perfect—finished, in fact.

Yes, but the frame for your picture isn't. I don't start things I don't finish. He laid his knife down and put a drape over the wood laid out on the workbench.

I won't look. Do you know I've never seen the painting? It's still in that hidden closet you built.

Think I did that bad a job, huh?

No! I mean, that isn't it at all. It'd be painful for me after all the hours we spent together while you worked on it.

I figured Coulton made you forget all that.

We've been over all this. Papa won't allow me to see you. Coulton comes to the house a lot, on business mostly.

Mostly?

Some. Look. He's nice to me. He doesn't yell at me and say hateful things.

Just remember who caused me to say those things. Think why I said them. Think for once how I hurt. I hadn't figured on Coulton coming into the picture again.

Again?

I knew him once.

You never mentioned it.

It isn't altogether a pleasant memory.

Was a girl involved?

You might say that.

I see.

No, you don't see at all, and I don't want to tell you about it—not now anyway.

Fine. Have it your way. I just came to get my dress.

Dress?

My mother's wedding dress. The one I wore for the painting. I left it hanging in the closet along with the painting. If you'll excuse me, I'll take it and be out of your way.

I'll be finished with the house, soon now.

Good for you. I'm sure you're eager to be rid of the Lovetts.

Oh, God, Annelise. How can you be so cold? Don't you know how I feel about you?

Tears rolled down her face.

And I you, Seth, and I you, she said as she walked to his embrace and he buried his face in her hair.

What are we going to do?

I don't know. I just don't know.

Elise staggered to her room and collapsed on the side of the bed. She closed her eyes and lay there while she regained her composure. Taking a deep breath, she stood and hurriedly pulled on her shorts and sneakers, noticing how tan her legs had become. She tied a blue shirt in a knot under her bust and jerked the elastic from her ponytail, fluffing her thick blond hair with her fingers. As she hurried down the stairs, she called to her parents but was out the door before they could say anything.

Elise had never been the new girl in town before. She wouldn't have imagined that as she watched the town's residents, they were observing her as well.

From behind the counter, Peyton saw Elise coming down the sidewalk. "Walkingest girl I ever saw. Let me tell you, she's wearing out some shoe leather."

"You'll have to sell her mother your store so she can afford to keep her in shoes, Peyton." Bobby rather enjoyed the standoff between Peyton and Margaret and never lost an opportunity to remind Peyton of the business transaction Margaret had proposed.

"I'd rather sell it to the girl. Get her off her feet awhile," he said with a laugh.

"Well, she seems nice enough," Bobby said. "She don't

bother nobody. Maybe I'm crazy, but it's almost like she belongs here. She don't seem to be a newcomer like the rest."

"No, she doesn't, does she? Nothing like her mother coming in here like she owned me. I wouldn't mind selling out so much if it wasn't to the likes of her."

"Did you ever meet the husband, Peyton? I wonder what he's like."

"Oh, he came in with her once. It was your day off. Big guy. Not the kind you'd care to cross. Didn't say anything. Just stood with his hands in his pockets looking around. He was casing the joint. Didn't fool me. Not a bit. I wasn't born yesterday."

"Look out, Peyton, here comes the daughter in the door. You make her a deal now. Offer to sell her the store."

Elise didn't need to buy anything, but she wanted to establish herself with the townspeople apart from her parents. She knew she was changing. It was almost physical. She was coming into her own, and she wanted to be a part of this town.

Peyton pretended to tip a hat when she walked in. She smiled broadly and saluted. Life was good! She looked around at the assorted merchandise—the purses, the racks of earrings and pins, a turnstile of sunglasses. Her mother would have called it a boutique. She felt sure that for Peyton it would never be more than a shoe store. Elise decided to buy a pair of sunglasses. She chose the most expensive pair she could find and took them to the register. "Sure that's the pair you want, miss?"

"Yes, sir, I'm sure." She tilted her head to one side and looked up coyly. "And that's all I want. Not the entire store."

Peyton laughed. "Thanks for telling me." He wiped his forehead with his forefinger. "That's a relief."

"Mr. Roberts, I'm sorry if my mother offended you. That's just her way."

"Call me Peyton, darling. And don't you let anything that

passes between your mother and me worry your pretty little head. I got a tough hide, and I imagine your mother does too. Used to having her way, is she?"

Elise nodded, her long hair obscuring her face for a moment. "I know there are people here who resent the newcomers like my family, but I wouldn't trade living here for anything. I hope I'll come to be accepted."

"You're already accepted, darling. We could use a dozen more just like you."

"I so enjoy exploring the town. It's different, more real than anything I've known before. It's more than glass and steel and highways."

"See, I told you we could use a dozen more just like you. You see what the natives see and love. You'll come to love it too."

"Oh, I do already."

"Then we can count ourselves lucky every day that you grace us with your presence." Peyton didn't smile and with all solemnity gave a deep bow.

Without meaning to, Elise found herself making a quick curtsy before she started toward the door.

Look at that baby. Annelise be only six years old and she curtsy as good as her mama.

Elise stopped and cocked her head to one side, listening.

"You okay, darlin'?" Peyton asked.

"Yes, thank you. Just getting my bearings."

"Well, you come back soon now, you hear? Bobby and I would love to have you visit anytime, wouldn't we, Bobby?"

Bobby looked at Peyton slack-mouthed but cleared his throat and said, "We surely would, Miss . . .?"

"Elise."

"Elise?" Peyton said thoughtfully. "A beautiful name."

"Thanks. I like it too. Well, I'll be on my way and not take any more of your time."

"I wasn't joking, Elise. You come back now, you hear?"

"I will. I promise." She stared at him a long moment. *Does he know about the curse on our house?*

Peyton cleared his throat. "Something more I can do for you?"

"No, sir, I was just remembering something." She waved and left the store.

"Well, that beats anything."

"What, Peyton?"

"I've sold a lot of sunglasses in my day, but that's the first time I ever had a woman buy a pair without even looking at herself in the mirror."

"Maybe she's the kind that thinks she looks good in anything."

"I don't think so. Don't think that at all. Just plain odd. But she seems nice enough. I'll give her that. She's a looker too, in her own way."

Elise found a kind of contentment through walking. She lost her pallor and grew softly tanned. And she learned that people wanted to talk to her. It was difficult at first. People in her neighborhood in Atlanta weren't inclined to idle chit-chat. She was learning, though. She remembered to wave and was comfortable speaking to strangers. They seemed to expect it, and gradually she did too.

Only Nadine Fletcher insisted she stop and visit awhile. Rain or shine, they sat on her porch. Today, she found Miss Nadine settled in her old padded rocker. The porch floor was a shiny gray that showcased multiple pieces of antique wicker.

Nadine didn't go in much for flowers but had an assortment of ferns.

"I taught school too many years," she told Elise, "to have time to fool with flowers the way some people do." She gestured toward her neighbor's garden. "I dealt with inquiring minds every day. I couldn't be bothered with black spot and aphids and that nonsense."

With the passing days, Nadine demanded more and more of Elise's time. She assumed the role of teacher and treated Elise as if she were the pupil, never allowing her to leave without some parting bit of information. She took to calling her "Miss Gone with the Wind."

"Well, Miss Gone with the Wind, I guess you think Atlanta has the corner on history."

"You have to admit, Miss Nadine, it has its fair share. *Gone with the Wind* lingers like a promise on Atlanta's tongue."

"Huh?"

Elise shrugged. "I see things differently than other people."

"Well, be that as it may, don't ever sell Apalach short. But for Apalach's own John Gorrie you wouldn't be living in the comfort of an air-conditioned house. Bet you didn't know that, did you?"

"Yes, ma'am. I've been to the Gorrie Museum. But, Miss Nadine, I'm wondering if we have something more than air conditioning in our house. Have you ever heard anything about a curse?"

"Curse?"

"Yes, ma'am, a curse on our house."

"Where'd you hear that nonsense? I don't know what you did in Atlanta, but we don't practice witchcraft in Apalachicola."

Elise shifted in her chair. The heat was building on the porch, and Nadine's voice droned on like a mosquito buzzing in her ear. Elise nodded, aware of the changes she was making in her own life—one step at a time—as she explored Apalachicola. Unlike the street that ran past Miss Nadine's house, some of the roads were still unpaved and dusted her shoes with a silky gray powder.

She saw homes that had been abandoned and others that should have been. Ragged curtains blew from unscreened windows. Broken lawnmowers and outboard motors littered rotting porches. Bit by bit, heat and humidity, Florida's indigenous vultures, were eating the very hearts of the neglected shrines. Only half listening, she heard Miss Nadine say, "That big three-story house on the bluff overlooking the river is haunted, not cursed, mind you. Haunted."

"Haunted?" Elise stiffened and pressed her fingers to her lips.

Nadine laughed. "Don't you think every town should have a haunted house? Gives it a little character, makes a good thickening for the soup, I always say."

Elise looked at Miss Nadine's steel gray hair and square, yellowed teeth. *You add your own bit of thickening, Miss Nadine.*

"You must have noticed it. I haven't been down there in years, but I wager it's still an attention getter. My daddy used to say it was a real showpiece in its day. Even had a ballroom on the second floor. That's where the tragedy occurred."

"Tragedy?"

It was some minutes before Miss Nadine answered, and Elise was afraid she'd just stopped talking. She did that at times.

"Oh, yes, it was a tragedy all right. Some people invite tragedy, you know. Annelise Lovett drew it like a magnet. Story goes her first love was a murderer. He'd been accepted by the whole town until he was found out. Talented young man they say. Could draw and build like a master. Fled before the mob got him. She got over him though. She was young enough to forget and wed the man of her dreams.

"There was a fancy reception and dancing in the ballroom. She was so happy, so beautiful, dancing the night away when her long hair caught in the flame of one of the wall sconces." Miss Nadine threw her arms high over her head, and Elise looked up, imagining the bride's hair reaching out to the flame.

"The last dance of the evening and quicker'n she'd fallen in love, flames engulfed her, and she ran down the winding stairway heading for the river, for water. Her new husband finally caught her and smothered the flames, but he was too late. Drew tragedy like a magnet. Daddy said she lived less than twenty-four hours, and her husband never left her side, just sat there, telling her he'd love her for all eternity. Eternity."

"How sad." Elise felt a catch, nearly a sob, in her throat.

"I'll say it was sad. Her family never recovered. Never. How could they?"

"Is she buried here?"

"Of course she is. This was her home. There's an old cemetery some place. On the outskirts of town my daddy always said. They were looking for high ground, you know. Cemeteries need high ground. Even though I never laid eyes on her, I grieve for her anyway. So sad. Sad."

Get away from my wife! How'd you get back here?

I'm smothering the flames, you idiot.

Coulton gave Seth a vicious push with his shoe and threw his own body on top of Annelise. When Mr. Lovett reached his stricken daughter, only Coulton was there.

Nadine shook her head. "Eternity's a mighty long time. I've heard tell there's still an odor of ashes, drafts of cold air, even screams." Glad now to have Elise's rapt attention, she added another tidbit. "The sound of her feet running down the stairs. Course, I never heard anything personally, but I do know that during the war . . ."

"War?"

"Why, World War II. You don't think I meant the Civil War, do you? Back then we had blackouts. You know, practice in case of a real air raid. Jenny and Lacey . . ."

"Jenny and Lacey?"

"The sisters who live there, Annelise's nieces, eccentric and suspicious as the day's long. Anyway, they were always being cited by the air raid warden for having a light in the upstairs window. Oh, they were very indignant, insisting there wasn't a light on in the house except where they had blackout shades. It got to be such an issue they started turning all the lights off and sitting in the dark until the practice was over. One night the warden saw a light and went inside to check. Sure enough, the place was dark as a cave, but maybe they turned the light off when they heard him coming. Who's to say?"

Mesmerized by the story, Elise left Nadine's in a daze. She walked past the three-story house on the bluff and stared at it a long time, wishing there were some way she could go inside. But unlike Miss Nadine's friendly invitations, she feared none would be forthcoming from the sisters.

Disturbed by the conversation with Miss Nadine, her pace slowed but followed a direct line to the shoe store.

"Well look-a-here, Bobby. Twice in one day. Bet you didn't like those glasses after all, did you?"

"Oh, no, they're fine. It's just. I . . ." She watched Peyton stare at her with a puzzled look on his face. She let out a heavy sigh and blushed. "The house down on the river. Is it really haunted?"

"That's what I've been told. I can't prove it, but then I can't disprove it either."

"Kinda like believing in God?"

"Yeah, I'd say so, just about like it, darlin'."

"I'd like to think it's haunted."

"Why's that?"

"I don't know. It'd be exciting, romantic, completely unexplainable."

"It'd be all those things and more. Sort of a second chance for somebody."

"Oh, that's it exactly." Elise looked around and wondered if she should buy something else.

Peyton smiled, sensing her unease. "I'm an old timer here. Anytime you want to know something, just ask. If I know it, I'll tell you. No secrets."

"Thanks. Don't be surprised if I'm back with more questions."

"I'll be waitin'."

Elise's imagination was fueled by the thought of a haunted house. She couldn't quit thinking about it. It hadn't taken any convincing on Miss Nadine's part for her to believe it added to Apalach's charm, but her parents didn't share her view.

Edwin bristled. "You're being ridiculous, Elise, listening to the morbid tales backward people tell. They're trying to scare you. It's a game to them. Don't give them the satisfaction."

"But, Dad, I can feel it. I really believe that house is haunted. I've even heard our . . ."

"The only haunting," her mother interrupted, "comes from those sick old women who live there. Why in the world would you want to believe in ghosts?"

"Why would you want to believe in God?"

"Don't be ridiculous. That's no comparison."

"Why not? They're both belief systems. I've never seen a ghost. You've never seen God."

"I can't believe that you're thinking, much less saying these things."

Elise's words seemed to hang in the air, truth swirling in dust motes of irreverence.

"Ghosts are imaginary," Margaret said in a disgusted tone, "the stuff of fairy tales. God touches our lives, influences our behavior."

"If you believe . . ."

"Just stop it!" Margaret interrupted. "I don't intend to listen to any more of this nonsense. It's creepy. You need to be in college, that's what."

At the mention of college, Elise started backtracking. "I'm sorry. I don't know why I brought it up. It just occurred to me."

"Well, don't let it occur to you again."

"Your mother is right, Elise. Don't talk like that. People don't know you here. They'll think you're strange."

"I'll try to be more careful."

Edwin smiled, pleased that for once she was actually going to take his advice.

9

*E*lise widened her explorations, walking farther and farther past the outskirts of town, looking for a hill, for high ground, for a cemetery. That's how she came upon the house.

Afterward she would remember that despite the warmth of a sunny day, she'd felt a chill and hugged her arms about her the first time she saw it at the end of the long, dusty road. There was a service station and a fruit stand and then nothing until she came upon the rambling two-story dwelling. It was on the outermost part of town, the road curving and climbing upward to the only home for miles around. There was an eerie silence, as though it was out of space and time, a black and white picture in a Technicolor world. It was a plain, serviceable house in need of a coat of paint. She'd seen other houses more ornate and beautiful, some more rundown; but this place spoke to her. It called to her as surely as if it had a voice.

She'd never approached any of the houses without having been invited, but without the slightest hesitation, she opened the gate and started up the steps. And then she saw him sitting in the porch swing and knew it wasn't the house that had called to her at all. Her mother would think she was imagining things, but the moment she saw him, she felt her heart contract, and something inside her began to live, something no longer concerned with a cemetery.

He was a tall, slender man, with a look at once quizzical and amused. As so often happened lately, he seemed somehow instantly familiar. She noted the pale blue of his chambray shirt, the navy pants, and that his pale brown, nearly blond hair was thick and needed cutting, one lock hanging over his forehead. The hair was a perfect complement to his smooth, olive complexion. Embarrassed for staring, she stopped short halfway up the steps and realized he stared as intently at her, his eyes an incredible green, reminiscent of emerald roundels.

An older woman appeared at the screen door, wiping her hands on an apron.

"Hello, dear, can I help you?"

Elise was struck by the kind, gentle voice that conveyed concern, so genuinely interested in helping her. She was a small woman but plump. Everything about her was rounded and soft as a biscuit. Elise didn't know how to answer. She didn't know what she wanted. The only thing she knew at that moment was that she didn't want to leave. The woman smiled. "Don't be afraid. He won't hurt you."

Won't hurt me? What a strange thing to say. She didn't want to stop looking at him ever but forced herself to turn toward the woman, all soft and faded, who had by now walked onto the porch.

"Are you lost, honey? We don't often see people walking this far out."

"No, ma'am. I'm not lost. We're new here, and I like to explore the town. I was looking for an old cemetery."

"There's no cemetery up here, honey. I thought for a minute you might be a social worker or something. Child, you're white as a sheet. Have a seat and I'll get you a glass of tea."

Elise's knees were about to buckle as she staggered toward the swing and its handsome occupant. She dropped beside him but still he didn't say anything. The nearness of him was a joy and a torment. It was as though she'd waited all her life for this moment. She took a deep breath. *Pheromones.* She hadn't thought of pheromones since that day with Ronnie. She was sure she could feel all the molecules in her body shift. She had a nearly uncontrollable urge to place her hand on his thigh. Almost as though he knew what she was thinking, he moved away from her toward the far end of the swing.

The woman returned with the tea and introduced herself as Mrs. Myers. "And your partner there, that's my only boy. My only child. Aren't you, sweetheart?"

Elise felt another chill that had nothing to do with the glass of iced tea she held. She turned and looked directly at him, hoping he'd speak. She stared into his eyes and smiled, assuming an amused expression herself. "Does he have a name?"

She waited for him to say something, but he didn't move or acknowledge that she'd spoken.

Mrs. Myers laughed. "Course he does. We don't often have company, and I forget. His name is Lawrence. When he was born I told his daddy I never wanted anybody calling him Larry or anything but Lawrence."

"Lawrence, really? That's always been a favorite name of mine too!" She felt him pull even farther away.

"I'm Elise, Elise Foster." She offered him her hand, but he ignored her.

Mrs. Myers turned a rocker to face the swing and sat down. "There was a problem years ago, and he doesn't talk anymore."

"Not at all?"

"I'm afraid not. Not even to me. My husband is dead, and it's just the two of us. He's good company despite it. I talk to him even if he don't talk back. Does what I ask him to, and I'm never afraid with him here."

Elise stared at the floor, embarrassed, but unable not to ask, "But he did talk? Before the problem?"

Drops of tea splashed on Elise's shorts as Lawrence snatched the glass from her hand and took two large gulps. He shoved the glass back in her hand and bounded down the porch steps and out of sight around the side yard.

"I'm sorry, honey. He's got a lot of anger in him."

"No, ma'am, I'm sorry. We sit here talking about him as though he can't hear us." Elise turned the glass in her hand, slowly gliding the tip of her tongue over the place where his lips had been.

Mrs. Myers twisted her apron nervously and several times seemed on the verge of saying something. Finally, "He talked until the accident. He was in the boat with his daddy—a floating log . . ." Her voice trailed off, and she wiped her eyes with the corner of her apron.

Worried that she was making Mrs. Myers uncomfortable, Elise said, "I really must be starting back. I think I've come a lot farther than I realized." As she started toward the steps, she saw the cat.

"Why, Mrs. Myers, I saw that cat at the inn where we stayed when we moved here."

"Not that cat, honey. It's never far from Lawrence."

"Oh, but I'm sure. It's an orange tabby just like the one I saw. It even has the same white star on its forehead."

"That's a wonder all right, but this cat never leaves the yard. I'd know if she wasn't here."

Elise continued down the steps, gripping the banister to steady her shaking legs. She looked toward the side yard where Lawrence had disappeared. "Mrs. Myers, may I come back and visit? I don't know many people." *Please say yes. Please say I can come back. How can I stay away?*

Mrs. Myers looked puzzled but smiled kindly. "Why, child, I'd love to have you. We seldom have visitors. You're welcome any time, any time at all."

So strong was the pull, it took a physical effort to move away from the house, but she turned and waved to Mrs. Myers. And there was Lawrence standing at the corner of the yard, the cat at his feet. Lawrence picked the cat up and stroked its fur, staring at Elise. He didn't wave or smile.

Elise walked home in a daze and went directly to her room. She clung to the new emotions that gripped her and could think of nothing but Lawrence Myers and her need to see him again. She spent a restless night and woke the next morning under a layer of frost that chilled the very marrow of her bones. So sure it was frost, she touched her arms and face for proof that wasn't there. She put on a heavy robe and went to the kitchen where she sat huddled at the table. *How long should I wait before going there again?*

Her parents came in from the sunroom and found her staring at the mug of coffee she clutched with both hands.

"Elise, are you ill?"

"No, ma'am, I don't think so."

"Then why are you wearing that heavy robe in the dead of summer?"

"I'm cold."

"Apparently." Margaret went over and felt her forehead. "You don't seem to have a fever."

"I thought perhaps the thermostat was broken."

"No, the temperature seems fine to me. Doesn't it to you, Edwin?"

Edwin was getting a cup of coffee and didn't turn around when he snapped, "Of course it's fine. It damn well better be after what we paid for that heat pump."

Sweat beaded on Elise's brow, and she threw off the robe. "I'm warm now."

The spoon clanged against Edwin's cup as he turned to Elise and said, "We're always grateful for small favors."

What's gotten into him now? I've tried so hard to be the kind of daughter they want. Elise closed her eyes and the drone of her parents' voices made her drowsy. Her reverie was broken when she heard her mother say, "Dallas."

"She's a genteel woman, Edwin, and that's nothing to take lightly considering she's lived here all her life. She's widowed and has agreed to lease some space to me. Thank God I won't have to deal with that awful Peyton Roberts any more. Dallas's husband ran the only hardware store in town, and since he died a little over a year ago, the building's been empty. The inventory is gone, so we can just gut the place and be in business. Frankly, I think Dallas will sell eventually. Right now it's like hanging onto her husband. She even offered to work in the store if we ever need extra help."

"If the business does as well as you think, we'll need her for sure."

"Elise, you look a million miles away. Have you heard a word we've said?"

"Sure. Yes, ma'am. I was just thinking about how busy y'all are going to be."

"Want to come help us out?" Margaret laughed. "Well, don't go pale and faint on me. I was joking. No offense, but you're such a dreamer, you'd just get in the way. Anyway, I'm thankful to be busy. Your father and I need this. It's a good thing you enjoy exercise. You could go stir-crazy once you're settled in a town this small. I know you're being friendly to the people here, Elise. People have mentioned you and tell me what a polite girl you are. I appreciate that. It'll be good for business."

Resentment rose like bile. "That isn't why I talk to them."

"Of course it isn't, but it helps nonetheless."

After her parents left the house, Elise walked to town. She saw their Jaguar parked in front of one of the vacant stores and to avoid being seen, turned down the street that ran along the river before doubling back to Peyton Roberts' shoe store.

"Well, for goodness sake, look who's here."

"Hello, Mr. Roberts."

"Don't be like your mother, hon, call me Peyton. You need more sunglasses or you want Bobby to fix you up with some new shoes?"

"Actually neither. I have another question. You've lived here a long time . . ."

"All my life."

"I want to ask you about someone, a man named Lawrence Myers."

Peyton whistled. "You covered some territory if you got out to the Myers' place. You must have thought you'd reached the end of the earth. I haven't driven by there in years."

"I didn't realize I'd walked so far. It was a long way, but it's pretty, the house sitting so lonely on top of that hill."

"I'm surprised that old house is still standing. That was one sad story."

"The boat hitting a floating log?"

"Yeah. That should never have happened. Hindsight has twenty-twenty vision. But how'd . . ." He stopped and looked toward the door.

Elise turned to see Margaret.

"I didn't see you come this way, Elise."

"I wasn't coming here," Elise stammered nervously. "I was down by the river but then decided to look at some shoes. Mine are getting worn."

"I do believe, Elise, that shoes are in the back of the store."

Bobby appeared from nowhere. "I already tried several pairs on her, ma'am. She decided to wait until our next shipment comes in."

"I see." Margaret looked at Peyton accusingly.

Peyton's eyes lingered a moment at her bust, just long enough for her to notice, and he asked, "Want Bobby to see if he can find a glass slipper to fit you," he hesitated briefly and continued, "Margaret?"

"Very funny. Actually I want some socks. I brought plenty of shoes with me from Atlanta. I hadn't realized Apalach was so modern as to be able to support a shoe store."

"My, yes. People in Apalach been wearing shoes for years now."

As Margaret turned to snatch a pair of socks out of the case, Elise made a quick exit. "I'm off now. I'll come back when that shoe order comes in." She walked hurriedly to the corner and then hesitated briefly. She wanted to turn left toward the Myers' but went in the opposite direction. Miss Nadine would talk her ear off and keep her mind off Lawrence Myers.

When she didn't see her on the porch, Elise walked up the steps and squinted to see through the screen door. She could just make out her form bent over a stack of papers. When Nadine saw Elise she ran to the door, still holding the red marking pencil. She pressed her face to the screen and appeared confused.

"Who is it?" She pushed the door open. "Oh, Miss Gone with the Wind. I thought for a minute you were one of my former pupils. I never know when one of them will drop by. All these years and they still come to see me." She tucked the red pencil into her hair and motioned to Elise to sit beside her in one of the porch rockers. "Your folks pretty well settled now?"

"Yes, ma'am. I'll feel like a native soon."

"No you won't. That takes years, years of living and loving and knowing everybody's business!"

Elise laughed.

"Don't you believe me?"

"I believe you. I absolutely do."

"Have you ever thought of being a schoolteacher?"

"No, ma'am, I don't think I have."

"If you taught school you'd get to know everybody a lot more quickly—a whole lot more quickly. The parents will tell you everything about their children and believe me, the children are only too quick to tell you everything about the parents." She laughed, throwing her head back, revealing her large, square teeth.

"You really miss it, don't you?"

"Miss what?"

"Why, teaching."

"Oh yes. I miss it. Every day of my life."

"I hope someday to find something I love that much."

"It can be a curse to love too much. A real curse." She smoothed her skirt and took the red pencil from her hair, rolling it back and forth between her palms like a piece of clay. Elise wondered if she'd forgotten she was there when Nadine looked up and said, "You think you're getting to know Apalach as well as you did Atlanta?"

"Better, I think. I feel like I belong here, as though I've always belonged here."

"Ready to trade in *Gone with the Wind*, huh?"

"Apalach feels like home."

The red pencil fell and rolled across the floor. Elise grabbed it before it rolled down the steps.

"I've been grading papers."

"Grading papers? Are you doing some substitute teaching?"

Nadine laughed. "No, I go over some of the old papers. Look to see if maybe I made mistakes. Once in a while I'll change a grade. Some of those papers are so marked up they look bloody. It's like I've waged a war on 'em. A teacher ever give you a paper back that looked like it was bleeding?"

"Maybe just a small flesh wound." Elise laughed.

"Smart, huh?"

"I don't know how smart, but I did okay."

"I never had a red mark on one of my papers. Not one. If they were bloody, it was real."

Elise wasn't sure what to say. "I'm sorry."

"No need for you to be sorry. It's water under the bridge now. My daddy was good at drawing blood."

"Oh, Miss Nadine, how awful."

"It was awful for my mother, all right. Now she was smart. Just wasn't smart enough not to marry my daddy. He was her undoing."

Elise saw tears sliding down her cheeks and leaned over and patted her hand. "Don't think about it. Don't let it upset you."

"No, I can't let it upset me, not anymore."

They sat without talking for a time before Elise cleared her throat. "Miss Nadine, you know so much of Apalach's history, I wonder if you could tell me something about the Myers family. Something about a boating accident."

"Lord, child, that was so long ago, but how could anybody forget something like that? Luther Myers." She shook her head. "Poor man wrecked his automobile and never walked again, but he was determined not to let his affliction hold him back. They had only the one boy, and Luther wanted to be everything to him a father should be, legs or no.

"When he took him out fishing that day it looked like he forgot he didn't have use of his legs. There'd been a bad storm that made them late getting away. It was near dark when the storm doubled back, and them with only one life preserver." She paused and appeared intent on smoothing her dress over her lap. "Luther had rigged up an old truck so he could operate it with his hands, a comical looking thing with no sides or anything so he could hoist his wheelchair in and out real easy. They were rushing cause they had such a late start, and one of the life preservers fell off the truck.

"It was too late to go back when he discovered it missing. Right then the boy said his father insisted he put on the one remaining." Nadine waved her hand in front of her face as though to shoo a fly or mosquito.

"Most of the men around here know that river like the back of their hands, but Luther hadn't figured on hitting a submerged log. Storm churned things up, you see. Probably had the motor wide open when he hit it. That poor youngster bobbed in the river and watched his daddy sink like a rock and nothing he could do. What a terrible thing for a child."

Nadine leaned back in her rocker and closed her eyes. Elise knew this signaled the end of the conversation. She patted her hand and started down the steps.

"Don't be a stranger," Nadine called softly.

"I won't. I'll see you soon."

Elise intended to walk past the haunted house but felt the pull on her feet, taking her to the Myers', to Lawrence. To assure her welcome, she bought some fruit for the Meyers', but her heart sank when she reached the gate and saw that he wasn't in the swing, but she'd just started up the steps when he came around the side of the house. He took one look at Elise, dropped the trowel he was holding, and began wiping his hands on the sides of his pants. His smile broadened and he took long strides toward her. Without warning he stopped in his tracks, and his face looked stricken. Elise waited, unable to move as he turned from her and, taking the steps two at a time, disappeared inside the house.

She felt something brush against her leg and looked down to see the orange tabby pushing itself against her, purring. When she tried to pet it, a pear rolled out of the basket of fruit she'd bought, and the cat ran away. "Now see what you made me do? I'm bruising the fruit."

She heard someone say, "Are you in the habit of talking to cats?" and felt his smile. Goose flesh crept up her arms as she turned to see Lawrence standing just inside the screen door. It was as though her blood chilled and slowed its course through her body. Her head rang with the sound of bells and then voices.

There you are, Flynnie! Annelise lifted the orange tabby cat and held it in front of her face. *I've been looking for you all morning.*

Do you always talk to cats?

Annelise whirled around and looked at the young man carrying a box of tools. His dark blond hair was thick and tousled, and his green eyes piercing.

What's it to you if I do?

Nothing. I just wondered.

What is your business here, sir?

Mr. Lovett hired me to build a new stable for his horses.

You must be Seth. I've heard him talking about you. Are you as talented as he says?

You be the judge of that after you see the new stable.

Elise cleared her throat. "No, I don't usually talk to cats."

"What's that, honey?" Mrs. Myers walked around Lawrence to the door.

"I, uh. Nothing. I brought you some fruit."

"You didn't! Now isn't that sweet? See what beautiful fruit, Lawrence? Come on in, honey. I was just making sandwiches for lunch. You're welcome to join us."

Lawrence stepped back into the dark shadows of the house.

"Are you sure it's okay?"

"Well, now, I wouldn't have invited you if it wasn't."

"I mean, will Lawrence care?"

"Why would he care? It'll be nice to have company for a change. It's been a long time, believe me."

They walked to a large, old-fashioned kitchen. A worn oilcloth covered the table and straight chairs with ruffled cushions on the seats completed the comfortable setting. The kitchen curtains were of the same fabric, and the room was as sunny as the living room had been dark. Mrs. Myers busied herself putting the fruit in a bowl and then turned to cut thick wedges of bread from a homemade loaf. Lawrence leaned against the doorframe, his right hip at a slight angle from his body. He stared at Elise. She longed to stare back, to drink in the very sight of him, but she didn't dare. He touched a wellspring of desire she hadn't known existed. Mrs. Myers put the bread, cold sliced chicken and mayonnaise on the table. "Lawrence, I haven't had company in a long time, and I like it. Please sit down."

He started toward the table but then turned and went out the back door. Elise walked to the window and watched as he took great strides across the yard, the cat running to keep up, chickens scattering before them. He walked with an easy, fluid motion and hardly breaking stride, scooped the cat up and under his arm.

"You'll have to excuse us, dear. He's not used to being around people."

"You don't owe me an apology. I feel bad. I mean, I'm keeping him from eating."

"He'll get something later. I can afford to be selfish once in awhile. Like I said, I enjoy your company."

"I don't want to cause a problem, Mrs. Myers, but I hope you'll let me come back—often. I'm trying to think of a major for college. I've thought of social work, working with the disabled . . . or maybe psychology. I don't know. Maybe being around Lawrence, with his problem, you know, could help me determine my career choice." *Where did that come from? Well, it needn't be a lie. It could be true.*

"Why, that's a wonderful idea. I'd like to think Lawrence could help somebody. So many people have tried to help him, and it's surely fine with me. Oh, I'd love to think he could help you. Like I said, people have been so good to him."

She walked to the door and looked outside. Satisfied they were alone, she sat at the table across from Elise. "It'll help you to understand better why Lawrence acts the way he does if I explain some things. Lawrence's daddy, Luther, drowned in a boating accident."

"Yes, ma'am, I heard about that."

"Lawrence wasn't but nine years old, but he blamed himself for what happened. He was never the same afterward. For a time that's all he could talk about, how his daddy drowned. And then finally he quit talking about it, quit talking at all." She closed her eyes for a moment and drew a ragged breath.

"I took him to doctors in Tallahassee and all over, but nothing helped. They told me he had some kind of personality disorder. And you know how cruel children can be. Lawrence was tall for a nine year old, but when they saw he wouldn't fight, they tormented him unmercifully. He finally quit school, but some teachers got together. They took turns coming here to the house. Came for years. He wouldn't talk, but he'd listen, and he'd write. He got his diploma."

"Was Miss Nadine Fletcher one of the teachers who came out?"

"Miss Fletcher? No, I don't remember a Miss Fletcher. What they did was a blessing though. Books became his salvation. How that boy loves to read. I just think of all the knowledge he has in his head and never says a word."

"How sad."

"Yes, in a way it is sad. I'd have loved him to marry and have a family and enjoy himself, but I can't think but what he's found contentment. At least he never had to go to war and kill somebody or do mean things he didn't want to do. The only life he has is through books. To me he's still a child. It helps me to deal with it."

Her voice broke and she fanned herself with her apron, obscuring her face for a moment. "But the way I go on! You'll have to stop me, hon. Lawrence won't talk, and I can't seem to stop, but come see us as often as you like. Time long since quit having meaning for us, and I'd appreciate your giving us the company. Well, now, I've got to get back to my stove. I'm putting up some preserves so I'll leave you be. Just make yourself at home."

Elise walked to the front door and saw Lawrence sitting in the swing.

"You can go eat now. I won't bother you."

He stood up, his back to her, and faced the road. "I assure you, you can't help but bother me." He turned then and walked past her into the house.

Elise followed him to the kitchen eager to tell Mrs. Myers he'd spoken to her, but his fierce look silenced her. She went back to the porch swing and wondered if she were going mad. Maybe she only imagined he'd spoken.

A little later she could feel his presence. She knew he was close to the front door but hidden in the shadows where she couldn't see him. The atoms and molecules, every cell in her body sensed his presence. She started talking, pretending he sat beside her. "My family is new in town. We moved here from Atlanta, and my parents are opening a shop that will sell writing paper and soap that smells good. Not as good as you smell, though." She gasped with embarrassment and quickly covered her mouth with her hand. "I'm so sorry. I didn't mean to say that. I've always been sensitive to odors. I read once that before people had names, they identified each other by smell. I can believe that because your pheromones speak to me whether you do or not."

She could tell he was still behind the door listening and hoped he'd ask what pheromones were. But he didn't and to cover the silence she continued her nervous monologue. "Please let me keep coming here. I've been lonely and unhappy all my life. I think I could be happy here though." Nearly out of breath with nervousness, she leaned over to stroke the cat, but it ran from her. She felt Lawrence moving away as well. When she went inside to tell Mrs. Myers goodbye, he was nowhere to be seen, though she was sure she heard voices in the distance.

Mr. Lovett, they a young man at the door saying you been asking for him.

Thanks, Ruby. I'll talk to him on the porch. Bring us a couple of glasses of lemonade if you would, please?

Seth Mitchell?

Yes, sir.

Kyle Lovett. He extended his hand and noted the calluses on the young man's palm.

You've earned yourself quite a reputation around town, Seth. People think you have a real talent for working with wood.

I'd like to think so, sir. I love finding the beauty in something as un-yielding as a piece of wood.

Do you have formal training?

No, sir. There was never enough money for that. I just studied and learned from other people.

Do you think you learned enough to build me a beautiful stable for my horses?

A stable? Well, sure, I could build a stable.

I don't mean just any stable. I want something outstanding, something to make me the envy of everybody who owns a horse.

I hope you'll let me try, sir. I'd like to show you what I can do.

Well, order the materials and put the bill in my name. Hire the help you need, and some of the men here on the place can help out too. When can you start?

Seth stood up. Now, sir. I'll draw up the plans this afternoon.

✑

MARGARET SAT ON A WOODEN box pulling on her new socks. Edwin tapped on walls and tested the floorboards, rocking back and forth on his heels.

"The building seems sound enough, Margaret. I think it's a great find, considering the possibilities around here."

Margaret looked up. "Elise was talking to Peyton Roberts when I walked in the store to buy these socks."

"So?"

"She knows I can't stand the man. He said she was looking for shoes. I don't believe that for one minute."

"For God's sake, Margaret, what else would she be looking for?"

"I don't know. That's what concerns me."

"My advice is to forget about it. Elise is an odd duck, but

she hasn't caused us any real problems, and there's no reason to
think she'll start now."

"No, but there's something about that Peyton Roberts that
makes me uncomfortable."

"Uncomfortable?" Edwin appeared more attentive. "In
what way?"

"I don't know." Margaret hesitated a moment, refusing to
admit that in some perverse way she found him physically at-
tractive. "It's nothing I can put my finger on."

Edwin pulled up a box and sat in front of her. He laid his
hands on her knees. "Did anyone ever tell you that you have
beautiful knees?"

"Only you," she laughed.

He cleared his throat. "Margaret, we need to talk. The psychiatrist told me we should talk this out, but I didn't have the
nerve before."

"Edwin, don't. You don't owe me explanations."

"Yes, I do. I owe you a lot more than explanations. I don't
have to remind you that we've been through a lot. And that
business when I was sick, well, I think it left you feeling betrayed
again. Maybe you have a hard time trusting people like this Peyton guy because you can't trust me. I let you down."

"No . . ."

"Let me finish. I wasn't myself. I was somebody neither of
us knew. I'd kept things buried so long, too long. I should have
known they'd have to surface sometime. Jesus Christ couldn't
carry that kind of guilt forever. I felt like I'd been wrapped in a
black cloud. I simply couldn't function. I know how hard it must
have been for you because I still looked the same, but my personality, my memory to some extent, vanished."

"Edwin, you shouldn't . . ."

"Yes, Margaret, I should. I've never talked to anyone about

this but the psychiatrist said he thought talking to you about it too would help clear the air, so to speak. We just went on pretending nothing had happened. But something had happened, and I want you to understand. A clinical depression is a serious, life-changing event, not a popular pill-popping illness. Looking back, I realize I felt it coming on. There was nothing but darkness waiting for me. But I had no control over any of it. I couldn't grasp what was happening, and that's why I fought so when you sent me to the hospital. I thought you were the one who was nuts."

"I know, and I admit I was frightened, but I was determined to get the best help possible for you."

"And you did. If you hadn't, I wouldn't be sitting here on a wooden box in the middle of nowhere."

"The move was the doctor's idea, Edwin. Oh, I know he didn't say, 'You should move to Apalachicola,' but he did think we should get out of the house where it all started. I just took it one step further and decided we should get totally away and start over."

"You were right, of course. And now that we're in a new place, we need to start over with that clean slate. Looking back, I think I always felt it was still Gene's house; all the memories of Gene were still there. Maybe you felt the same way. After awhile I couldn't suppress it any more. I just couldn't handle it, and I let you down. Margaret, please be honest. Do you love me? Truly love me?"

"What a question, Edwin! But you're right about our past being there with us. We should have left the house long before a doctor suggested it."

"But do you love me?"

"Yes, of course, I love you."

"I guess I'll never feel comfortable with that. I'll always feel I set you up, forced the issue."

"We've had a good life. Don't question my love, Edwin. Love is a snowflake, unique to each of us and all the same, all snowflakes." Margaret took both his hands in hers, leaned forward and kissed him gently on the mouth.

"Well, there's never been any question about it, Margaret, I love you. I guess I always did."

"We love each other. Now let's get some work done."

10

As often as she dared, Elise went to the Myers'. Impossible as it seemed, she knew she'd fallen in love with Lawrence the first time she saw him. It overpowered her in much the same way the black depression had seemed to consume Edwin. And like Edwin, she was unable to resist its control. Lawrence became her reason for getting up in the morning. She guarded her time with him so jealously that she tried to avoid doing anything to arouse suspicion in her parents. She quit watching the people on the screened porch and began joining Margaret and Edwin at home, most often in front of television in the evening. This newfound devotion wasn't lost on her mother though.

"You seem so changed, Elise."

Edwin heard them talking and looked up from his paper. "Good lord, Margaret, I imagine we're all changed. We aren't exactly operating off Peachtree Street these days."

"Don't be ridiculous, Edwin. That has nothing to do with it."

"Doesn't it?"

"No, it doesn't. It's just that Elise seems different somehow. I've never known her to be so much for television either."

"I'm just tired of reading all the time."

"Well, your father and I are usually too tired to read at night as well. Watching television is even a bit of an effort. Your taking on the responsibility for preparing our evening meal has been a big help, Elise. I want you to know that. Funny thing, I never knew you could cook."

Elise smiled to herself recalling all the time Mrs. Myers spent teaching her to cook, hearing her say, "You're like a daughter, honey, and it's so nice to have you here hanging on my every word. You didn't know you had a sister now, did you, Lawrence?" She'd smile at Lawrence sitting at the table, and most of the time he'd leave the room. He'd spend small bits of time with them so long as he was ignored. Say anything to him, and he was gone. Elise would gaze at the chair where he'd been only a minute before, sometimes passing her hand over the warmth his body left on the cushion. *I don't feel a bit sisterly toward you, and I surely hope you don't feel brotherly toward me.*

THE FOSTERS HAD JUST FINISHED another of Elise's home-cooked meals. Margaret gathered the plates and stacked them in the dishwasher. She stifled a yawn with her hand and started toward the cozy alcove where they'd placed the television. She stopped and looked back. "Why don't you come down to the shop tomorrow, Elise? The shelves are pretty well stocked, and we'll be able to open our doors soon. Dallas comes by 'most every day, and she'd like to meet you."

"Yes, ma'am. That'll be great. It's been awhile since I've seen what you've done. I'll stop by tomorrow," she hesitated, "for a little while."

"Oh, you'll spare us a little of your time," her mother replied sarcastically, already forgetting that her stomach was warmed by the good food Elise had prepared only hours before. "What's so important that you have to do?"

Elise clenched her trembling hands inside her pockets.

"Nothing that's so important, but I've gotten into a schedule of walking and visiting, and I want to be done in plenty of time to prepare a good dinner for you and Dad."

"Don't argue with that, Margaret," Edwin added genially, "she's getting to be a better cook than you are." He smoothed the bulky pages of the *New York Times* that had come in the mail.

"I've never pretended to be a master chef, Edwin. I have other talents."

"Of course you do, and I've surely got enough girth to prove your worth in the kitchen. But it's such a nice surprise coming from Elise."

"That's because she used to be such a dreamer. You're not a dreamer any more, are you, Elise?"

Elise shrugged and picked up the *TV Guide*.

MARGARET WAS STILL FRUSTRATED BY her inability to hire domestic help, and Elise had pretty much assumed the task. When she had things in order the next morning, she took a quick shower and then stood in front of her closet. More concerned with her appearance now, she reached for a dress but put it back when she remembered the heat of the long walk to the Myers'. She selected a one-piece shorts outfit she'd never worn. She hesitated briefly, drew a deep breath, and took a glimpse of herself in the bathroom mirror, hurriedly applying lipstick and fluffing her hair. Then, closing her eyes, she ran her hands down the sides of her hips, pretending they were Lawrence's hands.

A gust of cold air wafted up from the floor, and she opened her eyes and trembled. *Drafty old house!* Would she always have to pretend? Her love had become not only her greatest pleasure but her greatest pain as well.

She left the house full of the excitement that had entered her life. At the bottom step she hesitated and looked at the carriage stone. The grass had been neatly trimmed so that it rested at the edge of the lawn, dark and menacing. She stared for a moment and wondered if its fascination was wearing thin. It seemed to repel her somehow. She walked rapidly, for the sooner she saw Margaret's shop, the sooner she'd be with Lawrence. When she reached the block where the shop was located, she took a quick detour and ducked into the shoe store.

Peyton stepped back, feigning surprise. "Whoa, Bobby, look who's here."

Elise smiled. "When I came by the other afternoon, I forgot to thank y'all for helping me out the day my mother found me talking to you. I haven't mentioned Lawrence Myers to my folks, and I didn't know how she'd feel about me prying into their business."

"And," Peyton smiled and raised his eyebrows, "you weren't at all sure how she'd feel about you talking to me."

"Well, you two haven't seemed to exactly hit it off."

"That's just a matter of opinion. Frankly, I rather enjoy your mother. Gets my adrenaline going."

"I have a feeling it must do the same thing for her. But I have to run. She's expecting me to come see what she's done with the shop."

"I thought I'd pay a visit there one day myself, maybe buy some of her fancy soap. I'll smell so good she won't be able to resist me."

"I don't mean to be rude, Peyton, but I think it'd take more than soap."

He laughed and slapped his hand on the counter. "I knew I liked you. And I'm sure you're absolutely right." He was still laughing when she looked at him solemnly and said, "Mr.

Robe . . . Peyton, I heard someone say there's a curse on our house. What did they mean? What kind of curse?"

"Oh, darlin', don't worry your pretty head about curses. Enjoy your house. My old flame used to live there, but I guarantee you I never put a curse on it."

Elise smiled. "I can't imagine you putting a curse on anything."

"Well now, young lady, don't go underestimating me. I might could cook up a doozy of a curse if I put my mind to it."

Elise laughed. "Well, please don't."

Peyton winked. "I promise. Just for you."

"You must think I'm always prying."

"Not at all, darlin'. I'll be your answer man any day of the week. We'll do most anything to get you to come visiting, won't we, Bobby?"

Bobby gave Peyton a stern look. "That's right, Miss Elise. You're always welcome."

Elise waved and started out the door when she stopped short, nearly bumping into the girl she'd seen playing Monopoly on the porch.

Jill smiled and said, "You're new here, aren't you? I'm Jill Simpson."

"Yes, I guess I'm still new. My name's Elise Foster."

"If you weren't born here, you'll always be new, I guess." She laughed. "Well, see you around." Jill turned and crossed the street.

Elise looked back and saw Peyton watching her. She waved again and continued down the sidewalk.

"I really like that girl," Peyton commented to Bobby, "but something bothers me. I just can't figure out what it is."

"Maybe it's her mother that's really bothering you."

Peyton raised one eyebrow and hesitated. "Nah. But something isn't right. I can feel it."

"Why didn't you tell her about the house?"

"I couldn't. I wanted to, but it wouldn't come out. Guess I just want her to be happy."

"She's bound to find out."

"I know, but I'll deal with it when the time comes, I guess."

Elise looked back, wondering if Peyton was still watching her. He wasn't, but she hesitated a moment, feeling caught in one of her waking dreams.

Seth, you're doing such a beautiful job. Papa must love this house. He was just foolish over the stable you built. And now this—a paddle wheeler.

Well, he made his fortune off the water. I thought it might appeal to him. And I knew you'd love it.

Annelise turned in his arms and looked into his eyes.

He smiled down at her. Don't forget, darling, you were my inspiration. I feel guilty as hell though, letting you come here and see it.

I'll never let on. I wouldn't take anything for our time here together.

Nor I, Annelise, nor I. Be careful now, don't trip. I want to show you the secret stairway I built.

Elise shook her head to clear her thoughts and circled back around the block so that if she were seen, it'd look like she was coming from home. Just as she approached the main street, a blue pickup went speeding past her. She sighed. *Another redneck.* All the windows were down, and music was blaring. This wasn't unexpected. What was surprising was that it was something from Rachmaninoff. The truck halted at a stop sign, and she saw a dark-haired young man lean out the window and look back at her. Two hounds in the back of the truck looked too. *The wonders of Apalach*, she thought, and continued toward the shop.

A bell chimed when Elise opened the door. Margaret turned and said with surprise, "Elise!"

"Remember, I said I'd stop by."

"I know. It's just that you look so, so . . . I mean your hair and the lipstick. You look very nice."

"Your shop looks nice too. Wow! You've done so much since I was here the last time." Elise looked around the room and couldn't deny that her mother had a knack for decorating. She'd done everything in yellow and white with green accents. Margaret had scoured the countryside picking up old pieces of furniture that Edwin then painted, and now ivy and dried flowers spilled out of shelves and drawers, breaking the merchandise into neat little sections. She even had an old claw-foot bathtub with an arrangement of bath items and candles. There were bars of soap wrapped in lace and tied with green ribbons. Elise slipped one in her pocket for Mrs. Myers. After all those good meals, her parents owed Mrs. Myers big time. "Mom, the old bathtub is a wonderful touch. How . . ." At that moment the bell chimed, and in walked Dallas. Elise felt a pang of guilt to know so much about a woman she'd never met.

Margaret walked up behind Elise and put her hands on her shoulders. "Well, Dallas, here's my absentee daughter, Elise, you've been wanting to meet."

"This certainly is a pleasure," Dallas drawled. "I was beginning to think your parents had just made you up."

Elise smiled and reaching for her hand found it surprisingly cool and soft. "I've heard so much about you from my mother, Mrs. Anderson. I've wanted to meet you too."

"Dallas, honey. Call me Dallas. Everyone does."

Dallas still held her hand so Elise squeezed it and said quietly, "Dallas."

Dallas cocked her head. "Elise is such a beautiful name, a favorite of mine."

"Thank you. It came to my mother in a dream."

"Oh my, how romantic!"

Margaret was completely flustered. "Elise, you shouldn't tell people things like that. You make me sound like a perfect ninny."

"But, Mom, you did . . ."

"That was a long time ago, and it was probably just hormones."

Dallas laughed. "Whatever it was, it suits her, and I think it's perfectly charming that it came to you in a dream." She threw her arms wide. "Don't you think your folks have done a marvelous job with their boutique? Who'd ever guess it had been a dusty old hardware store. I guess you know my husband owned this place. I loved every nail and tool in it, but I'm glad not to recognize it any more. There's nothing of my Tom here now, and that's the way it should be. I refuse to grieve and be maudlin the rest of my days."

"I'm glad to hear that, Dallas," Margaret put in. "It makes me feel good to think we've helped you through a difficult time. You surely helped me by leasing us this space. You don't know what grief you saved me in not having to deal with that awful Peyton Roberts."

"Oh, Peyton's not so bad, once you get to know him. He loves to affect this pure cracker persona, and you just have to accept how he is. His family goes back a long way here, and that gives him a sense of pride he didn't earn. There's nothing more debilitating than inherited pride. But Peyton's a smart man. Don't let that cracker accent fool you. He's educated too, but you'd never guess it to hear him talk. He can discuss Shakespeare in one breath and paranormal phenomena in the other. Peyton's a talented man, but he's had an unhappy life. He could never please his father, and the only woman he ever loved married someone else. He never got over it."

Elise tucked a long strand of hair behind one ear. "Which didn't he get over?"

"Sarah. He never got over loving Sarah. He gave up trying to please his father. I think that's why he started playing the cracker role. He's done it so long now I sometimes think he believes it himself."

"Uh, Mrs. Anderson, Mom said you've lived here all your life. Maybe you can answer a question for me."

"Dallas, honey. Please. Makes me feel younger. Don't let these gray hairs fool you. They're premature, I swear to God. But what's this question you have? If I can't answer it, I'll bet nobody else can either, except maybe Peyton."

"I was wondering about the house down on the river, the one that's supposed to be haunted."

"Elise," her mother began.

"It's okay, Margaret. I know all about that. Yes, it's supposed to be haunted. I believe it is. And why shouldn't it be? If ever a house deserved to be haunted, that one does. You've heard the story?"

"I know about the bride who was burned on her wedding night."

"That's what happened. It was before my time, but that memory has been kept alive by those who told the story down the years, that and the screams and footsteps that have become part of the very fiber of that house."

"You've heard them?"

"No, but that doesn't mean others haven't. If I catch the scent of honeysuckle, I don't have to see the vine to know it's there."

Elise smiled. "I'd dearly love to go inside, just to see it."

"Elise!" Margaret scolded. "I can't believe you'd be so forward."

"It's a natural curiosity, Margaret. Who isn't fascinated by something supernatural?"

"I, for one," Margaret replied dryly.

"Well, I'm with Elise, and I can get you in that house any time you like. The women who live there, Aunt Jenny and Aunt Lacey, are distant relations of my husband. Very distant, but his folks always treated them like family. Tom's father ran a café here, and Mr. Anderson was always sending something good to eat up the hill to his kin. And then years later my Tom took up the mantle with the hardware store, always making little repairs or something for them."

"Dallas, I'm sorry. We don't mean to pry. I'm sure Elise doesn't want to impose . . ."

"She's not imposing. Not at all. I wouldn't offer if I didn't want to, believe me. Good lord, Margaret, what have I got any more if it isn't time? I'm ashamed to say I haven't been to see them but once since Tom died. Elise is doing me a favor. It's time I went, and I'll take you with me, Elise. I'll call you in a few days."

"Oh, thank you so much, Mrs. . . . ." she stopped when someone knocked on the door. Dallas turned and said, "Louise! Margaret, you don't mind if my friend Louise Montgomery comes in, do you? The girls in my bridge club have been dying for a look inside here. Louise's house is just a few blocks from yours, you know."

"No, I'm afraid I didn't know."

"Not nearly as grand as yours, Mrs. Foster, and shame on me for not having called and introduced myself before now. But welcome. It's nice having neighbors in the boat house again."

Dallas turned then and said, "And this is Margaret's daughter, Elise."

"So pleased to know you, Elise. You must be about my

daughter Debby's age. You should come over sometime and get acquainted. Debby and her friends keep a wicked game of Monopoly going." She laughed. "I think it's the same one they started in junior high."

Dallas cleared her throat. "She might be more interested in meeting your handsome son, Louise. Elise, you'd adore Stan. He's away at college at the moment."

"Not to brag, but I'm a proud mom, Elise. Stan's coming home soon, and I'll just bet Dallas will see that you meet him. She loves to play cupid."

Elise blushed, thinking of Lawrence, and stammered, "I . . . I'm really glad to have met you both, and I'll look forward to seeing you again soon, Mrs. Anderson."

Elise started out the door, calling back, "I'll buy some vegetables and fruit so we can have a cold salad for dinner, Mom. It feels too hot for anything else."

"Sounds good to me." Margaret waved, but Elise was already hurrying along the sidewalk.

II

*E*lise's head reeled at times with all the things that interested her, most of all Lawrence Myers. Much as she tried to stay away from him, she couldn't seem to help herself.

She walked with purpose now, moving swiftly to close the distance between them. By the time she reached the eastbound highway the sun seemed to climb as fast as she walked. Her stride broke momentarily when she heard classical music. A truck pulled to the far side of the road and the dark-haired fellow she'd seen earlier called to her.

She held her hand to the side of her ear and shook her head.

He turned the music off. "Can I give you a lift?"

"Thank you, no. I'm fine."

"I'm not dangerous," he called.

"I didn't think you were."

"Well then, let me give you a lift."

"I need the exercise." She noted from the corner of her eye that the truck inched along the highway, keeping pace with her.

"In this heat? Come on. I live here. I don't bite."

"Really, no."

"Please?"

Elise ignored him and continued walking. A short distance ahead, she saw him park the truck under a tree. When they were nearly level, he got out of the truck and crossed the road.

"I can't believe this," Elise muttered.

"Neither can I, but how else can I get to know you?"

She stopped. "What about your dogs?"

"They'll be there when I get back. How far we going?"

L.L. Bean she thought to herself as she took in his faded red plaid shirt, jeans, and short black boots. He was older than she'd thought though, maybe twenty-three or twenty-four. "WE aren't going anywhere."

"Careful. You're liable to hurt my feelings."

"As if I care." She stood her ground, arms akimbo.

"Aw, come on. I just wanted to meet you."

She extended her hand. "My name is Elise." She turned to leave, but he continued holding her hand.

"Around here it takes two names for an introduction."

She sighed. "Elise Foster."

"No, I meant you should know my name too." He put his other hand on top of hers and said, "It's Ty. Ty Roberts."

"Oh! Any relation to Peyton?"

"Second cousin. You know Peyt?"

"I've been in his store a few times." She slipped her hand from between his and continued up the sidewalk.

Ty went back to his truck and drove slowly beside her. The dogs stretched their necks over the side of the truck and never took their eyes off her.

"Sure you don't want a ride?"

"I'm sure."

When she crossed the street to the fruit stand, Ty pulled over and stopped too. "You sure come a long way for some fruit."

Elise just smiled.

He bought a bag of boiled peanuts, but she lingered over the fruit until he gave her a mock salute and got back in the truck. When he was out of sight, she started up the road to see Lawrence.

Just like the first day, Lawrence was in the swing, not waiting for her, but seeming to defy her for disturbing his routine.
The minute she started up the steps, he walked toward the door.
In the beginning she'd call to him, begging him to wait, but now
she knew better than to waste her breath. It only made him an-
grier. Today, though, he stopped with his hand on the door.
With his back to her he said, "Leave us be. You'll destroy what
we have here . . . please."

"That's the last thing I want to do. I just want to be a part
of your lives."

"That isn't possible."

"It is if you'll allow it. I think I've waited all my life to be
here. It's like I never lived until now. I've always been on the
outside looking in. And no one cared."

"No one cares now. You don't realize what you're doing. I
wish things could be different, but they can't."

"But they can! Just give me a chance. Please!"

"I can't. Not even if I wanted to."

"And I can't help wanting to be here. I can't help how I feel
about you . . ."

"Don't . . ."

"Don't? I told you. I can't help myself. Do you think I enjoy
feeling this way? And anyway, your mother likes having me
around. And I think you're mean not to talk to her. You don't
have a problem talking to me."

"I don't have a problem talking to you. I have a problem
with you. From the first day you came here . . ."

"Well, I have a problem with you too. That's why I can't
stay away."

"How did you get here?"

She laughed. "I walked. How else?"

"Then you walked a very long way."

"Yes, I did. That should be proof that coming here is important to me."

He nearly turned to face her but then continued inside the house.

"Try smiling once in awhile," she called after him. "Maybe it'd make you feel better." The words were no sooner out of her mouth than she could hear her mother saying the same thing to her. This was different though. Totally different.

Mrs. Myers came to the door and looked puzzled. "Were you talking to someone, hon?"

"Just Lawrence. He talks, Mrs. Myers. Don't you ever doubt it."

"I pray to God you're right, but still I can't believe it. Talking to you helps me though. Honey, you don't know how wonderful it is to have you here. I didn't realize how much I missed the company. But mostly, I'm thankful for you talking to Lawrence, taking such an interest in him and all. You talk to him just like he's anybody else, like he cares what you say. I appreciate that. You give him dignity."

"He doesn't need dignity, Mrs. Myers. But there's such a stubborn streak in him."

"It's not that he's stubborn, dear. It's his illness."

"Maybe so. But I'm determined to find a way to get through to him."

Elise followed her to the kitchen, picked up a pan of green beans and began snapping them. "Have you always lived here, Mrs. Myers? Is Apalach your home?"

"Law, no. I came here as a bride from North Carolina. I was a mountain child. But that was so long ago, Apalach is home now."

"Did you ever hear about the house that's haunted, the one on the river?"

"My, yes. Who hasn't heard that story? And we have sort of

a connection to it. My husband was a distant relative of the young man who built Mr. Lovett's stable and later a house for his daughter. His own design, they say. But then he was accused of murder.

"It was a terrible thing. Nobody in Apalachicola suspected he was a fugitive, especially not Mr. Lovett's daughter. Word was she was kind of sweet on Seth. That was the young man's name, Seth. Mr. Lovett nipped that in the bud though. Talent or no, he wasn't good enough for Mr. Lovett's daughter, and she was forbidden to see him anymore."

The kitchen door slammed and Elise looked up to see Lawrence glaring at his mother, green eyes blazing.

She felt a ringing in her head, heard voices and worried she might faint.

Mr. Lovett, I don't know how to tell you this. I should have recognized him sooner, but then with the rumors I did remember. It's more than rumor, Mr. Lovett. The man who built your beautiful house is guilty of murder. I was there. The young woman was a distant relative. For God's sake, protect your daughter.

"It's okay, Lawrence," his mother said, "this isn't gossip. It's ancient history. Elise lives here now. She might as well know what the rest of us have heard about for years. It's part of the very air we breathe. Come sit with us, son." She pulled a chair out from the table, but he turned and went out the door.

She sighed. "Like I said, dear, he don't mean to be rude. But as far as I know all the stories about the house being haunted are just that. Stories. I've never been inside the place, but there's been plenty of talk over the years, and you know how people will add a little bit here and a little bit there to make a story more interesting."

"It's so terribly sad, Mrs. Myers, that young girl to be so much in love and then to die that way. I even dream about it sometimes." It wasn't until she said it that Elise realized that more and more frequently her dreams became nightmares about the young bride. A chill passed over her and the pan of beans nearly slipped from her lap.

"You okay, honey?"

"Yes, ma'am. The pan slipped."

"It was a sad business. I grant you, it was enough to haunt a house all right."

Elise rinsed the beans and put them on the stove. "I think I'll walk around outside a bit, unless you need me to do something."

"Heavens no, child. You go ahead. You're company. If I need something, I'll call Lawrence."

Elise walked to the shade of the grape arbor and sat in an old chair where she'd watched Mrs. Myers rest and doze. She was so accustomed to talking to Lawrence when she couldn't see him that she spoke aloud as she sat alone under the arbor. "I've never known such peace. I could grow old here."

"You won't get the opportunity."

"Lawrence, you startled me!" Elise stared straight ahead, not turning to look back at him. "I didn't realize you followed me."

"Yes, I followed you." *I could follow you to the end of time.* "As often as you try to force me to speak, I try to convince you that you don't understand what you're getting into, and God help me, I can't bring myself to try explaining it to you. I don't want to hurt you the way you're hurting me."

"Hurting you? I would never do that."

"Oh, but you do. You'll hurt us all in the end. My mother and I have a measure of peace here, but you will be the instrument of our destruction. I wish I could make you understand, but I don't know how."

"I told you. I can't seem to help myself. And you have no right to deny me."

"Oh, but I do. I have every right, more than you'd ever imagine."

"Don't you think your mother has rights too? She likes my company."

"My mother is a fool."

"Lawrence! How can you say that?"

"Because she is. She has no right to encourage you. She's selfish, the way you are. Thinking of her own enjoyment."

"I won't make trouble for you, and your mother never hurts me the way you do."

"Hurt you?" He let out a painful cry. "Don't you know it isn't in me to hurt you?"

"You've hurt me in ways *you* can't begin to imagine." Elise stood up and turned to face him.

Lawrence stared at her a moment, not angry, just puzzled or maybe pained, then he turned his back to her. "Where did you come from? Really."

"I told you. Atlanta."

"No, you've come farther than that."

She walked closer to him and then turned away. They stood back-to-back, inches apart, until Mrs. Myers called. "Lawrence, will you bring some tomatoes for our salad? Please?"

"The woman you call a fool is preparing your lunch."

"Yes, even fools can cook."

Elise sniffed and wiped her eyes with the back of her hand. She let out a deep breath, something caught between a sigh and a sob.

"Don't cry! I won't have your tears on my grave!"

"Lawrence, what a horrible thing to say. How can you be so cruel?" She could hear his labored breathing, but neither of them turned around. She spoke through clenched teeth. "Get the tomatoes for your mother. I don't know how I can bear to love you." She drew in a sharp breath with the realization of what she'd said and started walking from him toward the house. When she reached the kitchen door, he hadn't moved and stood where she'd left him.

ELISE WAS MISERABLE FOR HAVING told Lawrence she loved him. *How could I have been so stupid!* She paced the floor of her room, wringing her hands. *How can I go back there and face him?* And the troubling dreams did nothing to ease her discomfort. In her dreams she no longer looked like herself but was a young girl with long dark hair. Only the emotions, the uncertainty, the terror were her own. Someone stood at the end of a lonely road, a figure in white who frightened her. Once she woke in the middle of the night breathing hard as though she'd run a long way. And she wasn't in her bed. She was in the hall outside her parents' room, and in the dim shadows her feet looked gray with dust. She stayed awake the rest of the night, and when the sun came up she ached with longing to see Lawrence. She couldn't bring herself to face him, though. Not yet. Still, later that morning, just for the comfort it brought her, she walked toward the Myers' for a bit before turning back toward town.

She was deep in thought about Lawrence when she realized she was at Miss Nadine's. She started up the steps before she saw her in the rocker, sound asleep. Elise turned to go, but Nadine called, "Don't you go leaving without speaking to me."

"I didn't want to wake you."

"I wasn't asleep. Besides, I can sleep any time. Come on and have a seat. Tell me what's going on in your life."

Elise sank into the rocker with a heavy sigh. "I'm still exploring, Miss Nadine, meeting new people, and dogs."

"Dogs?"

"I don't know what made me think of those dogs. I met a guy recently, and he goes everywhere with these two hounds in the back of his truck. I always expect them to jump out, but they don't."

"There used to be a man here had a dog that rode on the hood of his car."

Elise laughed. "On the hood of his car?"

"Yes, ma'am, took that dog all over the place, and I don't know that he ever fell off. Don't know who was the bigger fool, the man or the dog."

"Nobody can say that people here are boring. They're so interesting, so real and honest."

"We're that all right. Real honest and real mean."

"Why, Miss Nadine! I haven't met anyone who's mean." *How about Lawrence Myers? Don't you think he's mean?*

"Then you never met my daddy."

"No, ma'am, I haven't."

"He's dead. Long dead. Seems like though I can remember those times better than I can what happened yesterday. People say you shouldn't talk bad about the dead, but I always say, why not? Being dead doesn't change what you were when you were living. If I didn't respect somebody when they were alive, why in hell should I respect them when they're dead? 'Scuse my French. My daddy always brought out the worst in me."

"Maybe that's just fathers and daughters. I don't get along that well with my dad either, but then he's not my real father. He . . ."

As though Elise hadn't spoken, Nadine cut through her words and continued with her story. "He was better to me than he was to my mother, though. I wondered why she didn't leave him. But where would she have gone? Her daddy left her the grand sum of one dollar when he died. The rest went to her brother and sister. My grandfather was a good man, but his word was law. When he forbade her to marry my daddy, he meant it. Daddy thought he'd get over it, never dreamed he wouldn't inherit big money some day. Stuck in his craw that she came from more than he did. His whole goal in life was to be somebody. He was somebody all right. Somebody tight with his money, somebody who didn't hesitate to leave bruises on my mother's body.

"She taught school and had to have clothes, but he begrudged every stitch she ever bought. She hadn't been brought up to do for herself. Her family had a woman come to the house to do their sewing, and my mother wasn't good with a needle. She tried but ended up buying most of her clothes. If he thought she paid too much for something, he'd march her right down to the store and make her return it. Oh, the shame of it, and her a schoolteacher."

"You followed in her footsteps then?"

"How's that?"

"Becoming a teacher, just like your mother."

"I sure didn't want to be like him. He tried to buy me, always giving me things. He never figured out I'd have rather he do things for my mother. Doesn't seem fair we pass this way only once and then to have somebody's life be a pure living hell that one time through." She shook her head from side to side.

"I know somebody like that. Miss Nadine, do you think it's possible to love someone with every ounce of your being and that person will never love you back?"

"I guess. I'm not sure my daddy ever loved my mother. I

think he loved the idea of her inheriting money some day. I was luckier than my mother. When I loved, he loved me back. I never doubted that for one minute.

"He was such a beautiful young man. Those Greek men are like gods. The sun turns their bodies to pure gold. Course, it'll turn on you, the sun will, and next thing you know those Greek gods are made of leather. Not Nick though. He was always my golden boy."

"If only I could be that lucky."

"Luck has nothing to do with it. If it's meant to be, it's meant to be. There's nothing more to it."

"But what happened? Where's he now?"

"Why, he's here, of course."

"Here? You mean in Apalach?"

Her voice grew deep and quiet. "He's with me."

"He lives with you?"

Nadine grew flustered and her eyes looked wild. She thumped her chest with a trembling fist. "He's here in my heart where he belongs, where he's always been."

nother week passed and Elise still hadn't heard from Dallas. Elise quizzed her mother to see if she'd been to the shop. "Of course I've seen her, but I'm not going to be bothering her about taking you to some old house. I've found Dallas to be a woman of her word, but time moves by a different clock in a fishing village. And by the way, we're having an open house at the shop on Tuesday."

"You are?"

"Yes, we are, Elise. Surely you expect me to open for business. I'd planned something more elaborate, but I don't want to seem pushy, too Atlanta. I've learned that I have to pace myself if I want to be accepted here, so we'll just keep things simple. I'll float helium balloons out front and have light refreshments. I would appreciate it if you'd be on hand to greet people and serve punch. We'll open at ten that morning. I have an announcement coming out in the paper. I've ordered soap samples with the name of the shop on the wrapper."

And it'd never occur to you to tell me this important news.

"Is it a secret or can you tell me?"

"Tell you what?"

"The name of your shop."

"Didn't I tell you? A Touch of Class."

Ouch! "Your idea or Dad's?"

"Mine, of course. Remember, this is my baby."

"I'll be glad to help if you need me."

Margaret looked at Elise critically. "I believe I just told you I would."

"Then I'll be there."

"And don't wear shorts."

Elise's face burned, and the hurt stung like tears. *You know I wouldn't. Why do you have to be so mean? Mrs. Myers would never be so unkind. What about shoes, should I wear shoes too?* Aloud she said, "I won't embarrass you."

By the time Tuesday came, Elise's fingers felt numb from tying ribbons on the tiny soap samples. She couldn't help but admire what her mother had done with the shop, though. The antique cash register gleamed, and a crystal bowl filled with punch rested on a bed of ivy and yellow hibiscus blossoms. Elise wondered if Peyton would show up and was surprised to see him come in with Dallas.

"Margaret, Elise, you know my friend Peyton Roberts. You're neighbors now!" Margaret gave a pained smile and nodded.

"I'm not adding shoes to the inventory, Mr. Roberts, so I won't be competition."

"I guess I can sleep better at night now," Peyton said a bit curtly. Dallas punched his arm. "Be good now. This is a party." Elise raised her eyebrows, and he smiled at her.

Edwin walked toward them and Dallas extended her hand to him, "And, Mr. Foster, so nice to see you again too."

Come on, Dad. Tell her to call you Edwin. No? It's your loss.

Dallas turned and touched Peyton's elbow. "My friend Peyton Roberts." The men shook hands, but neither spoke. Dallas looked from one to the other and said, "I'm bringing all my friends, Margaret, to see what you've done with a dusty old hardware store."

When Peyton wandered over to a display of stationery, Margaret said, "If you don't see anything you like, let me know, and I'll include something for you in my next order."

"How bout some blue lined tablet paper?"

"I beg your pardon?"

"You know, a tablet. A plain old tablet. But never mind. I can find that at the drugstore."

"You can probably find soap too! Oh, forgive me. I don't mean to be rude. I'm sure I can find something to please you, Mr. Roberts."

"I doubt it, Mrs. Foster, but we'll see."

Dallas called to Margaret and she turned to greet Dallas's friends. "My bridge pals and oldest friends, Margaret. Frances May, and you'll remember Sue Carter, and Louise Stone, your neighbor." Margaret greeted each of them and guided them toward Elise for punch. When she turned toward the window, Margaret saw Peyton wave from the sidewalk. "I suppose he's returning to his store," she remarked.

"Why, Mother, you sound disappointed he left so soon."

"No, Elise, I'm not disappointed at all," she snapped.

Before she left, Dallas reached behind the counter and brought out a bottle of expensive champagne. "My compliments, Margaret. The Fosters can celebrate tonight! Peyton wanted me to tell you it was from him! Isn't that just like him!"

"You mean taking credit for someone else's generosity?"

"Now, Margaret. He was joking. You just don't know him yet."

"No, I guess not, but I know you, and that's enough. We'll toast you tonight. You can count on that."

Elise stopped with the punch ladle poised above a cup when she realized she was enjoying herself. She really was enjoying herself! She noticed that nearly all the area merchants came in and looked around. A lot of the local people came and even some of the people from the island. It was St. George Island, but to the locals, it'd always be "the island."

Elise's heart sank when Dallas left and made no mention of the haunted house, but a few moments later she came back and stuck her head in the door. "Elise, I haven't forgotten. One day soon. I promise."

Later, when they were cleaning up, Elise said, "Mrs. Anderson is the nicest lady."

"She surely is," Margaret said. "I wish we could be friends."

"Why can't you?" Edwin asked.

Margaret paused and said a bit sadly, "I don't know."

WHEN ELISE HAD ALL BUT given up hope that Dallas would remember, there came the early morning blaring of a car horn. She looked out her bedroom window, and Dallas called from her car, "Do an old lady a favor, Elise, and don't make me come inside. Let's go visit that haunted house before the sun gets any higher. Hey, Margaret," she called, when Margaret waved from the front door. "I'll take good care of her. See you at the shop later, you hear?"

Elise hurried downstairs and ran to the car. Dallas waved to Margaret and made a U-turn in the middle of the road. She looked over at Elise. "Nobody's going to say anything," she said. "I know every man on the police force. Most of them aren't dry behind the ears. There was a time years ago when the chief was sweet on me. Don't look so shocked, honey. I was desirable."

Elise laughed. "I'm sure you were, Mrs. Anderson, uh, Dallas. You're very pretty."

"A woman never minds a compliment, honey, but I wasn't fishing for that, really I wasn't. But I know I look like my mother, and anybody will tell you she was a fine-looking woman. Lady. I'm a woman. My mother was a lady. Even after I gave up ciga-rettes, I never deluded myself into thinking I was a lady." She made a sharp left turn. "Peyton Roberts tells me you've been in his store from time to time. He seems awfully fond of you."

Elise blushed. "He's nice to me. He and my mother don't get on much, but there's something about him I like."

"There's plenty to like, Elise. He was one of the smartest students to ever graduate from our high school and probably has more education than anybody in Apalach, other than a few M.D.'s. I'd put his brains up against anybody's. Peyton's no slouch, but he could win an Academy Award for acting the part."

Elise laughed and wished there were some way she could approach Dallas about the story of the riverboat house, but she hesitated. *One house at a time.*

They were quiet for a few moments with only the sound of Dallas humming softly. Elise remembered the song from Tues-day night bridge. *"Things are seldom what they seem . . ."*

"I met someone the other day who says he's a relative of Peyton's."

"Ty?"

"Yes, ma'am."

"About the only relative Peyton has left. Nice boy. His par-ents are dead so he's alone except for Peyton. Ty was adopted, a nephew of the Roberts actually. He was just a baby when his parents were killed in a car wreck. Poor little Ty had to be pried loose from his mother's arms. Maude and Earl weren't young, and they'd never had any children. Didn't matter though. They took him in without a thought. They couldn't have had a more devoted son if he'd been their own though. Ty is okay. You should get to know him."

Dallas made another sharp turn. "Let's detour a little and ride along the river. The smell of the water clears my head."

"I love Apalach," Elise said shyly.

"Why how sweet, darlin'. There's a lot to love, isn't there?"

"I think so. Much more than I'd ever have dreamed from a fishing village."

"That what your folks call us? A fishing village?"

"Yes, ma'am."

"I guess that's what they see. I see a way of life. But fishing village is okay too. Has a nice ring to it."

"I think that's what they liked, the sound of it."

Dallas laughed. "Yes, I can just see Margaret rolling that around her tongue like a piece of toffee."

As they drove past Miss Fletcher's they both looked, but she wasn't on the porch. "That's the saddest thing," Dallas said.

"Oh, I think so too," Elise replied. "I don't think she should have retired."

"Retired?"

"From teaching. She has so much knowledge, and she just lives to share it with somebody."

Dallas slowed the car and looked around at Elise. "Nadine Fletcher never worked a day in her life."

"But she told me she did," Elise insisted. "She's always talking about her students. She misses them so."

"Elise, I was born and raised here. Nadine Fletcher was already in trouble by the time I started school. But I know one thing. She never graduated."

"But . . . I don't understand."

"We're almost there. I don't have time to go into it now. We'll talk about it on the way back. Or get Peyton to tell you. He's the town historian. Not much ever went on here that he doesn't know about. But now, I want to tell you about the

Lovett sisters. Aunt Lacey is the shy one, and you can tell from the pictures on the living room wall that she was a pretty little thing when she was young. Aunt Jenny was plain and never forgot it. There was Lacey so slender with long blond curls and poor Jenny, stocky with coarse black hair that hasn't been tamed to this day. When Aunt Lacey's husband died and she moved back home, Aunt Jenny wasn't a bit happy about that turn of events. She'd had all her daddy's attention until then. Lacey was his pet." Dallas tapped the horn and waved to an elderly man.

"Aunt Jenny hasn't made life easy for her sister. Claimed she had to be tough to make Lacey snap out of her grief. Looks to me like she's still trying to make her snap out of it," Dallas said wryly. She eased the car up the incline and parked on the spacious circular drive, tapping the horn lightly before getting out. "Want to let them know somebody's here. They don't get many visitors."

As they went up the steps, Elise had trouble taking a deep breath, and she rubbed her chilled arms.

Dallas paused and said, "My Tom repaired these porch railings before he died. He was always doing things for them." When they reached the door, Dallas raised the brass bridle that hung from a cast iron horse's head, but the door opened before she could make a sound.

Two withered old women stood just inside the open door. "Why, Dallas Anderson," the larger of the two women said and hugged Dallas. "Oh, Dallas, you are a sight for sore eyes."

"Aunt Jenny, Aunt Lacey, forgive me for neglecting you. I just haven't been myself since Tom died." She reached behind Aunt Jenny and clasped Aunt Lacey's hand.

"Well, child, you're here now and that's what matters. But come in, come in. I wished I'd've known you was coming. Lacey would've baked a cake, wouldn't you, Lacey?" Lacey nodded but didn't utter a word.

"I didn't tell you 'cause I didn't want you going to any trouble."

They started into the house when Dallas looked back and saw Elise standing mesmerized, staring at the winding stairway from the open door. "Aunt Jenny, Aunt Lacey, forgive me. This is my new friend, Elise. I told you I wasn't myself. Here I am being rude and leaving the child standing alone on the porch."

Elise found herself with unaccustomed poise and maturity. "I'm so pleased to meet you, and what lovely names. I've never known anyone named Lacey before."

"It was a pet name," Jenny scoffed. "My father called her that because she wanted lace on all her dresses. The name fit 'cause she got all the lace she wanted. She was always silly that way." Aunt Jenny pushed her glasses firmly on her nose and looked closely at Elise. "I think I've seen you walking past the house."

That it was more of an accusation than a comment wasn't lost on Elise. "Yes, ma'am," she replied, "you may have. We moved here from Atlanta, and I'm busy exploring." *So someone was staring at me from behind the curtains.*

"Lord, help. I forgot I brought you a fresh coffeecake. Elise, honey, would you mind getting it from the back seat of the car for me?"

Elise figured Dallas hadn't forgotten. She just wanted to fill the old women in on her and her family. As Elise walked leisurely down the steps, she felt a rush of cold air and thought of the young bride fleeing the steps on her wedding night. It was as though a cloud covered the sun, and she was unaccountably sad when she walked back into the room with the coffeecake. She heard Dallas say, ". . . in the riverboat house."

Aunt Lacey patted Elise's hand and took the cake to the kitchen. "I'll put on water for tea and be right back," she whispered.

While Dallas and Aunt Jenny talked, Elise sat in a rocker facing the winding staircase. She tipped her head back in order to see the top of the stairs. Dallas and Aunt Jenny were engrossed in conversation when Elise stood up and walked to the stairway. She put her foot on the bottom step and then turned, looking over her shoulder, embarrassed. "I, I'm sorry. I just . . ." She couldn't finish the sentence. She really had no explanation for her action.

Aunt Lacey came back in the room then. She looked at Elise's foot on the step. "That's where our father was sitting when his sister came running down the stairs."

"That's enough, Lacey," Aunt Jenny interrupted, but Lacey continued. "He was just a little tyke, and he was sleepy. The adults were upstairs dancing, and he sat there in his blue velvet wedding outfit sound asleep with his head against the railing. He woke up to see a flaming white figure dash past him. He thought it was a fiery angel. And in a way it was. My poor father never got over that moment. He carried that image to his grave. His beautiful sister, flames feeding on her wedding finery. Such a terrible tragedy."

"Is the ballroom still there?" Elise ventured.

"I figured you'd heard the story," Aunt Jenny said, making no attempt to hide the disgust in her voice. "Of course the room is still there. It's never been used since that night, though. We keep it dusted, that's all. The door is closed on those memories."

Elise drew a deep breath for courage. "I hate being rude, being so bold, but could I see it?"

She saw the stony look on Dallas's face but pushed ahead. "Please?" She was beyond being polite. *One way or another, I have to see that room.*

Dallas cleared her throat. "Elise, Aunt Jenny and Aunt Lacey don't give tours of the ballroom. I've never seen it myself."

Aunt Lacey stood and raised her head defiantly. "Jenny, I think we should let her see it."

"No, Lacey. We've heard more than enough out of you today. Mind your own business."

"But, Jenny, I feel it. Something tells me it's what we ought to do. Maybe it's her name, but I think she should see it. Our aunt's name was Annelise, you see, like a part of yours."

Dallas murmured, "I'd forgotten. Yes, Annelise."

Aunt Jenny never said a word, and her mouth turned down at the corners, but she led the way up the stunning stairway. At the top of the stairs, she removed a key from a small shelf inside the case of a grandfather clock. She inserted the key, hesitated a moment, and opened the massive double doors.

Elise caught her breath. The floors were pale as honey and huge gilded mirrors lined the walls on either side. "There used to be sconces," Aunt Lacey whispered, "but our grandfather had them all removed when Annelise died."

A current of cold air seemed to pull Elise into the ballroom. The last thing she heard was a small cough from Dallas before the music began. Elise glided onto the floor. She twirled and dipped and danced with abandon, she who'd never felt a moment's grace in her life. She whirled past the gilded mirrors, her own image lost among the blurring colors she glimpsed. The music coursed through her veins, carrying her faster and faster around the room, and then it stopped as suddenly as it had begun. She nearly fell with the suddenness of it, and then slowly, gently collapsed at the feet of the three women.

They watched her in fascination and horror. She looked up at them and burst into tears. "I'm so sorry, so very sorry. I don't know what came over me. It must have been the music."

"Music?" they inquired in unison.

"Yes, ma'am. The music. It was hypnotic."

Dallas spoke sternly. "There was no music, Elise."

"Oh, but you must have heard it. I heard it so clearly, a beautiful lilting waltz. You heard it, didn't you Aunt Jenny? Aunt Lacey?"

Both women shook their heads ever so slightly from side to side.

"But I can't have imagined it. It was so real. It was the music. Otherwise I would never have danced like that. Could never have danced like that. I've never been a good dancer."

Dallas replied dryly. "You could have fooled me."

"That's the tea kettle whistling," Aunt Jenny said sternly. "Lacey, go make tea, and I'll lock up."

Elise was horrified at what she'd done, but at the same time she felt it had been beyond her control. When she and Dallas were in the car again, she kept apologizing and trying to explain to Dallas. Finally she said, "Maybe it was just my imagination, about the music, I mean. All the stories, that beautiful room, maybe I just thought there was music."

"That's probably it," Dallas conceded. "But there's something I'd better tell you. I suppose your family is the only one in town who doesn't know it, but the house you live in was built for Annelise."

Elise didn't correct her. She listened to the story over and over, gleaning from each telling another bit of information.

"Annelise loved riverboats. Her father bought the plans from a young admirer of his daughter and had him build the house in the shape of a boat for her. She never saw it. Everyone kept it a secret. Some day it was to be a wedding gift. When she became engaged, her father asked her fiancé not to spoil the surprise, to save it for their wedding night. When she died, Coulton—that was his name, Coulton—said he'd never forgive himself for not letting her see it.

"No one was allowed inside, and then Coulton declared

he'd sleep there one time. Imagine, him in the bridal bed alone. People thought he'd kill himself for sure. Oh, but I don't want to talk about it. So much hurt and anger, and Annelise dead.

"It was rumored there was a painting of Annelise in the riverboat house, a wedding gift for Coulton. No one knows what happened to it."

Elise swallowed hard. "Do you suppose he saw it?"

"Who can say? Years later a local family bought the place, but by then the house had reverted to the Lovetts. No one ever saw Coulton or the painting again, not that they didn't look for it. They searched every place they could think of. It disappeared as sure as Coulton did."

"I wonder what happened to him?"

"Oh, there were stories that he became a riverboat gambler. Others said he died an alcoholic. I don't suppose anyone ever really knew, but it was like he left a curse on that house. I hope your family, not being from here, can change all that."

"I hope so too. I appreciate your telling me and for taking me to meet Aunt Jenny and Aunt Lacey. I'm truly sorry if I humiliated you. I don't know what came over me. You've been very kind. My parents, my mother especially, are so grateful for all you've done. Please don't tell her what happened today." *Please don't tell the bridge club either.*

"I wouldn't dream of it. Let's just try to forget it."

"I'd like that." Impulsively and totally unlike herself, Elise leaned over and kissed Dallas on the cheek before getting out of the car. "I really am sorry," she said and ran from the car, tripping over the carriage stone. Dallas got out of the car to help her up. "Are you okay?"

"I know that's there." Elise stared at the dark shape. "I begged Mom not to take it up, and here I go and trip on it—

again. It's like it gets in MY way! I'm okay. My knee's skinned a little is all. Nothing that'll keep me from dancing," she said, and laughed. *Oh God, where'd that come from?*

But Dallas laughed too and drove off feeling a little less strange about the day's events.

Elise stood awhile looking at her home, feeling its sorrow. Inside she climbed the grand stairway to her parents' rooms, to what had undoubtedly been the bridal suite. She walked slowly across the room toward the front window, trying to avoid looking at the ornate cheval that had come with the house. The real estate agent told Margaret that Sarah had moved to a small place in Tallahassee and couldn't accommodate the mirror. With her artistic eye Margaret was thrilled to get it and had positioned it at an angle to the bed so that it reflected the giant oaks in the front yard. As Elise walked past the mirror, she started to avert her gaze when something caught her eye. There had been a momentary reflection of long dark hair in the mirror, she was sure of it. She took a step backward, but she couldn't bring herself to look. She ran down the hall and reached the bathroom just in time to lose her breakfast.

At about the time Elise was being sick, Dallas was walking into Peyton Roberts' store. Peyton looked up from the register and whistled. "Here comes the prettiest girl in town."

"Not today, Peyton. We need to talk." She called to the back, "Hey, Bobby, can you watch the store while your boss treats me to a Coca-Cola?"

"Whoa now, Dallas, I'm the invitee. You should be buying the drinks."

"I'm not in the mood for jokes today, Peyton. Let's just get out of here so we can talk."

They started walking down the street when Dallas stopped. "This won't do. Let's go to my house."

"This offer just gets better all the time. Maybe I should go back and tell Bobby to lock up now."

"Peyton, I keep telling you this is serious."

They walked to Dallas's car without speaking. She pressed her keys into his hand. "Here, darlin', how bout driving for me?"

"You really are rattled, aren't you?"

"Frankly, yes I am. I'm hoping you can help un-rattle me."

"Well, I have a preferred method for that, but I'm not sure it's what you have in mind."

"Honest to God, Peyton, I don't know what I have in mind. I just know something isn't right."

Peyton parked the car under a large oak in Dallas's front yard. "I love this house. It's nothing big or showy but has wall-to-wall charm. I always envied Tom coming home to this every night." He raised his eyebrows when Dallas let the remark pass. She really was upset.

As they walked up the steps, Peyton remarked, "You ever consider painting this place blue? I always thought it cried out to be blue. I even told Tom that once, but he just laughed at me."

"No, I never did. If I felt better, I'd laugh at you too. Have a seat, and I'll put on some coffee, or would you rather have a Coke too?"

"No, coffee's fine. The way you're acting I might even need something stronger than coffee."

"I have some wine cooling. Let's have that. And I'll fix us a couple of sandwiches if you haven't had lunch yet."

"Sounds good to me. I haven't had a home-cooked sandwich in a long time."

"If you're hinting for a meal, that could be arranged too."

The kitchen was the color of butter cream with a pale blue breakfast nook set in a bay window. "We'll eat here since you're so fond of blue."

As they sipped their wine and ate ham sandwiches, Dallas told him what had happened that morning. "I don't know why it disturbed me so, but it did. Peyton, I truly believe she heard music. You should have seen her."

Peyton whistled. "She's a sensitive girl, and I guess she's taken all these stories to heart."

"And remember, she lives in Annelise's house."

"That's true. Does she know that?"

"I told her. Today. But it wasn't until after the business with the music, on our way home."

"I've studied a lot of the paranormal literature, Dallas."

"I know. I didn't bring you here just because of your good looks."

"You think I'm good-looking?"

"Stop it. This is serious."

"There are lots of things we can't explain, Dallas, not by any means we understand. It's like religion. We've got no proof. You take it on faith or you don't. Some say there's energy left from traumatic experiences. This energy can be picked up by living people. I'd say Elise would be especially susceptible. She even asked me about Lawrence Myers the other day."

"You've got to be kidding. How would she know about him?"

"She's walked out to the house. That's all I know."

"Way out there?"

"That's what she said. I've gotten her to open up to me a little. Turns out she's never dated much. Never had a real boy-friend. She puts herself down a lot."

"I'm glad she has you to talk to, Peyton. I don't think she and her mother have a very close relationship. Margaret's cer-tainly a handsome woman but no one I'd call warm."

At the mention of Margaret, Peyton's face reddened.

Dallas noticed and said, "Oh, I know you don't like her. Elise told me you two didn't hit it off."

"That's putting it mildly. But I like Elise. I like her a lot, and I don't want her to get hurt."

"I don't know what we can do to protect her. I, for one, won't be taking her back to the Lovetts'. Keep letting her confide in you, Peyton. Let's pray this blows over. At any rate, I feel better for talking to you. I tell you, it was eerie. I've lived a long time and never experienced anything like it."

"Let's hope you don't again. You want to give me a ride back to the store, or do I have to walk?"

"I'm sorry, darlin'. I'll drive you back."

When he was getting out of the car, Peyton said, "Why don't we take in a movie sometime?"

Dallas smiled and waved, and he didn't know if she heard him or not.

13

*E*lise couldn't quit thinking about her experience in the ballroom and pretended to have a stomach upset, not leaving the house for days. *Lawrence must think he's rid of me for good. Well, he's in for a surprise.* But she had fitful, uneasy dreams that made her even more reluctant to go to the Myers'.

Feeling trapped inside the house and unable to shake the feeling of Annelise's presence, she became obsessed with finding the long-lost painting. Like those before her, she began in the attic and spent the greater part of an afternoon there while Edwin was away on business. Hot beyond words, it was creepy and dimly lit, but she took a flashlight and wore rubber gloves. She inched her way around the perimeter of the house, pushing at beams, running her gloved hands down the rough sides, but there were no hidden walls or secret doors. All she got for her effort was a bump on the head and a splinter that pierced her glove. Still, she wasn't deterred.

She could hardly wait for Margaret to leave the house the next morning. She had only one more day before Edwin returned from Atlanta. She checked every inch of the parlor. Nothing. She spent hours in Edwin's study, moved all the books from the bookcases, and lifted the carpet in as many places as she could. Next she tackled the kitchen. If she didn't finish before Edwin returned, she wanted rooms that had fewer places of concealment. She knocked on walls and ran her hands along smooth surfaces searching for something, anything that would move.

She'd completed her search of the downstairs rooms and was on her way to the shower when she stopped midway up the stairs. She turned and went back down and, kneeling on the floor, began knocking on the panels at the back of the staircase. She thought she detected a hollow sound, but she'd knocked on so many walls she doubted her hearing. Still, she was sure there was something . . . She pressed the panels, pushed with the heels of her hands and began trying to shove them from side to side. One seemed to give a little. She wrapped a towel around a hammer and finally it moved, revealing an empty space under the stairs. She aimed the beam of the flashlight from floor to ceiling, but it was empty. She walked around bent over, pushing, knocking, running her palm over every inch of space. It was such an ideal hiding place, but she was convinced nothing was there.

Much as she wanted to keep searching for the painting, Elise thought she'd die if she didn't see Lawrence. Just thinking of him made it difficult to draw a deep breath. Before Edwin arrived home the next day, she left the house and started walking to the Myers'. When she reached the highway, she heard music. Ty Roberts pulled his truck over to the curb and turned the music down.

"I've about worn the rubber off these tires hoping I'd run into you. I thought maybe you'd moved back to Atlanta."

"No, I've been home."

"I didn't think you could do without all that exercise."

"I had a virus," she lied.

"On your way to the fruit stand, I guess."

"As a matter of fact, I am."

"Get in. I'll take you there."

"But you're going in the opposite direction."

"Doesn't matter. I like your company."

As he came around to open her door, Elise noticed that even in black boots he bounced along like he had springs in his feet. He smiled broadly as though he knew he had beautiful teeth and an infectious smile. *So full of himself. Where did I hear that? So full of himself.*

"No dogs?"

"Too hot. I left them home today, not that they didn't want to come with me. You have a dog?"

"Me? No. I've never had a pet."

"Not even a goldfish?"

"Not even a goldfish. You can't believe how fussy my mother is about the house. She used to be an interior decorator, and we're like mannequins in a showroom."

"You don't look like a mannequin to me."

"I sure feel like one at times."

Ty reached over and ran his hand lightly down her arm. "No, you're a real, live girl."

Elise shrugged. "Thanks for the vote of confidence."

Ty laughed and when they got to the fruit stand, he raced around to her side of the truck and stood with his face in her window. "I'll wait for you. You've been sick so I'll give you a ride back."

"Oh, no, please don't wait. I'd feel rushed, and I need the exercise, I really do." She tried to open the door, but he held it shut.

"Come on. Let me take you home."

"No! I don't want you to wait for me."

"Okay, I'll leave on one condition."

"What's that?"

"How 'bout going to a movie with me Saturday night?"

"A movie?"

"You must have noticed there isn't much else to do around here."

"It isn't that. It's just . . ."

"Oh, come on. It won't kill you to spend an evening with me. I'm not leaving 'til you say yes."

"You don't take no for an answer, do you?"

"Nope. I don't usually have to twist a girl's arm to get her to go out with me either."

"I bet you don't."

"Saturday night then. Seven o'clock?"

"Fine. Do you want to know where I live, or should I just walk out to the highway and wait for you?"

"It'd be kind of cute for you to do that. We usually meet at about the same place, but I know where you live. Seven o'clock then." He gave a little salute and said, "Later."

She bought some fruit for Mrs. Myers before starting up the road. She thought she heard Ty's truck, but when she looked back, the road was clear. *He's becoming a real nuisance. I'll go to a movie and that's it.*

When she reached the Myers', she hesitated a moment before she opened the gate. The road continued to climb for maybe a quarter of a mile, and then there was an expanse of weeds and woods. Could there be tombstones among the weeds? Maybe Lawrence would help her explore.

She turned back to the gate and felt chilled by the stillness. Everything was quiet, too quiet. She felt a moment of panic and called, "Lawrence?" She heard footsteps running down the stairs inside the house, and for a fleeting moment she thought of Annelise. At the screen door, the footsteps stopped abruptly. Lawrence stood there, a shadow behind the screen.

She was so happy to see him, she was unable to speak. She didn't care how angry he was at her for coming. Just to see him . . .

"It's you."

"I suppose you thought you were rid of me."

"Maybe."

Mrs. Myers came around the corner of the house then. "Why law, child, where've you been? I've missed you something terrible."

"I've missed you too, but I had some things to do at home and couldn't get away."

Lawrence pushed the screen door open and stared at her. Something had changed between them. She knew it. The dark recesses of her body tingled and grew moist. Without taking her eyes off his face, her arms grew weak and she let go of the bag of fruit. She watched numbly as rosy fuzzed peaches and clusters of marbled grapes fell at her feet. She stood motionless as Lawrence walked toward her and knelt to pick up the spilled fruit. Had she been able to move, she could have put her hand on top of his head. He was so close, the nearness, the very scent of him was intoxicating. Then he seemed to swirl with the fruit, moving in a circle round and round her feet. She could hear Mrs. Myers crying, "Catch her, Lawrence, she's going to faint." When Elise opened her eyes she was lying on a bed. She knew it was his when she saw all the books lining the walls. Mrs. Myers was patting her hand.

"Oh, I'm so embarrassed."

"You fainted, honey, nothing to be embarrassed about."

"I forgot to eat," she replied weakly.

Elise looked toward the window where the cat sat on the ledge and saw Lawrence leaning against a bookcase watching her, knowing it wasn't hunger that made her faint.

"I'm a strong believer in hot tea, even on a day like this. Lawrence, keep an eye on her, and I'll be back in a few minutes."

"I've missed you," she whispered. "I think you missed me."

He walked to the foot of the bed and looked down at her.

"It doesn't matter if I miss you. I have feelings the same as you do, but it makes no difference. It can't, and you're just stirring things up that you don't understand."

"Is there someone else?"

"Someone else?"

"Another girl in your life."

He gave a harsh laugh. "You might say so but not in the way you mean."

"I don't understand."

"I know you don't, and I can't explain it to you. I've tried to convince you not to come here any more. What you want from me isn't possible."

"Oh, but I love you so. It has to be possible."

"Don't say that!"

"But it's true." She tried to stand, but her knees buckled. He grabbed her before she fell and for the briefest moment held her body tight against his. She thought he might have pressed his lips to her hair, but she couldn't be sure because in nearly the same instant, he pushed her roughly to the bed.

"You do care. You do," she whispered.

"I can't. Don't you understand? A million times over, I can't."

"I'll never believe that."

"Believe it."

Mrs. Myers returned with the tea and a thick slice of buttered bread. "This will make you feel better. Here you bring me fruit and you not eating anything yourself. I've never met your mother, but she has to be a fine person to raise such a sweet girl. You just rest now. You've got a long trip home yet today, and I don't want you fainting on the way."

Lawrence walked to the window and sat beside the cat, never taking his eyes off Elise.

"I'll leave you two now. Call, honey, if you need anything. That tea'll do wonders. Just you wait and see."

When his mother left the room, Lawrence turned and stared out the window, as though he could no longer look at her. Accustomed now to addressing his back, Elise said, "Lawrence, a terrible thing happened to me the other day. Mrs. Anderson took me to the Lovett house, the one they say is haunted. When they showed me the ballroom . . ."

He turned and looked at her then and something like panic in his eyes made her stop talking.

"You went to the ballroom!"

"Yes, I couldn't help myself. And I heard music. It was like someone took over my body. I danced in front of strangers, Lawrence, in their house! And the worst part? I was the only one who heard the music. I keep thinking that's how it must be for you, how it's so difficult for you to talk, as though someone else controls your body. Someone controlled my body. I know it."

He walked to the bed and looked down at her with such a pained expression, she said, "Oh, Lawrence, I didn't mean to hurt you. I thought you'd understand."

"I do understand. I wish I didn't." He closed his eyes briefly and without another word left the room and went downstairs. Only the orange tabby remained on the windowsill watching her.

When she felt stronger she took the cup and saucer to the kitchen, but Mrs. Myers was nowhere around. She walked to the porch and found Lawrence in the swing. She drew a deep breath and sat beside him.

"I don't mean to make you angry. Believe me when I say I can't help myself. I've never been in love before. All my life I've been miserable. There's so much you don't know. Don't deny me the chance for happiness."

"It's hard to say this, but you leave me no choice. Not everyone is meant to be happy. Maybe not even you." He turned to her then and placed his forefinger on her lips. "Don't go on with this. You'll only be hurt."

"Too late. I'm already hurt. Just seeing you hurts." She felt herself drawing near, wanting to kiss him, when, unmistakably, she heard classical music. She looked toward the road just as Ty's truck drove past the house, made a sharp U-turn and came back. A cloud of dust enveloped everything. He stopped the truck when he was even with the front gate. Like dry mist the dust began to settle, and the truck came into full view. He turned the music off. "I didn't know they sold fruit here."

"They don't, Ty. They give it away."

"What are you doing way out here anyway? You ready to go now?"

"No, I'm not ready to go."

"Suit yourself. You be ready Saturday night though. I'm counting on it."

Her hand was shaking, but she waved and he drove off, dragging a cloud of dust behind him.

"One of my admirers," Elise said and laughed, but when she looked around Lawrence was gone.

As she walked home that afternoon Elise felt tense, always worrying that Ty would be around the next corner. She was deep in thought when she reached the house but paused for a moment and stared at the carriage stone.

Edwin came to the door. "You okay, Elise?"

"Yes, sir, just lost in thought. You been home long?"

"Awhile. Come on inside and get something to drink. You look flushed. I'm busy with some paperwork in my study, and Margaret will be late tonight. She called to say she got a new shipment of soap and wants to get everything unpacked before she comes home."

◌◌

WHEN FIVE O'CLOCK CAME, MARGARET locked the door to her shop and went to the back room to begin checking an order of soap. The scent of so much soap in the enclosed room was making her sick, so she opened the back door for fresh air. She was kneeling before one of the boxes when a shadow fell across the floor.

"Oh!" she gasped. Then, "Peyton, it's you."

"You okay?"

"Yes, I'm okay. Or I was. You frightened me."

"I guess you're down there praying."

"No, I'm not praying! I'm unpacking soap and opened the door because the perfume was giving me a headache."

"You're planning to sell stuff that will give people a headache?"

"I don't suppose you ever sold a pair of shoes that pinched! What am I saying? Of course this perfumed soap won't bother anybody. But put enough of it in a small space, and it can get to you. What are you doing here anyway? Customers usually come in the front door."

"I'm not a customer. I was out dumping some trash and saw your door standing open. I just came over to be sure everything was all right."

"Thank you. Everything is all right." She was aware that the opening of her blouse gapped as she put her right hand on the floor to boost herself to her feet. She pressed her left hand against the blouse and nearly fell over before Peyton stepped forward, grasped her arms and helped her to her feet.

For the briefest moment he didn't move, and the closeness of him nearly took her breath away. Unbidden, she felt a rush of passion and drew a deep breath full of perfume and lust. He still gripped her arms, and she didn't move.

Peyton smiled and raised his eyebrows.

Margaret was furious that he might have sensed her unease and pulled away from his grasp. "Well," she said briskly, "I suppose Dallas was right. You really are a gentleman."

"You'd doubt Dallas?"

"Not any more. Well now, Mr. Helpful, I guess I'd better get back to my inventory, or I'll be here all night."

She waited for a smart remark that didn't come. He just turned and started for the door.

"Peyton," she called to his back. He stopped but didn't turn around. "I do appreciate your concern. I really do. Thank you."

He turned and faced her. "Oh, it was nothing. I just felt in the mood for a headache."

"Here." She tossed him a bar of French milled soap. He caught it in one hand and pressed it to his nose. "Do you suppose I could ever smell this good?"

"I doubt it, but you can try anyway." She laughed and closed the door behind him. Her hands were shaking.

MARGARET DIDN'T MIND THE LATE evenings at her shop but regretted she wasn't able to be home on Saturday when Ty Roberts was taking Elise to a movie. "A date?" Margaret questioned. "Your dad and I didn't think you knew any young people."

"I wish I didn't know this guy, but he keeps pestering me to go out with him, so I'm going, just this once. He's a cousin of Peyton Roberts."

"Oh," Margaret said, the familiar flush moving up her neck.

"Don't sound so disappointed, Mom. He seems nice enough, despite being Peyton's cousin, if that's what's worrying you. And anyway, I told you I don't have any real interest in him."

"Where does he work?"

"I've never asked. Part-time on construction, I think. I told you—I don't have any interest in him."

At seven o'clock sharp, when Ty parked his truck in front of the house, Edwin and Elise were on the front porch. Edwin raised his eyebrows. "A redneck?"

Elise laughed. "I don't know. If he is, he's a redneck with a taste for classical music."

When she was in the truck, he said, "Don't you know you're supposed to keep me waiting?"

"Only if I'm trying to impress you."

"Ow! That hurt."

"What do you expect when you force yourself on someone?"

"Okay, I deserved that. Can I help it if I like you? Most girls would be flattered."

"I'm not most girls."

"Maybe that's what I like about you."

In the movie she shoved her hands in her pockets to avoid any awkward maneuvering. Ty wasn't to be discouraged, though. He reached over, pulled her hand from her pocket and laced his fingers tightly through hers. Her face burned with fury while she kept comparing his hand to Lawrence's that was so much bigger. When the movie was over he continued holding her hand all the way to the truck.

"I'd like to go straight home, please."

"I'll get you home early, but first I want to take you to a pretty little spot where we can see the moon on the water."

"You've never learned to take no for an answer, have you?"

"Not if I can help it."

"You're so, so . . ." and then she heard herself repeating what she'd overhead Dallas say, "full of yourself."

He laughed. "That what you think? Give me time and I'll prove you wrong."

"I don't think so."

"I think so, because you are wrong."

"But I'm not going to give you the time."

"Man!" He hit the steering wheel with both hands. "Why can't we ever just have a decent conversation? You spend so much time at that spooky old house you forget what it's like to be with a red-blooded American boy."

"How dare you! You have no right to talk about the way I spend my time or who I spend it with."

"Is that right?"

"Yes, that's right."

He started the truck. "I'll get you home. I wouldn't want all this talk to tire you out too much."

When they reached her house, he leaned across her to open the door but then pulled back. "Shit!" He walked around, opened her door and walked her as far as the steps. "Elise," he hesitated and said, "Oh, never mind," and walked back to his truck. He didn't have springs in his feet this time. Before she reached the door, he had Beethoven's Ninth going full blast. She looked back and could see tail lights growing dim in the distance.

14

*B*efore she went to the Myers' on Monday, Elise stopped by the shoe store. Bobby was at the counter alone. "Hey, Miss Elise, did you really come to see shoes this time or you looking for Peyton?"

"I'd like to talk to Peyton if he isn't busy."

"He just went to the post office. Have a seat in his office. He'll be back in a few minutes."

"Office?"

"You didn't know he had an office?" Bobby escorted her to a small room at the back of the store with floor-to-ceiling book-cases and a scarred oak desk. There were leather-bound volumes of Shakespeare and the Oxford Classics. She was just beginning to check a section on paranormal literature when Peyton came in.

"This is really Bobby's office, you know. He just lets me use it."

She smiled. "Sure he does."

"Your mom tell you I about scared her to death the other night?"

"No, sir, she didn't say anything. At least not to me."

"It was nothing. Her back door was open, and I thought maybe she'd forgotten to lock up or something. Scared her when I walked up on her unexpected."

"Must not have scared her too much."

"Maybe not," he smiled. "Guess I'm well on the way to

showing her what a nice fella I am." He laughed. "Want me to get you something to drink from the drugstore?"

She shook her head. "Thanks anyway. I just stopped by because I hadn't seen you in awhile."

"I'm flattered."

"And I'm impressed by your library."

"I read a lot. Got a lot of curiosity. Thought maybe I'd write a book myself one of these days. Being dubbed the 'town historian' and all, I feel kind of obligated to give Apalach her due."

Elise smiled. "Mr. Roberts," she began, and he had the good sense not to correct her, "something happened to me recently. I'd like to tell you about it, in confidence."

"Why I'd be privileged to have you share a confidence." His acting skills were so honed, it wasn't difficult for Elise to accept his shock at her account of what happened that morning in the ballroom of the Lovett house. She told it just as Dallas had, but Elise trembled as she spoke. "I haven't told my parents. I thought maybe you'd understand. I think Dallas is angry."

"I'm sure she isn't angry, hon. That isn't Dallas's way. If anything, she'd be worried about you. I don't know that I can say anything to shed light on the subject. You've heard the stories about that house. I can't explain it, but maybe you really did hear music."

Elise closed her eyes briefly. "Thank you. Maybe I'm not crazy after all."

"No, I don't think you're crazy. I do think you are a highly impressionable young lady, though. You may be sensitive to things the rest of us miss. It can be a gift or a curse. Depends on how you use it."

"I'd like to reverse what happened to Annelise."

"Darlin', we'd all like to do that."

"But I want to try. If they'd let me back in the ballroom,

maybe I could hear music again. Maybe I could finish the dance for her. It sounds crazy, I know. But it's no crazier than other things, the voices I hear, the music . . . I just have this overpowering feeling that had she finished the dance her hair would never have caught fire. Miss Nadine said she was dancing with her new husband, the last dance of the evening."

"Nadine told you that?"

"Yes, sir. It's so important that I get back in the ballroom and try to reverse things for her. It was her last dance."

"Oh, darling, that's a wonderful thing that you want to do that, but I don't know that you could manage it, no matter how strongly you feel about it. Anyway, after what happened, do you really think they'd take you up there a second time?"

"Probably not."

"Don't get into something so deep that you get hurt. This isn't your wrong to right."

"Sometimes I think it is. I've become absolutely obsessed with finding her picture."

"You and lots of other people."

"I know there's supposed to be a hidden stairway."

"Don't waste your time. It was sealed shut eons ago. If that picture was still in the house, someone would have found it by now."

Seth unlocked the concealed door at the back of the stable and tucked the rolled canvas under his arm.

Elise cocked her head. "Did you hear anything?"

"No, but my hearing's not what it used to be."

"I know it wouldn't seem fair that after all these years a stranger should come to town and find the long-lost picture, but I can't seem to help myself. I've looked every place but the upstairs bedrooms. If I don't find it there, I suppose I'll stop searching—or start all over again. I've been very thorough, though. I did find a storage area under the stairs, but it didn't have anything in it but bugs and dust. Sometimes I think Annelise wants me to find her picture. The cold air that follows me, I think it's Annelise."

"Now, hon . . ."

"No, really. More and more I feel she's with me. At first I was afraid, but now I think maybe she's trying to tell me something—I mean, when I heard the music and all. That's why I'd like to finish the dance for her."

"I worry about you, hon. I'm afraid you're getting in over your head here. Nadine has no way of knowing she was dancing when the accident happened. There's plenty to do in Apalach without dwelling on the past."

Elise laughed. "There is?"

"Well, maybe not. But look at all the positive things that helped form Apalach. Have you been to the Gorrie Museum?"

"Oh!" She clapped her hand over her mouth.

"What's wrong?"

"I've been to the museum, but you made me think of something. The day Dallas and I went to see Aunt Jenny and Aunt Lacey, I happened to mention Miss Nadine's retirement, and Dallas said she hadn't retired, that she'd never worked a day in her life."

"That's right."

"But Miss Nadine told me she'd taught school here. And she surely talks like a teacher. I get a lesson in Apalachicola history every time I see her."

"She knows her history all right, part of it anyway. But Dallas is right. Mrs. Fletcher, Nadine's mother, taught school, but Nadine never worked. She wasn't able."

"Wasn't able?"

"No. When Nadine was in high school there was some trouble with a boy. She was a pretty young girl, very athletic, tall and lean, and had coal black hair that hung nearly to her waist. I was just a young'un, but not so young I didn't notice how pretty she was. I guess she could have had any boy in town she wanted. She could play sandlot softball on Saturday, and on Sunday she'd be in the choir singing like an angel. Her daddy, Sam Fletcher, worshipped the ground she walked on. He was a tough old dude with political ambitions, and he expected a picture book family to help him with his quest.

"Then the beginning of her senior year Nadine fell in love. Lots of girls were falling in love about that time of their lives, but Nadine fell for a high school dropout, son of a local fisherman. In a small town, back then especially, that amounted to political suicide, but Nadine wouldn't stay away from Nick no matter how much her daddy threatened her. She was Sam's own daughter, and she stood up to him, laughed at his threats. He kept her locked in her room for weeks, but she never stopped defying him. Finally he took her away. People could hear Mrs. Fletcher scream and beg him to leave her be. Sam came home alone, but a few months later he went after Nadine and brought her back. She wasn't the same girl he'd taken away. Her eyes were black as two dark holes, and she was docile. Didn't give him one bit of trouble. Meek as a lamb."

"So he had his political career back on track?"

"No. Nadine's mother jumped off a bridge. That ended Sam's career once and for all. And just to be sure she hadn't jumped for nothing, she sent a letter to the editor of the local paper. It was never published, but it didn't have to be. News travels faster than a printing press in a small town. And Nadine couldn't finish school. Sam tried sending her back, but she couldn't hold anything in her head long enough. But she remembered her history. She can quote Apalach verse and chapter. And she's gotten some better over the years. They say she takes books out of the library every now and then. And she'll go for long periods and seem almost normal. Mostly though, she talks about the past, about the time when she was a child."

"And Nick?"

"Disappeared. Never did find him. His family tried but they were poor people with a house full of young'uns. I figure Sam either paid him off or scared him so bad he never came back."

"What happened to Mr. Fletcher?"

"Heart attack about twenty years ago. Left Nadine well fixed. She wouldn't have needed to work if she could. And she's able to live there by herself. Such a headstrong young girl." Peyton shook his head from side to side.

"She still seems kind of headstrong to me."

"That right? Well, maybe she's at peace with herself. Eventually I guess we all find peace of some sort, one way or the other. I'm glad she's made friends with you. You can take that as a compliment of the first order. I haven't known anyone to go in that house since before her daddy died."

"Oh, we never go inside. We just sit on the porch."

Peyton stood up and looked down at Elise. "That's mor'en I've seen anyone else do. But be careful now and don't take this business with Annelise too seriously. You've got your own life to live."

Elise stood on tiptoe and kissed him on the cheek. "You don't know how much it matters to me that you care."

When Bobby came back to the office to see what was keeping him, Peyton still had his palm to his cheek.

All the way to the Myers', Elise kept listening for Ty's truck, but he was nowhere around. She walked rapidly, but it was a long way. As Peyton said, it might be the end of the earth. She took one last look down the dusty road before she opened the gate and started up the steps. She didn't see Lawrence anyplace, but his mother said she thought she'd heard him chopping wood.

Elise found him near the woodpile. He'd taken off his shirt and his tanned, muscled back glistened in the hot sun. He split several pieces of wood and then wedged the ax into a stump when she was sure he heard her behind him. He continued staring off into the woods, and she raised her hands, longing to touch his back, but stayed inches away, caressing the air. Embarrassed, she turned to go back inside.

"I'm begging now. You've reduced me to that. Don't come here again."

Without turning, she stepped backward until their backs touched.

"You can't mean that."

He sighed. "If you understood, you'd know I mean it."

She could see his fists clinched on either side of his body and pushed more tightly against him. He made no effort to move away. Growing bolder, she took a fist into each of her hands, slowly loosening his fingers. "Do you have any idea how absolutely gorgeous you are? How can I help but love you? Those Greek fishermen have nothing on you, Lawrence Myers. I ache, actually ache for you. I can't get close enough. I could melt right into your body. Oh, Lawrence, what are we going to do?"

"We aren't going to do anything. There's only heartache for meddling in something you don't understand. You can't keep coming here."

"You don't want that any more than I do. I know you don't."

"No. I want all the things you want, only more. You can't

know what it's like after all these years . . . but it isn't a matter of what I want." His hands squeezed hers so hard they hurt and she let out a low moan. He turned then and took her in his arms, kissing her lips, her eyes, her tears, pressing her to him and then pushing her away.

He spoke harshly. "That's what you've wanted, now go." He started off into the woods. "Leave us be."

"*H*ello there, Miss *Gone with the Wind*. Were you going to try snubbing me again today?"

"No, ma'am. I didn't see you." Elise tried to make her voice sound normal, fearful of betraying her newfound knowledge of Miss Nadine's circumstances.

"You weren't looking either, were you? How you been?" She didn't wait for an answer but proceeded to tell Elise about a book she'd been reading. "It's about time."

"I can't hear you, Miss Nadine."

"No wonder, standing way out there on the sidewalk. The book I'm reading. It's about time," she shouted. "Says time's a continuum, like everything that's happened is still there, back up the road a piece. I like to think that's true. I was just sitting here thinking of the boy who used to deliver groceries when I was a little girl. I remember that black bicycle as good as if he'd dropped my groceries off this morning. He was a teenage boy when I was just a tyke. Been dead years now, but I still like to think of him with that curly head of hair riding up the road—it wasn't paved then—with a basket of groceries for my mother."

"If only we could find a way to go back up that road," Elise said.

"That's the trick, Miss, getting back."

"I guess memory is the only road we have, Miss Nadine, but I have to go. I'm on my way to the Lovetts'."

"The Lovetts'? Why in the world would you go there?"

"I visited them with Mrs. Anderson, and I want to thank them for their hospitality."

"You're mighty polite."

"Thanks. I hope they think so. By the way, could I borrow that book sometime?"

"Book?"

"The one about time."

"Oh, yes. Sure."

ELISE'S STEPS SLOWED AS SHE neared the house, and her palms were moist on the box of cookies she'd baked that morning.

When Aunt Jenny came to the door, Elise smiled and said, "I brought you some cookies." Elise held the box in her outstretched hand, but Aunt Jenny made no move to take them. Aunt Lacey came up behind her and reached for the box, but her sister pushed her away.

"I understand how you must feel, both of you. I just want to apologize for what happened that day. You don't know how bad I feel."

"I don't care how bad you feel! You aren't welcome here. Ever!"

Before the door slammed in her face, she heard Aunt Lacey calling, "I care, Elise. I care." Aunt Jenny shoved her away from the door and snapped, "Shut up you old fool, or they'll have us both committed."

Elise looked down at the box in her hand. "They're still warm," she said quietly and placed the box on a table by the door. "They're still warm."

It wasn't until she reached the sloping lawn that Elise shivered and remembered the old saying, *somebody's walking on my grave*. She stopped and looked back at the house, realizing she'd retraced Annelise's painful flight. She strained to hear the whispered voice of a man say,

Oh dear God, Annelise. Oh my darling.

Elise closed her eyes tight on unshed tears, rubbing her hands down her cold arms. *I want to help you, that's all, but I can't even get inside the house.* She jammed her trembling hands in her pockets and followed the river road so she wouldn't have to pass Miss Nadine's again. The wind picked up, and she'd just become aware of the sweet smell of pot when a voice startled her.

"You make a pretty picture with the wind in your hair that way."

"Ty! Where'd you come from?"

"I could ask you the same question. I was here first." He sat with his back against a tree, looking up at her.

"This where you come to indulge?"

"Not so often any more."

"I used to know someone who said pot's no fun if you're by yourself."

"That right? Then come join me." He offered her the joint.

"No thanks. I never liked the stuff. Anyway, here come your dogs from the woods. I hope they're friendly."

"Actually, they're friendlier than you are."

"Touché. Do they have names?"

"The dogs?"

"No, the trees. Of course, the dogs."

"Well, the white one with the black saddle is Lady, and the one that's solid black is Trouble. Lady 'n Trouble."

"Very clever."

"I thought so." The hounds began sniffing her shoes and wagging their tails.

"Didn't I tell you they were friendly? Why don't you try pettin' em? You just might like it."

Hesitantly she reached her hand forward and touched one of the dogs on its smooth, rather pointed head.

"Don't you think it'd improve the looks of your house to have a hound dog on the front porch?"

"Knowing my mother, I don't think that's going to happen. I suppose you think some outboard motors and rusted buckets would look nice too. Maybe a few fishing nets."

"I never said that. Don't put words in my mouth. You just come from the Lovetts'?"

"How'd you know?"

"Where else would you have been down this way? You sure got a thing for old houses."

"Maybe."

"I got to say I admire those two old women living there in that house, living down the scandal with all the dignity they could muster."

"Scandal?"

"You know, about Annelise and all."

"Since when did dying become a scandal?"

"When you've just married a fine man, but you love someone else. Someone who's a murderer."

"I've heard there was a man accused of murder, but you know how stories grow over time."

"Yeah, we have our own little Greek tragedy. Annelise's mother was Greek. It just never made it to our schoolbooks."

"I guess I'd envisioned someone totally different."

"Story goes Annelise was a tomboy, and her doting papa indulged her whims for fast horses and anything else she wanted.

Then, when she grew up and was very beautiful, he expected her to behave like a lady. I imagine she tried, but there must have been something inside her that craved danger. She took to sneaking out at night to meet this guy who'd done some work for her dad."

"I think I heard that someplace too, but how would people have known that? How could they have found out?"

"From the Lovett servants for one. Then when this older man, Coulton, came to town and fell for the lovely Annelise, her papa couldn't believe his good fortune. But you know the rest."

Elise dropped to her knees beside Ty. "I've gotten the story in bits and pieces, and I keep thinking of her, but how awful for Coulton too."

"He had his own demons all right. He stayed with the Lovetts, all of 'em trying to console each other, I reckon, but after Annelise's funeral, he returned to the house built for his bride and walked over the threshold with empty arms and a deed in his pocket. You know which house, don't you?"

Elise nodded.

"It couldn't have been an easy thing for him to do, even with a deed to an architectural marvel. He must'a had a bad night. When the servants came the next morning, the front door stood wide open and no one ever saw him again. He didn't even take the deed. It was on the stairs, like he'd dropped it on the way out."

"That story gets more and more tragic."

You're no match for me, Coulton. I could break you in half.

Get off me, Seth. Maybe I can make this worth your while.

You mean that deed over there on the table? I don't think so. I earn my money. I don't get rich inheriting property from unfortunate girls.

I don't know what you're talking about.

I think you do. Where do you think I went when I left here? I wasn't running away like people thought.

"What's the matter? You look mighty deep in thought."

"I was just listen . . . remembering something else I'd heard."

Ty stood up and crushed the joint with the heel of his boot just as Trouble came over and pushed his head under Elise's hand.

"See, what you need is a dog. Mine are a real comfort. A dog can improve your life. You should try it."

"I wasn't aware my life needing improving."

"You got nothing better to do than hang around the old Myers' place, and you think your life doesn't need something more in it?"

"I don't think the way I spend my time is any of your business."

"No, it isn't. Wish it was though. I haven't made any bones about wanting to get to know you better."

"You sure haven't. And I haven't made any bones about not wanting to know *you* better." Elise stared up at him.

"I suppose it must be the challenge."

"What?"

"The challenge of getting to know you. You make it so damned difficult. Why else would I keep asking for your insults?"

Elise stood and brushed grass from her skirt. "Do you really like classical music or is that just a front you put on?"

"Regardless of what you think of me, my truck, or my dogs, I don't put on a 'front' as you call it. My mother gave piano lessons. Classical music was all I heard growing up. Fortunately, I liked it. Disappointed?"

"No. It's the most interesting thing about you."

"God damn! You got one mean mouth, you know that?"

"Not mean. You wanted to get to know me. I'm just being honest."

Ty sat down, leaned against the tree again and began laughing. The dogs ran over and nuzzled him under the chin and licked his face. He laughed all the harder and rolled on his stomach to get away from them.

"I don't know what's so funny. But enjoy yourself." Elise started walking away and Ty sat up.

"Elise," he called.

She stopped but didn't turn around, aware that she was assuming Lawrence's pose.

"There's a difference between being honest and being unkind. You probably don't know the difference. You people move in here and act like you own Apalach and our thoughts and feelings and everything about us. Well, you don't know jack shit. You don't know anything about me because you never bother to look beyond the end of your conceited little nose."

She whirled around then, furious. "That's not true! How dare you assume you know me! I'm not trying to be unkind. I know the people who invented unkind, the people who taunted me all the while I was growing up, the people who hurt my feelings again and again, the people who never liked me, who never tried to know me. Those people were unkind. I just want you to leave me alone." She was crying by the time she turned and started to run. Ty caught up with her and grabbed her arm.

"I'm sorry. Really. We always seem at odds with each other."

"All the more reason not to be together."

"All the more reason to get things squared away. So I'm not some ambitious blowhard. I like simple things like classical music and the silky feel of a dog's ear. That doesn't make me a doormat for you to wipe your feet on."

"I never . . ."

"You didn't have to."

She looked down at his hand still on her arm.

He followed her gaze and let his hand drop to his side.

"Elise, there's room for both of us in this town. Just don't be so quick to judge people."

"I could say the same thing about you."

"Maybe so. But if you're going to live here, let's at least try to be friends."

"I'll try, but I can't make any promises."

Ty laughed. "Do you really believe I thought you would?"

She smiled. "No, I don't suppose you would. You have more faith in those dogs."

"I guess I do. And with good reason. They're devoted and never fail to make me happy."

Elise appeared thoughtful and then looked directly at Ty, staring into his eyes. "Maybe I do need a dog."

"You could do a lot worse. Can I give you a ride home?"

"No, I . . ."

"I know. You need the exercise."

"See, you're getting to know me already." She waved and looked back to see him shuffling through the magnolia leaves, heading for his truck. "Ty?" she called.

"Yeah?" he answered hopefully.

"I've been wondering. How do you spell your name? T-e-i-g-h?"

"Nope. Just T-y. I'm glad to know you've been thinking of me. That's encouraging." He started walking back toward her.

"Don't let it be. I've just never known a Ty before. Does it stand for Tyler or Tyrone?"

"Neither. Stands for me. Guess they thought I'd be slow and gave me an easy name to deal with."

"I doubt that. Don't parents believe their children are brilliant right up to the time they get the results of an IQ test?"

"Is that your way of saying you think I have a low IQ?"

"If the shoe fits . . ." She laughed. "I didn't say that. All I know is that you're relentless."

"Relentless in my pursuit of you?"

"I didn't say you were pursuing me."

"That's what you meant though."

Elise smiled, waved again and continued on her way.

Ty started back toward his truck, mumbling, "She's thinking about you. That's progress."

Elise thought of going to the Myers', but because Margaret closed the shop at noon on Wednesday, she tried to make it a point of being home in the afternoon. When she walked in the house, Edwin called to her from the breakfast room off the kitchen where he and Margaret were having lunch.

"Join us, Elise, or did you have a repast of fruit at the Myers'?"

Elise froze. *How does he know about the Myers?* "I haven't had lunch." She ignored the reference to the Myers. "I've been re-paying some social obligations. It's good for business," she said, looking at Margaret.

"Your mother and I think you're spending far too much time out there."

"What do you mean?"

"I mean we've heard how you spend most of your days at the Myers' place. That isn't healthy. A young girl has no business out there. It could be dangerous."

Dangerous? How? And who's carrying tales?

"You can give me all the dirty looks you want. People are starting to talk. They aren't blind, you know. They make innu-endos about your long walks to the Myers'. What do you suppose they think? Your mother has a thriving business now, and I won't have you destroying that. We live here. We have reputations to uphold. We expect you to remember that and act accordingly."

The Atlanta Edwin was back. Maybe he'd never left. The cold, gruff Edwin.

"It seems to us you've developed a strange obsession where

the Myers are concerned, or you're pretending it's the Myers. People wonder what you're doing out there."

"I'm trying to decide on a major for college."

"What's that got to do with going to that spooky, old place?"

"It isn't spooky, and it has everything to do with it. I'm trying to think things through, decide what I want to do with my life."

"Why, Edwin, I think that's very smart of Elise. See, I told you there was nothing to worry about. So you did write to some schools, Elise?"

"Yes," she lied, promising herself she'd get letters in the mail right away.

"Well, I still don't like it," Edwin grumbled. "I don't like it a damn bit."

Stunned, Elise stared at him. She'd heard him say the same thing before, in other circumstances. There was the familiar blinding flash in her head, and she saw herself, just as Miss Nadine saw the boy on the bike, sitting on the floor outside her parents' bedroom crying and sucking her thumb. But her parents then were Gene and Margaret. And she could hear Edwin saying, "I don't like it a damn bit."

The next thing she knew Margaret was shaking her by the shoulders. "Elise, are you okay? What's wrong?"

Elise sighed. "I was just deep in thought."

Margaret's voice trembled. "You looked like you might be having a seizure or something."

"No," she looked at Edwin, "I was just remembering something." She turned and ran upstairs to her room.

"What's she talking about, Edwin? She frightens me."

"How should I know what she's talking about, for God's sake? No telling, considering the way she chooses to spend her time. I don't think we should let her keep going out there, Margaret. I don't like it. There's something about her that's changing."

"Maybe. But, Edwin, you seem awfully hostile lately. I think we should see the doctor about adjusting your medication again."

"Dammit, Margaret, quit trying to push it off on me. It's Elise that has the problem, not me!"

"I think I've made my point, Edwin."

"You've done nothing but make me angry. Let's just drop it, shall we?"

⌒♪⌒

ELISE WAS LYING ON HER bed staring at the ceiling when Margaret came into her room.

"I'm sorry, Elise. Since his depression, Edwin's had a short fuse. I hope it's nothing more than his medication needing some adjustment. It's pretty bad when depression seems preferable to his hostility. He scares me at times. He's sharp in ways he didn't used to be, frightening, something more than depression."

"I'm sorry if he worries you, Mom, but for me, well, he isn't really my father."

"How can you say that! He's the only father you've ever known."

"No he isn't. You've just never wanted me to talk about my real father."

"You were so little, Elise. You can't really remember Gene."

"But I do. I remember lots of things." At that moment it was bravado, but she felt she would remember—soon. Something was moving forward in her memory, a coin on the verge of dropping out of the bank where it had been imprisoned.

"While you're remembering, remember how good Edwin has been to you! Gene was a scoundrel." She gasped. "Oh, Elise, I'm sorry." She started to cry. "He was your father. I swore I'd never say anything against him."

"A scoundrel?"

"I didn't mean that. But I'll be honest, being married to Gene wasn't a bed of roses."

"Is that what you've had with 'Uncle Edwin'?"

"No, it hasn't been a bed of roses, but it's been a good marriage—on the whole. Oh, Elise, what choice did I have?" She ran out of the room and left Elise more puzzled than ever. *What choice did she have?*

Elise pleaded a headache and stayed in her room the rest of the day. Let her mother cook for a change! Sometime after dark she thought she heard Ty's truck and music, but she couldn't be sure. Then, without knowing why, she pulled her nicest gown over her head and draped her grandmother's pearls around her neck. She looked down at them, thinking they looked like something Annelise might have worn. She pushed her fingers through her thick hair, lifted it upward and let it fall over her shoulders. She started toward the mirror but paused and turned back toward the bed. Like a rosary, she kept sliding the pearls through her fingers and then laid them on her nightstand before getting into bed. She stared at the ceiling until her eyes were sore and dry. She didn't remember falling asleep, but finally the headache was gone, and she was at peace.

There's no way Edwin can keep me away from Lawrence. I'm not a child any more, frightened of his displeasure. I'm not like my mother; I have a choice, and I won't let him destroy my happiness. She walked to the Myers', all the while hearing classical music, but never seeing Ty's truck. When she walked through the gate, she noticed again how quiet everything was. And again Lawrence came running down the stairs, but this time he came right up to her and took both her hands in his. He was unbearably close and pressed her hands to his lips.

"What's come over you?"

"You. You've come over me."

"Mrs. Myers?" she called, her heart a drumbeat in her ears. "Is your mother here, Lawrence?"

He continued holding her hands to his lips and slowly shook his head, his green eyes filled with mischief.

"She must have gone into town?" He nodded and a faint smiled played about his mouth. Without a moment's hesitation, he took Elise in his arms and carried her up the stairs to his bedroom. His eyes never left hers as he leaned forward and began unbuttoning her blouse. He slid her bra straps off her shoulders and kissed the top of her breasts. She moaned and slipped out of her shorts and underwear. Oh, dear God, that this could happen. Elise moved her hands down Lawrence's lean, hard body as she unbuttoned his shirt and slid his pants to the floor. On his bed, next to him, her body brimmed with the warmth of happiness. Even to someone as naïve as Elise, she found it hard to believe he wasn't an experienced lover. Yet how . . . and then she ceased to think or wonder about anything beyond the feel of his body against hers. His hands were gentle and caressing, and his lips seemed to devour her. The ecstasy of the moment was like a glowing white light. Her back arched and she cried out. But the voice wasn't hers. Long, dark hair lay over Lawrence's pillow. Long dark hair that belonged to someone else. Annelise! Lawrence had made love to Annelise! She could see her lying there beneath him. Not Elise! Annelise!

"How," she whispered, "How? You can't have him! You're dead."

And then she saw two skeletons on the bed, one on top of the other.

She cried out and sat up in bed, rigid with fear, her fine gown drenched with perspiration even as she shook in the chilled air. She pressed the edge of the sheet to her breast and felt something hard. She was wearing the pearls she remembered leaving on the bedside table.

"Finish your own dance," she sobbed. "I've quit caring." As she pulled her damp gown over her head, the dream returned so vivid, it seemed more than a dream, and she shivered in the drafts of cold air. "I can't see you," she whispered, "and that makes me afraid. But you can't have Lawrence. I won't let you!" She didn't go back to bed, determined to be out of the house before Edwin came downstairs the next morning. She left a note secured with a magnet to the refrigerator.

Gone for a walk
Be back for lunch

Let them think she was at the Myers'. They wouldn't find her there. Not today.

Careful not to wake her parents, Elise eased the door open and rushed down the front steps, again reminded of Annelise's feverish flight toward the river. The trees, wet with morning dew, were filled with the sounds of jays and cardinals and the rustling of sparrows. She took a deep breath and hurried away from the house and Edwin. She crossed Avenue E and walked aimlessly, finally pausing to look in the window of a coffee shop she hadn't noticed there before. She stared without seeing when Ty pushed the door open.

"Elise! What are you doing here this time of day?"

"I could ask you the same thing."

"Having some java. When I make coffee, it tastes like diesel fuel. Come keep me company."

Without a word, she followed him inside. Ty's lone cup of coffee was on a table near the window. The other tables were crowded with men in plaid shirts and heavy boots, everybody talking about the work that lay ahead of them. They rubbed their hands across oilcloth tabletops smoothing out their ideas, their schedules, and plans for the day. Steaming cups of coffee vied for space among plates of grits and eggs and sausage. Elise and Ty sat down, and Gladys Sexton appeared at their table.

"Business is booming, Gladys."

"Sure is, handsome. What can I get for your girlfriend?"

Ty looked at Elise, but she just stared expressionless. "Just coffee, I guess." Gladys started away and Ty called, "and a plate of toast. Bring us some toast. Please." He looked at Elise. "Unless you want something more."

Elise shook her head.

"I don't want to take up one of her tables and not spend some money. She's got lots of competition with all these bed and breakfast places springing up all over town." He took a sip of coffee. "You're mighty quiet. Sure you're awake yet?"

"I'm tired. I didn't sleep well last night."

Ty knew the men were watching them, but he didn't care. He waved and turned back to face Elise. He couldn't help but feel good to be sitting at the same table with her. She sat with her head bent and her hands folded in her lap. Obviously she wasn't taking the pleasure in the moment that he was. Service was slow, and he could see why. Gladys had hired mature women, inexperienced as waitresses. They worked their way single file among the tables, each carrying one dish. Ty couldn't help but smile. He hadn't realized Elise was watching him until she asked, "What's so funny?"

"They act like bridesmaids," he said, "carrying bouquets of grits and eggs."

"Classical music and now metaphors. You bring a whole new meaning to redneck."

"Hey," he started, but Gladys came then with Elise's coffee. "The toast'll be here in a minute. You need water or anything?"

"Thanks, Gladys, but we're fine, I think. Elise?"

She didn't answer so he flashed his most engaging smile and said, "Like I said, we're fine."

"This old building's been here forever. Gladys bought a lot

of history with this place. Back in the 1800s it was a bakery, Mrs. Emily Bell's bakery. Quite a lady, Mrs. Bell. She ran a hotel, too, after her husband was blinded in the Civil War." Elise didn't comment but did sip her coffee. He felt like every eye in the place was on them, and he tried to pretend everything was okay. "Guess you're not interested in commercial buildings, no matter how old they are."

Elise glanced up and gave him a withering look.

He blew on his coffee and said, "This will probably become my favorite hangout in the near future. Yep, I'll probably be joining these guys full-time soon." He looked at Elise for a response and wasn't sure she'd even heard him. He was thankful for the diversion when a waitress brought their toast.

"I guess you can hold your curiosity about what I was trying to tell you while we have a bite to eat. I can see you're just dying to know what I'm talking about, though." He let out a heavy sigh. "Elise, please do me a favor and eat a piece of toast. I have a bit of a reputation here." The words were no more out of his mouth than the door opened and a pretty young girl came in. She stood for a moment and looked around the room before going out of her way to walk past Ty's table. Elise looked up at her, but the girl didn't acknowledge her presence, saying very pointedly, "Hello, Ty."

Ty flashed his smile again and said, "Morning, Jess. Nice place your mom has here."

"Isn't it just?" she said, looking back at Elise now before going behind the counter to speak to her mother.

"Your girlfriend?" Elise asked dully.

"No."

"Too bad. She's pretty."

"You're prettier."

"But I'm not your girlfriend either."

"No, you're not. More's the pity."

"Ty, would you have time to take me by the Lovetts'?"

"But you were just there yesterday!"

"I know. I wouldn't ask you, but I feel too tired to walk."

"I don't suppose being up at the crack of dawn would have anything to do with it."

"Probably."

"I always have time for you." He took another bite of toast. "You should know that by now. But as I was saying, I'll soon be joining these guys here mornings." Seeing she still wasn't paying attention to what he was saying, he reversed course. "Do you mind my asking why you'd want to go to the Lovetts'? I swear you must have a thing for old houses."

"I have an obsession with ghosts."

"You believe that stuff about their house being haunted?"

"Oh, yes, I believe it."

"I guess it's people like you who keep stories like that alive."

Elise shrugged and drained her cup of coffee. She started to stand up and Ty said, "I'll pay the check and be right with you." As they walked out the door Jess called, "See you around, Ty."

"Yeah, Jess. See ya."

"Bet she'd be your girlfriend if you wanted her."

"If I wanted her."

They rode in silence until they reached the Lovett house. "I'm sorry to be such a bother." Elise hesitated with her hand on the handle of the door but then got out of the truck. She stopped by Ty's window. "I won't be long."

Her knees felt rubbery as she climbed the steps. She drew a shaky breath and was about to knock on the door when she saw something out of the corner of her eye. Her box of cookies was still on the table, alive with ants. She seemed unable to look away when the door opened and Aunt Lacey was there, staring at the white box crawling with ants. "Oh, my dear, I'm so sorry. You'll have to forgive Jenny. Do come in."

Just as Aunt Lacey stepped back to let Elise enter, Aunt Jenny, old as she was, came down the stairs so fast she might have been fleeing a fire herself. Still in her nightgown, she went straight to the open door. She knocked Lacey aside and pushed Elise backward, nearly knocking her over. "I thought I made it clear you weren't welcome here."

"I hate to trouble you, but I'm having a problem. I need your help. Please let me come in."

"What kind of problem?" Aunt Jenny snapped.

"I," she hesitated, "I think it's Annelise."

"You may have a problem," Aunt Jenny snorted, "but I assure you it isn't Annelise."

"Then why did I hear music, that beautiful waltz, in your ballroom?"

"You didn't!"

She thought she heard Aunt Lacey pleading, saying Elise had heard music, when the door slammed in her face. A breeze picked up and cold air swirled about her legs. Elise looked at the long flight of porch steps, sighed and spoke into the breeze, "You're here as sure as I am. I know you are. I just can't see you."

Ty started the truck as Elise came down the steps. "I see they didn't invite you in for tea."

"Please, Ty, don't."

"Sorry. Where to now?"

"No, I'm the one who's sorry. Here you're providing free taxi service, and I behave like an old grouch."

"I'm not sure how free it is."

"What?"

"Nothing. Never mind. Want to come to my place for a while, unless you're worried about your reputation?"

"You mean my parents' reputation. I seem to have ruined mine already. I really want to go to the Myers'."

"Elise, I'll take you any place you want to go. I'll take you to Tallahassee if you want me to, but I really don't want to take you out there. I can't understand . . . oh, never mind."

Elise's eyes narrowed. "Have you been talking to Edwin?"

"What? Your dad? Why would I talk to him?"

"I just wondered. I guess that settles it then. I'm not up to the walk, that's for sure."

"Boy, you must be tired! You've hardly insulted me today. I'm not used to you being so docile."

"I'm tired of so many things, Ty. My dad especially."

"Anything I can do?"

"No, but you're sweet to offer."

"You have no idea how sweet I can be if you'd give me half a chance."

Ty pulled up in front of her house and jumped out to open her door. When they reached the steps, he could see Edwin standing behind the door. Elise squeezed Ty's hand. "Thanks again." Before he could answer, she was out of his reach and up the steps. Edwin stepped aside to let her pass. "Margaret's at the shop, Elise. We were worried about you."

Elise didn't answer and started up the stairs to her room. Edwin shouted at her, "I'm talking to you!" The only sound was her door closing. She lay back on her bed, unable to escape the weight of her dream, a pressure that tormented her. *I have to rest, regain my energy so I can deal with this.*

16

*D*allas had just finished a late lunch when she heard a car pull up in her front yard. She went to the door and was surprised to see Aunt Lacey getting out of a taxi.

"Why, Aunt Lacey, what an unexpected pleasure. Do come in." She leaned over to kiss the old woman on the cheek. Lacey gripped her arm and whispered, "It's not a pleasure call, Dallas."

Dallas waved the taxi driver away. "It's okay, Henry. I'll give her a ride home."

"HERE COMES THE LAST OF the big spenders, Bobby," Peyton called when Dallas came in the shop.

"Don't you wish? Hey, Bobby." Dallas waved and walked over to a turnstile that glittered with brooches. "This new?"

Peyton grinned. "Want to get my hand in before the competition beats me to it."

"We just expanded on the stuff we already had, Miss Dallas. Bet you'll find something there you like."

"I'm not buying today, Bobby. Just looking. I feel restless."

"I got a sure-fire cure for restless," Peyton said.

"Peyton Roberts, do you ever get your mind out of the gutter?"

"Not if I can help it, darlin', not if I can help it."

"How 'bout buying me a bottle of Coke and a package of peanuts? I want something cold that fizzes, and I need to talk."

"I can talk to a pretty woman 'til the cows come home, but you'll have to buy something so I have money."

"Peyton!"

"Okay, let's get that bottle of Coke. It's all yours, Bobby."

As they walked past Margaret's shop, she was placing a sign in the window. In fancy script it read, A TOUCH OF CLASS.

"That sticks in my craw," Peyton said. "Makes it sound like the rest of us don't have any class."

"Do we?"

"You know what I mean."

"I'll admit I envied her when they first came here. She's so beautiful and seems to have such a charmed life. But any more, I don't know. Despite all she has going for her, she doesn't seem happy. The more I get to know Margaret, the more I feel sorry for her."

"I don't feel sorry for her," Peyton muttered.

"What?"

"Elise is the one I feel sorry for."

"Me too, but she's young. There's still time for her. Say, let's give some business to one of our own. Did you know Gladys Sexton opened a coffee shop?"

Peyton laughed. "Where do you think I get my coffee every morning, one of those fancy bed and breakfast joints? I'm glad Miz Bell's old place is in the food business again."

"Umm," Dallas murmured and looked around. Gladys's barebones establishment reminded Dallas of her own childhood passion for playing café. She looked around at the wooden tables covered with blue checked oilcloth and the long table with a cash register that served as Gladys's counter. Open loaves of bread spilled out on a worktable in the back, with jars of mayonnaise and mustard in plain view. The light on the Coke machine winked at her from the back wall. Gladys, Dallas thought, hadn't gone much beyond playing herself.

"What's on your mind, Dallas, that's making you so restless?"

"I had a visitor today." She opened the bag of peanuts and poured a generous amount into the bottle of Coke.

"Anybody I know?"

"Aunt Lacey. She had Henry bring her over in his taxi."

Peyton whistled. "Aunt Lacey?"

"Don't think I wasn't surprised. She said I was the closest thing to a relative they have. She can't talk to Jenny. All they do is argue. While Jenny was taking her nap, she called Henry to come get her. Their first stop was the old family cemetery. Turns out Elise went to their house this morning asking for help. She thinks Annelise is haunting her or something, and Aunt Lacey believes her. Believes Elise heard the music too, so she paid Henry to pull some weeds and clean Annelise's grave up a bit. Sounds like she's trying to bribe a ghost into leaving Elise alone. Aunt Lacey insists Annelise still comes to the house, but Jenny says she'll have her put in a mental institution if she ever tells anybody."

Dallas lowered her voice. "Jenny's taken out a restraining order on Elise. Doesn't want her near their property. I think it's more to get back at Lacey for taking Elise's part than anything, but she swears she'll have Lacey committed if she sees Elise near their house again. Poor soul's scared to death. And, get this, Aunt Jenny's been threatening to go to Edwin, if she hasn't already."

"You're kidding!"

"Not in the least, darlin'." Dallas hesitated a moment before she said, "Peyton, I hate to ask you, but will you be a dear and talk to Margaret? All that child needs is to have on her conscience that she was responsible for having Aunt Lacey put away someplace."

"Yeah, sure, but I'll have to think how to approach it." He stood and picked up the little green ticket Gladys left at their table. He paused a moment and looked down at Dallas. "Why don't you and me go out for oysters on the half shell some night?"

"You really know how to get turned down for a date, don't you? You know good and well I can't stand raw oysters."

"Like I always told you, darlin', they go down like a bad cold. But I'm willing to compromise. I'll eat 'em raw, and you can have yours fried."

"Let's do that, but first let's settle this business with Margaret. No point in going for a bout of indigestion."

"Okay. But soon. You can't stay in mourning forever." Peyton tipped his imaginary hat to Gladys, and when he returned to the table, Dallas stood and gave his hand a quick squeeze. "Thanks, Peyton. Don't know what I'd do without you."

"You don't have to, you know."

"No, I don't, do I? That's what's so nice about being friends with the landed gentry."

They stepped outside the door, and Peyton's voice took on a husky tremor. "You know what I mean."

"Do I?" She laughed and jangled her car keys from her upraised hand as she crossed the street to her car.

MARGARET LOOKED UP FROM THE cash register when she heard the shop bells on the front door. She moistened her lips and gave Peyton a dazzling smile.

Peyton feigned interest in some stationery until the last customer left the store.

"You won't find what you're looking for over there. I haven't put it out yet." Margaret reached under the counter and drew out a simple but elegant tablet of lined paper. The lines were silver on a blue gray background. The cover was of nubby cream-colored paper. She held it out to Peyton. "A gift for being such a nice neighbor and checking on me the other night."

"Do I owe you a pair of shoes now?"

Margaret gave a disgusted sigh. "I'm only trying to be nice. Give it back if it makes you uncomfortable."

"I'm sorry. I appreciate it, really. I'm just a bit concerned about something right now. You ever take a break from all this good smellin' stuff?"

"I suppose I could close for a few minutes. Do we have some kind of emergency?"

"We don't, but there's something I need to discuss with you."

"You seem so serious."

"I am serious, Maggie. It concerns Elise."

"Oh." She didn't know whether she was more shocked by him calling her Maggie or his reference to Elise. She pulled an ornate fan from under the counter. The word "Closed" was lettered on the front, and she propped it in the front window. "Lead the way."

"Maybe we could just sit in the back. Do you have any kind of office?"

"Nothing elegant, but I'm working on it."

"Well, I don't want a headache, but we need some privacy."

"I'll give you a headache," she threatened as she walked toward the back room.

"You already do," he said softly.

"What?"

"Nothing. Talking to myself."

They sat facing each other in antique rockers. For a long

time Peyton didn't say anything, trying to calm himself and collect his thoughts. "Maggie, I don't know how to put this. It sounds crazy, but Elise has developed an unwholesome interest in people around here, people who've been dead for years."

"But what . . .?"

"Hear me out. This is hard enough. I'm not in the habit of betraying a confidence, and I don't want anything Elise may have confided in me to leave this room. Still, for her sake I have to talk to you. It's crucial that she stay away from the Lovetts. Aunt Jenny has taken out a restraining order."

"She's what! I don't understand. What do the Lovetts have to do with Elise?"

Peyton sighed and rubbed his hand across his hair. "Remember when Dallas took Elise to see the Lovett's?"

Margaret nodded.

"Well, Elise asked to see the ballroom where Annelise was dancing on her wedding night. Dallas said they unlocked the doors, and Elise glided into the room and danced like an angel."

Margaret stifled a laugh. "Elise doesn't dance. I could never even get her to take lessons. She was too much of a tomboy."

"Well, she did dance and claimed she danced to music. No one heard music but Elise. Believe me, everyone was shook, especially Elise."

"I wish you'd told me. It's all so so . . ."

"I know. I wish I had too, but Elise confided in me, and I tried to honor that confidence. And now she's been back to the Lovetts'. After she went there again this morning, trying to get them to let her inside, Jenny took out a restraining order. Told her sister she'll have her committed if Elise shows up there again."

"Have Elise committed?"

"No, she'll have Aunt Lacey committed because she's taken

Elise's part in all this. Poor old thing's terrified. None of us, especially not Elise, should have that on their conscience."

Margaret walked to the window, wringing her hands. "What's wrong with her? What am I going to do? How can I tell Edwin?"

"Maggie, stop! Listen to me." Peyton got up and stood behind her, unable to resist the temptation to grip her shoulders. "We'll handle this somehow, but I'm begging you, please don't betray the confidence Elise has placed in me."

Not since Edwin's illness had Margaret felt so numb with disbelief. She didn't want to move, to have Peyton take his hands from her shoulders. She leaned her head back slightly and her hair brushed his face. Unable to prolong the moment any longer, she turned and stood before him, closer than was comfortable, struggling to take a deep breath.

"You okay?" he asked, his voice hoarse.

"Not really," she whispered before returning to her chair. "All these people, dead and alive, seem woven into some gruesome tapestry."

Peyton stood, looking down on her for a moment and went back to his rocker. "I never thought of it like that, but in a way, I guess they are. Aunt Jenny might not follow through with her threat, but she could stir up a peck of trouble for Elise. For all its influx of foreigners, Apalach is still a small town. It could get real unpleasant."

"Surely this Aunt Jenny isn't serious! She wouldn't have her own sister committed any more than she'd bother with Elise. And anyway, who in this day and age would believe this garbage about a girl who's been dead for over a hundred years?"

Peyton leaned forward and rested his head in his hands.

"Oh, Peyton, you don't believe it, do you?"

"What I believe isn't important. The issue here is that Elise believes it. I don't know, Maggie," he passed his hand across his mouth, "it's almost like Annelise waited all these years for the right person to come along . . ."

"Now stop! You're sounding crazy too." She reached forward and touched his knee. Not until he covered her hand with his did she realize what she'd done. It was such a natural gesture.

"Yeah, I guess I do, but don't ever underestimate the power of the mind or its byproduct, the imagination. It's a force that can make us believe things that aren't true, the same as it can help us understand things that are true." He squeezed her hand and leaned back in his chair.

She appeared thoughtful for a moment. "I can see Elise being captive to her imagination in this setting. But back to this Aunt Lacey. Did she ask you to tell me all this?"

"No, Dallas did."

"Dallas!" Margaret sat up straight, sliding her hand from Peyton's knee.

"Aunt Lacey went to her with all this."

"I suppose Dallas didn't want to embarrass me by telling me herself."

"I'm not sure what her reasoning was. She knows you and I haven't exactly hit it off, so it was a big favor for her to ask of me."

"Yes, I can see it would be. You two have known each other a long time . . ."

"Forever."

"So she'd feel comfortable going to you for help."

"I'm flattered to say yes to that. She's special in so many ways."

"She is. She really is." Margaret sat for a time not saying anything, and Peyton tried to lighten the situation.

"I'd say you smell good, but I can't tell what's you and what's soap."

"It doesn't really matter, but for your information, Mr. Roberts, I do smell good."

"I never doubted it for a minute, not a minute."

"Damn, but I hate to go to Edwin with this. He's been so short-tempered lately, not just ugly to Elise but to me too."

"Elise told me he'd been ill a while back."

"It seems she tells you a lot."

"She has to talk to somebody . . . Maggie, I really care about Elise. She's probably the closest thing to a daughter I'll ever have. I was drawn to her the first time she came in the store. I had this overpowering need to protect her. She seemed so vulnerable . . ."

"I've never seen her as vulnerable, just difficult."

"Maybe you don't understand her."

"I'm her mother, for God's sake."

"Yes, you are." Peyton gave Margaret a penetrating look, and she turned away.

"Okay, so I haven't been the ideal mother, but I've tried. Truly I've tried."

"I'm sure you have. Parents aren't any more perfect than their children."

"I'm glad she's able to talk to you. She surely isn't getting along with Edwin these days. To be honest, they were never close, never had much of a relationship. I suppose she told you he isn't her biological father."

Peyton nodded.

"Elise was too young to know what was going on, but my first marriage . . . well, we had some trouble. It was ugly, and all these years neither Edwin nor I have ever really gotten over it. We thought we had, but it came back to haunt us."

"So you believe in ghosts?"

"No. That was just an expression! I most certainly do not

believe in ghosts. I don't think Elise does either. She's just confused, you know, moving from her home and all. I do dread going to Edwin with this. Better I tell him, though, than have him talk to that Aunt Jenny. You know, I can't help but wonder if she's talked to him already. He's been so angry."

"Could be, but she's pretty reclusive."

She sighed and closed her eyes briefly. "I have my work cut out for me this evening. I can't imagine how this is going to affect Edwin."

"I worry how it's going to affect Elise. I wish there were some way I could help."

She made a harsh sound. "I do too. I wish I could let you handle things with Edwin. I so dread facing him. He just isn't himself, and I don't know how he might react, but you've helped already, Peyton. You know you have." She leaned forward and cupped his hand in hers, remembering how she'd done the same thing to Gene, the way she'd kissed his palm when she told him she was expecting a baby. She lingered a long moment, turning Peyton's hand palm up when she heard him clear his throat. "Boy, this soap really gets to you, doesn't it?"

"Oh, I'm sorry. I was just remembering something." She released his hand, and Peyton stood up and started for the door. They'd crossed over into a new relationship Peyton was less equipped to handle than the old one. "I'm sorry to have been the bearer of bad news, especially that concerns Elise. If I can help, let me know."

"You really do mean that, don't you?"

"Yes, I mean it. Now I'm going to leave before I do something foolish."

He reached the door before she was out of her chair, before he could hear her say, "Oh, do something foolish, please do something foolish."

As it turned out, it was Margaret who was foolish. She thought her head would burst if she had to keep all the things Peyton had told her to herself, yet the evening got later and later, and Edwin was still on the phone with a client in Atlanta. By the time they finished dinner it was unusually late, and they were all tired. Still, Margaret was determined to have things out in the open. Elise started to her room when Margaret told her they needed to talk. She pleaded another headache, but Margaret was adamant. She did wonder, though, if Elise really might have a headache. She looked so expressionless. Edwin folded his paper. "Sure this can't wait until tomorrow, Margaret?"

"No, it can't wait one more minute." Keeping her voice as steady as possible, Margaret related the story, implying it had been Dallas who had talked to her.

"NO!" Elise jumped up from her chair. "That mean old woman. She's just like Annelise!"

"Elise," Margaret scolded. "You shouldn't speak of the dead that way."

"You mean like you shouldn't call my father a scoundrel?" She heard Margaret's indrawn breath but went on. "Being dead doesn't change what Annelise was. I won't go to the Lovetts' because I don't want to hurt Aunt Lacey, but," she looked at Edwin, "I refuse to stay away from the Myers."

Edwin stood up. "Margaret, you and Elise sit." Elise continued to stand, and he towered over her. "I said, sit!"

He was so angry all the color had drained from his face, making him look the way he had when he was cowed by depression.

"Please, Elise," Margaret implored.

Elise started to leave the room, but Edwin jerked her back by the arm and shoved her into the chair. "Now, if I have your attention. You are not, under any circumstances, to go to the Myers' place again. Never. Do we understand each other?"

"No! We don't understand each other. I told you, I won't stay away."

"Oh, I think you will. Your father spoiled things for your mother and me long enough. I won't let you do it here."

"Edwin!"

"Be still, Margaret. You know it's true. If Elise goes to the Myers' again, it won't be Jenny Lovett she has to worry about. She'll answer to me. Go there again, Elise, and I'll have that place condemned, torn down. It won't be the Myers' anymore."

Elise gasped and stared, openmouthed.

"I hate you," Elise screamed. "I've always hated you." She ran to her room, grabbed the pearls, went back downstairs and flung them hard at Edwin's feet. He flinched from the sting but kicked them aside and grabbed her before she could walk away. In one swift movement, he pulled her around and slapped her viciously across the face.

Margaret screamed and rushed toward Elise, but Edwin grabbed her, sobbing. "Oh, Margaret, I'm so sorry. I didn't mean to. I'm so sorry," he whimpered. Margaret was still trying to pull away from him when she saw Elise run out the front door.

Elise's first thought was to go to the Myers', but she was afraid Edwin would follow her. Fearful that he might make good on his threat, she walked in the opposite direction. She'd run a few blocks and then walk to catch her breath, all the while looking back over her shoulder for car lights. She avoided the main roads and walked in the shadows of trees, unable to bring herself to go home. She wandered without realizing where she was until she saw the lights from the screened porch where she'd watched Monopoly and bridge games. The Montgomery house. The familiarity of it attracted her like a moth. It was late and there were no games tonight, just a couple of guys talking. She stood in a stupor behind the camellia bush, not realizing at first that one of the guys was Ty. He seemed to be arguing with someone she hadn't seen before.

"You've always been strange, Ty. Here you're home again, and my sister is fairly dying to go out with you—her and a few others I could name. Won't you take her out just once?"

"I don't think so, Stan." Ty shook his head. "It wouldn't be fair to encourage her."

Elise kept trying to place the name Stan. Who'd mentioned a Stan? Then she remembered Dallas saying he was Louise Montgomery's son.

"Who knows, Ty. You just might enjoy yourself."

"Nah. I don't think so."

"Who's this girl you're so crazy about?"

"Nobody you know. She's new here."

"She live in Sarah's house?"

"Yeah."

"What do you see in her?"

"I see someone intelligent, sensitive . . . God. She's like music to me, a concerto I can't hear often enough. I can't believe how much I want to be with her. She draws me like a magnet."

"Like your music."

"Yeah. I don't understand it, but I'm crazy about her. Hell, Stan, it's not easy to explain. It's just how I feel."

"Let's have a beer and forget it. Debby would be crushed if she found out I talked to you and got nowhere. Didn't you notice how the girls left so we could be alone?"

"I hadn't really thought about it."

"Well, it was all part of the plan. I'll have to lie and tell her we talked about school and stuff."

Later, when Ty walked across the street to his truck, he couldn't help but think that he was being as silly as Debby. Elise Foster had made her feelings about him abundantly clear. He jumped in the truck and turned the music on before he realized he wasn't alone. "Debby?"

"Guess again."

"Elise! What are you doing here?"

"Hiding."

"Is this some kind of game?"

"I wish. I had a big falling out with my . . . with Edwin, and I can't go home now."

He started the truck and turned the volume down on the music. "I suppose you've eaten already. Would you like something to drink?"

"No. Thanks. I don't know if Edwin's looking for me, and I don't want to risk having him find me. Let's go to that place you wanted to take me before, where the moon shines on the water."

"You're different from any girl I've ever known. This is the first time a girl ever asked me to take her to Lookout Bay, and I know your intentions aren't what I'd like them to be."

"Thanks for understanding that."

They drove in silence, and when he parked the truck overlooking the bay, she still didn't say anything.

"Have you ever noticed how still and quiet this town is?" He didn't wait for an answer and continued talking. "I do love this place. I've always felt so lucky to have grown up here, but then, maybe everybody loves their hometown." He hesitated, inhaling the silence. "I just wish I could find some way to really say it, to find words that would describe what I feel."

It pained him to hear her rapid, indrawn breath, the involuntary leftovers from crying. He wanted to hold her hand, do something to comfort her. *No,* he thought, *you dork, you want to hold her in your arms.* Tentatively he touched her hand with his forefinger. "Elise, maybe it'd make you feel better to talk about it." The silence held, and he thought she wasn't going to answer.

Finally, "I can tell you I won't be going to the Myers' any more. Not because I don't want to. I've been threatened, forbidden."

"I'm sorry. I really am. I don't understand, but I know going there is important to you."

"The most important thing in the world. I know you think I'm weird, but, Ty, I feel absolutely haunted. That old house on the river has nothing on me. I feel Annelise's presence. I think she gets inside my body, or at least my head. I don't expect you to understand, but that's how I feel."

"I've never bought into that ghost stuff. I always felt there was enough mystery right here on earth without looking to the beyond for more."

"I never bought into it either until I came here. I was always aware that I never fit in. I was never popular or anything like that. I felt out of synch. But I didn't think of the supernatural, not seriously anyway, until we moved here. I think it began in earnest the first night I slept in Annelise's house. I've been plagued with dreams—nightmares really—ever since. Try to explain that."

"I wish I could, but you know I can't. What will you do?"

"I don't know. My parents will want to pack me off to college right away. That will be their solution, but it isn't what I want."

"I remember when I went away to school. How hard it was to leave here. I'd give anything to be able to help you, but I don't know how."

"I don't know either, Ty. But I appreciate your listening, letting me be here with you."

"You know how much I mind that, don't you?"

"I think so."

They sat for a long time staring at the water. Ty was both miserable and happy. Elise sat beside him, numb with grief and pain.

"Elise?"

"Huh?"

"It's long past midnight. It doesn't matter to me, but I don't want you to be in trouble."

"No chance of that," she replied hoarsely. "I'm already in trouble."

It was quiet in the truck, and they could hear the water lapping at the shore. Several hours later Ty woke up with a start. Elise was slumped against his shoulder, and he had a crick in his neck. He turned on the light in the truck. "Sweet Jesus, Elise, it's five a.m.!" She pulled back from him and rolled her head from side to side. The sharp intake of his breath shocked her awake. "Oh, Elise, what happened? Why didn't you tell me?" He touched his forefinger gently to her cheek and she winced. "Oh, baby, who did this?"

She spoke haltingly. "Take me to Peyton's." Unable to hold back the tears any longer, she began crying quietly. "I have to see Peyton."

"Okay, we'll go to Peyton's." He put the truck in reverse and peeled out. When they got to Peyton's house he said, "You stay here. I'll see if he's home." It seemed he'd hardly left before he was back in the truck. When they got to the shoe store, Peyton's truck was parked out front, but it was dark inside. "Sometimes he goes down to the Gorrie Bridge to wait for daybreak."

"I'll wait for him then."

"Let's drive around back. Maybe he's in his office." They could see a dim light, and Ty rushed around and opened her door. "I wish you'd let me help you."

"I wish I could too."

"I'd like to think you mean that."

"Really," she said, "I do." She turned then, and knocked on the heavy oak door. She looked back at Ty and was about to return to the truck when she heard the lock turning. He had a cup of coffee in his hand, his shirt wasn't tucked in, and his hair was uncombed. "Well, aren't we a sight?" Peyton said. "I can't remember when I've had a pretty lady call on me at this hour. Come on in."

He stuck his head out the door and waved to Ty as he started the truck and began pulling away. Elise followed Peyton to his office, and he pulled a chair over for her. "Ouch," Peyton groaned. "Ty didn't do that, did he?"

She touched her cheek. "Ty?" she asked, puzzled.

"Apparently you just got out of his truck. He's really smitten with you, but he told me he can't seem to get to first base."

"This has nothing to do with Ty." She touched the warmth of her cheek with her fingertips. "Edwin can take credit for this."

He whistled. "Your dad?"

"My Uncle Edwin."

"You aren't making sense, hon."

"Edwin was my real father's best friend. Before he and my mother married, he was Uncle Edwin."

"So that's how it is. Has he always made a habit of hitting you?"

"This is the first time. I said something mean that hurt him. He was very ill before we moved here, and he hasn't been able to control his temper since. He doesn't want me going to the Myers' any more. He said such ugly things. But, Peyton, I don't know how I can bear to stay away. He even implied Lawrence is dangerous."

"Lawrence Myers? What's he got to do with you?"

"Edwin's forbidden me to go there. He doesn't want me to see Lawrence. That's obvious."

Peyton ran his fingers through his hair and took a sip of coffee. "I'm afraid I'm not following you."

"I don't understand it myself, Peyton, but I'm in love with Lawrence, so desperately in love."

The color drained from Peyton's face, and his eyes widened.

"I know what you're thinking, but he talks to me. He really does."

"It isn't that, it's . . ."

"The age difference?" She gave a short laugh. "It doesn't seem to exist. All that matters is this overpowering love I have for him. He's all I think about."

Peyton got up from his chair and walked around to Elise. He knelt on the floor in front of her, taking both her hands in his. He held them for a long moment, then kissed her warm cheek. "Elise, honey, Lawrence, all the Myers—they've been dead for years."

Elise stood up so quickly she pushed Peyton backward and turned her chair over. "No! I see him all the time, and his mother has been so kind to me. You said yourself you haven't been by there in years. They're there. Just go and see."

"Elise, believe me, I want to help you. You have to have imagined all this."

"NO! Don't do this to me! I haven't imagined it. I thought I could tell you anything, that you'd be the one person who'd understand."

"I'm trying, hon, I'm trying. Ty thinks you just have some fascination with that old house. God knows everything is still there, but it has to be a mess, though the county keeps the weeds down and stuff like that."

"No, I'll prove it. I'll go see them right now. I have to see Lawrence." She rubbed her temples. "Even I know it sounds crazy, but, Peyton, I believe Annelise is in love with Lawrence too."

"Hon, she'd have more right. They're both dead."

Elise burst into tears. "Peyton, you of all people! I thought I could count on you—for anything."

"Dear Lord, I thought so too."

"I have to get out there. I need to get there right away." She walked toward the door.

"Wait. I'll take you. My truck's out front." Peyton's hands shook so badly he could hardly fit the keys into the ignition. For once he was at a loss for words. He drove slowly, trying to think what could have happened. The music and now this.

When they reached the house he thought how much it re-sembled nothing more than a charcoal painting. "See, it's de-serted. There's nobody here."

"It's early. They just aren't up yet."

His voice cracked, "Oh, darlin', please don't do this."

"Do what? Love the only person I've cared about my whole life?"

"Let me take you home. No, let me take you to Dallas. Dallas will give you a cup of good strong coffee, and we can talk about this some more."

"No, Peyton, I have to wait here. I have to see for myself."

"I can't leave you out here. You know that."

"I've been coming here for months. Why is today any dif-ferent?"

"For one thing, you've had quite a blow—a couple of 'em."

"Please trust me. Let me stay. I belong here. I really do."

"I'll have to tell your folks."

"No! Please. This one time. Let me have this time."

"Elise, understand. I feel responsible."

"I give you my word. No one will ever know you brought me here. And I'll be fine. I really will."

She opened the door to the truck and then turned back to kiss his cheek. The salt on his wet face tasted blue. "Everything will be okay. I promise."

Peyton drove to the end of the road and turned around.

The last he saw of Elise was through the rearview mirror. She was opening the gate. He was numb with disbelief. He didn't recall the drive back to Apalach except that he felt he'd been to the end of the world.

The first thing he remembered was knocking on Dallas's door. She turned on a lamp in the living room and came to the door wearing a robe of yellow silk. Her hair was tousled, and she looked so very appealing. When he saw her, Peyton's first thought was of poor Tom Anderson, to have had to leave Dallas. He didn't know if it was desire or grief but he caught her in his arms and laid his cheek on top of her head.

"Peyton? What's happened? What's wrong?"

"I don't even know where to begin, Dallas. How bout making us some strong coffee and letting me use your phone. I have to call someone."

He watched her walk toward the kitchen, noting the gentle sway of her hips beneath the silk. He held the phone a minute before dialing. "Ty? Thank God you're home. I was afraid you'd still be out."

"I was just about to leave again. Is Elise okay?"

"No. That's why I'm calling. I don't want to go into it now, Ty, but she's not well. I left her out at the Myers', and I'd . . ."

"You what!"

"I know. I felt I had no choice. She was so insistent. But would you drive by there and see if she's okay? Don't tell her I sent you or anything. I just don't know what she's liable to do."

"I'm leaving now. I don't know why in God's name I care about that girl, but I do."

"So do I."

"Yeah, Peyt, but I'm in love with her. I can't seem to get her out of my system, and I think she hates me. It's like having poison ivy in your blood stream."

Peyton couldn't help but laugh. "That bad, huh?"

"That bad."

"There may be a cure, but get on out there."

When he hung up Dallas was at his side with a cup of coffee. "Elise again?"

"Yep," he said wearily, "again. Dear God in heaven, Dallas, I don't know how to help her."

She put her arms around him and massaged his back the way she would a small child. "Here I'm always going to you for help, and you have your problems too, don't you, darlin'?"

THE PAIN IN ELISE'S HEAD was like a thing apart. It didn't belong to her, but she could feel its hurt. She stood at the gate a long time staring at her hands, afraid to look at the house. She trusted Peyton. He wouldn't lie to her, not intentionally, but she couldn't deny the days she'd spent with the Myers either. She started up the steps and noticed a rotting board she hadn't seen there before, and then way in the distance she heard Mrs. Myers.

"Elise, honey, is that you out there in the dark? Come on inside. There's a chill in the air this morning."

"I can hardly hear you, Mrs. Myers. You sound so far away."

"I know, honey, but I'm here. Lawrence will be there in a minute."

At the mention of his name, her knees grew weak, making it more like a dream. Was she dreaming again? Afraid of falling, she sat on the top step. She closed her eyes and tried to remain erect while she waited for Lawrence. She didn't know how long she was there before he was sitting beside her and took her hand in his.

"Are you okay?"

"Is this a dream?"

He laughed. "I don't think so."

"Oh, please hold me." *Of course, he's real. I can feel his arms around me.* "I can feel your heart beating."

"So can I."

"That's a good sign."

"It sure is. Let's go now, okay?"

"Where? I just got here."

"I'm not sure. Let's start with my truck."

Her eyes flew open then and she gasped, "Ty!"

"Who'd you think?"

"Where's Lawrence?"

"Oh, baby, don't ask me that."

They were as far as the gate now, and she started to turn back.

"No, Elise, not today. You aren't yourself. I'm taking you home. You can't stay here today."

"Ty, I'm so afraid."

"Is it your dad? Are you afraid of him?"

"In a way, but mostly I'm afraid of myself. Of what's happening to me. I can't seem to make sense of anything anymore. I need some answers, but I don't know how to get them."

"Peyton wasn't able to help?"

"No. Well, I'm not sure. I might as well go home and face Edwin. I can't stay away forever."

"Want me to come in with you?"

Elise looked at him. "You'd do that?"

"Sure. Why not?"

"You may have noticed that Edwin has a bit of a mean streak." She touched her swollen jaw.

"Yeah, well, maybe I could take some of the heat off you."

"Nothing will take the heat off me, but I appreciate the offer. I appreciate all the time you've given me."

"The pleasure was all mine, you know."

Ty parked in front of the riverboat house and wrote something on a slip of paper before handing it to Elise. "In case you need me. Any time, just call." He turned then to get out of the truck, but she put her hand on his wrist. "Don't, please. Not this time," and she rushed from the truck, misjudging the distance to the ground, and fell forward, hitting her head on the carriage stone.

17

*T*he doctor assured the Fosters that Elise's injury wasn't serious. "I expect she'll wake up any time now."

"Don't you think we should take her to a hospital?" Margaret looked at Edwin, but the doctor answered.

"Personally? I wouldn't move her if she were my daughter. Her pulse is good. Be patient."

"She looks so awful," Margaret whispered.

"She hit that rock pretty hard, Mrs. Foster. Be glad she didn't require more stitches than she did. The swelling will go down with time, and the bruising will begin to fade. A little plastic surgery might not be a bad idea. You might want to put an ice pack on her cheek too."

Elise felt that she was swimming through time, swimming toward light. But the light hurt her eyes, and she wanted the peace of sleep. She came closer to the light. Or was it another dream? She could see someone lying on a bed. A doctor approached and put a mirror close to her mouth. *Oh, I know. They want to see if she's breathing. Why, it's me! Oh, Lawrence, it's me!* Elise looked into the mirror and woke with a scream.

Margaret ran toward the bed just as Edwin came in the door. They reached Elise as she was throwing off the sheet, trying to get up. "No, darling," Margaret said, "don't sit up so suddenly."

"Your mother and I have been so worried, Elise. Thank God you're awake."

Her eyes were wild and frightened, and she looked from one to the other. Then her gaze settled on Edwin. "I remember now, Uncle Edwin. I remember why I hate you."

"Oh, Elise," Margaret pleaded, "don't. You aren't well." She winced as she looked from the bandaged head to the bruised and swollen jaw.

"No, Mom, I've been sick all my life. Because of him."

"What on earth do you mean? You're just confused. You had quite a blow."

"Yes, but it was a long time ago, about fifteen years, in fact."

"Fifteen . . .?"

"All this time I couldn't remember. But I remember now. Like it was yesterday." Tears rolled down her cheeks, and the pain in her head throbbed.

"Please, Elise, not now. Just rest." Margaret gave Edwin an imploring look, but he stood pale and stunned. Her lips moved soundlessly so he couldn't hear her say, "Have your depression, Edwin. Nothing more. Just a tiny depression."

Elise continued numbly, without inflection. "It was golf day for Daddy and Uncle Edwin. Surely you remember, Uncle Edwin, how you and Daddy played golf every Saturday. And just like always, Mom put me down for my nap. But this time was different. I heard something that woke me. I thought you were crying, Mom, and I went to your room. I opened the door, but you didn't notice me. Oh, no. You were too busy.

"Your bed was against the wall where I stood, and I looked in the mirror facing the bed. I could see that neither of you had on clothes. For years after, every time I tried to look in a mirror, that's all I could see. Uncle Edwin on top of you. I thought he was hurting you and ran to look for Daddy. But he wasn't home. I started to cry and went downstairs to the front door just as Daddy came in. He picked me up and asked what was wrong. I told him what I thought was the truth, that Uncle Edwin was hurting you.

"He didn't say a word. He carried me upstairs and sat me down. He put his finger to his lips and pushed me toward my room. When he went into the bedroom, I sat against the wall outside your door and sucked my thumb, something I hadn't done in a long time. You screamed, Mom, and Daddy and Uncle Edwin were yelling at each other. 'My best goddamned friend.' That's what Daddy said. Uncle Edwin, of course, said he didn't like it a damn bit. And, Mom, you just kept saying, 'What about me?' When Daddy came out, he ran downstairs and left in your car, didn't he, Mom? I can still hear the tires squealing. He wrapped your car around a tree, and I never saw him again. I hate you both!"

Margaret was pale and cold as stone. The Atlanta Margaret. "Are you quite finished, Elise? I wouldn't want you to leave anything out."

Elise's head throbbed and she began to retch. Edwin handed a basin to Margaret and walked to the window, his head bowed as though he might be praying.

Elise was limp and her face beaded with perspiration.

"I think you'd better rest now, Elise. Later I'll finish the story for you. I think you'll find it very interesting." Margaret turned to leave the room, pushing Edwin toward the door.

"You're going to tell her everything?" Edwin asked, cowed and shaky.

"Yes, everything. Why not? She'll just go on trying to hurt us otherwise. I'll run down to the shop now and see how Dallas is doing. I won't be long."

When she walked in the shop, Peyton and Dallas looked up guiltily. Margaret laughed nervously, "Here he is pestering the help."

"Oh, darlin', business is slow. He can be good company."

Peyton didn't smile or make his usual banter. "How's Elise? She any more alert?"

"Oh, she's very alert. She woke up about an hour ago, filled with venom."

Dallas looked at Peyton and raised her eyebrows.

Peyton hesitated. "She still angry about the business with the Myers?"

"The Myers?" Margaret laughed bitterly. "I'd almost forgotten that problem. Maybe she's forgotten too. At this point she's utterly consumed with something that happened when she was only three years old."

"Three years old?" Peyton asked.

"Oh, yes. That blow to her head opened a Pandora's Box of problems. But I don't want to bore you with our family's ancient history. I just came down in case you needed anything, Dallas, but I can see you're in good hands." She looked at Peyton and didn't even try to fake a smile.

After she left, Dallas said, "If I didn't know better, I'd say she was jealous."

"Jealous?" Peyton asked innocently.

"Yes."

"You must've hit your head too."

"No, I felt it when she walked in here. You sure you haven't been making goo-goo eyes at Margaret?"

"Would I do that?"

"Of course you would! Shame on you, Peyton Roberts."

"Now don't go accusing me. Just be glad we're friends now."

"Oh, I am. Margaret's been through a lot. Thank goodness Elise is awake, even if she is giving them hell."

"Do 'em good," Peyton said, tipping his imaginary hat and walking out the door.

ELISE'S CONVALESCENCE WAS SLOW. DESPITE her youth, she seemed unable to regain her strength. She assumed that was why her mother avoided returning to the story of her dad's death. She could just hear her. *Oh, Edwin, don't worry about it. We'll get it all sorted out as soon as Elise is stronger.* Elise didn't care. All the wanted was to see Lawrence. If she could see Lawrence, everything would be okay.

She trusted Peyton, but at the same time she knew what she'd experienced, and nothing he could say would convince her otherwise. But each time she tried to think it through, she was overcome with fatigue, and the headaches that continued to plague her. Her days were restless and her nights tossed with dreams. In one she saw Lawrence striding up the road, coming for her. And in another, the happiest of the dreams, she found the painting of Annelise hidden inside the cheval, a dream so real she wondered at times if she'd actually located it.

EDWIN WENT TO THE SHOP every day at noon so that Margaret could come home and have lunch with Elise. She never imagined the pain this thoughtful gesture brought her daughter. Elise nibbled at salads tossed with bittersweet memories of lunches shared with Lawrence and Mrs. Myers at her oilcloth-covered table.

They ate at the glass-topped table set with woven placemats and linen napkins. Margaret twirled some sprouts on her fork and looked up at Elise. "I saw Ty just as I was leaving. He said he'd stop by later. He and Peyton have surely been loyal visitors."

"They really have. Dallas came by the other day too."

"Really? I'm surprised she didn't mention it. What did she have to say?"

"Oh, the usual." *She didn't tell you because she didn't want you to know I'd pressured her to tell me more about this house and about the missing painting.*

As soon as Margaret left, Elise cleaned up the kitchen and went to the porch. She had just settled in a rocker when Ty pulled up. He started toward the porch when she called, "Let the dogs come too."

"Honest?"

"Honest."

Ty sat on the top step and the dogs stretched out on the porch. "See, didn't I tell you a couple of dogs would look good out here?"

"Oh, Ty, that seems such a long time ago." She dropped her hand, and Lady came over and laid her head across Elise's lap. "I have to admit this is sweet, Ty."

"She's been running in the woods this morning and probably doesn't smell too great. Needs a good dose of that soap your mom sells. If you like, I'll put my head on your lap instead."

"How do I know you haven't been running in the woods too?"

"You won't unless you let me put my head in your lap."

"You wish!"

"Yes, I do." He cleared his throat. "Elise, you never did ask what I was trying to tell you that morning in the coffee shop."

"I'm sorry, Ty. I don't remember."

"Don't guess I should expect you to. I wanted to tell you that I'm opening my own business."

"A music store?"

"Cute. No, I'm going into construction. I decided there's no use in letting all these people come in here and make a killing on the building and remodeling. I've developed my own company."

"That's great, Ty. I'm so happy for you, to know you've found what you want to do. And just think what a public service it'll be."

"Public service?"

"Sure. Exposing all your workers to classical music. Why they'll be hammering to Beethoven's Fifth and singing the Messiah every Christmas."

"Very funny. I did want to ask you to help me choose a name for the company, though."

"How about Classical Construction?"

"Be serious. I'll need customers."

"I don't know, Ty. That's something you should do yourself. You'll have to live with it a long time."

"That's why I want your help."

She bent her head and replied softly, "I'm not able to help myself or anyone else these days."

"I understand, but think about it."

"The gentleman's dilemma."

"Seriously, do you really think I'm a gentleman?"

"Seriously, Ty, yes. You've been much more than that to me, though. You have no idea how much I value your friendship."

Ty looked at her with a pained expression and started to say something but stopped and laughed. "Want me to take the dogs or leave them here the rest of the afternoon?"

"I'll be sleeping most of the time. Otherwise, I'd surprise you and say leave them."

"You're all right, Elise, you know that?" Ty kissed her on the cheek and bounded down the steps with the dogs.

Elise watched the truck until it was out of sight. She could hardly believe how comfortable she felt with Ty and how she'd come to depend on him in ways she'd never imagined possible. She went to her room and fell asleep thinking of him and his dogs. She hadn't slept long, less than an hour, when she woke with a start and jumped out of bed. She stood in the middle of her room, confused for a moment, and then followed a current of cold air to her parents' room.

Like a sleepwalker, she went straight to the cheval. She stood behind it, beyond the glass, and began a meticulous search. Time and again she ran her hands over the polished wood that secured the mirror. Finally, there it was. Her fingers touched the tiny recessed catch just as they had in her dream. The back slipped off the mirror. She gasped and clapped her hand over her mouth when she saw the nearly life-sized painting of a beautiful young woman in a long, flowing dress, white as bridal silk. She faced a mirror, her back to the artist, and she was turned slightly, looking back, long dark hair draping her shoulders.

"Oh, Annelise," she whispered, her eyes wet with tears. She blinked hard to clear her vision and saw that the mirror in the painting reflected the presence of a man. Annelise was looking back at the man! It was just a series of short brush strokes, hazy and indistinct but reminded Elise somehow of Lawrence. *It had to be Coulton! Oh, Lawrence, she thinks you're Coulton. Little wonder. The green eyes, just like Lawrence's.*

Turned over, the mirror was transformed into the painting. Flipped again, and there was the mirror, so lovely, so innocent, hiding its treasure all these years. The dark, sparkling eyes of the young girl were filled with amusement and adoration.

You're a girl in love. No doubt about it. It wasn't Seth you loved, though, it was Coulton. Is that what you want me to know?

A bone-numbing chill passed through her body. Her breath was shallow, and the room seemed to spin ever so slowly. With hurried movements, she started to replace the secret panel when something caught her eye. She stopped and looked carefully at the lower left corner of the painting. Only partially in the picture, but unmistakably, was an orange tabby cat with a star on its forehead.

Her hands shook as she struggled to replace the panel. Before leaving the room, she steeled herself and stood in front of the mirror. The reflections of Margaret and Edwin were no longer there, but neither was she. It was as though the painting had come through a mirror that could reflect no one but Annelise.

18

With what had become ritual, Elise spent more and more time on the front porch, not unaware she was emulating Nadine Fletcher. She was just coming inside when she saw a stack of mail on the hall table. Her name was on an envelope yellowed with age. She opened it and read the simple message. *Honey, we miss you.* Not I miss you, but we miss you. She pressed the note to her heart and slipped it in her pocket.

Later that afternoon she saw Peyton's truck pull up in front of the house. "You don't know how glad I am to see you," she called.

"Likewise. How's my best girl?" He stopped at the carriage stone. "You planning on leaving this here?"

"Oh yes. It's very special to me now. Provided a real breakthrough." She rubbed her fingers over the fading purple scar on her forehead.

"That right? Well, I guess that's good. Your dad here?"

"Probably. He spends a lot of time in his study. He gets work from his law firm in Atlanta. I'd just as soon we not let him know you're here."

"It's your call. I came to see you, not him." Peyton sat on the top step, almost at Elise's feet, just as Ty often did.

"Hon," Peyton cleared his throat, "I bring bad news."

Something froze inside Elise, and she had difficulty breathing. *Edwin! He made good on his threat! He had the Myers' home condemned.*

Peyton squeezed her hand. "It's Aunt Lacey, hon. She died last night. In her sleep."

Elise drew a sharp breath and licked the taste of relief from her lips.

"In a way it's a blessing." Peyton sighed. "She doesn't have to be afraid any longer."

"But, Peyton, I feel responsible for that fear. I know she wanted to help me, despite Aunt Jenny."

"That was between them. There was so much between them. And she died peacefully, in her own bed."

"How can we ever know death is peaceful? Don't you think it's something we say to make us feel better?"

"Maybe. I can't speak from experience, that's for sure. You seem to be getting stronger every day. Have you ever thought of getting away from here? Just a change of scene for a while?"

"You want to get rid of me too, just like my parents."

"No, that's the furtherest thing from my mind. I just thought you'd find it easier to put some distance between you and the things that bring you pain."

"Oh, Peyton, there's so much that brings me pain, but I can't talk about it here, not with Edwin in the house."

"Well, come down to the store sometime. We'll have another heart-to-heart." He stood up, kissed her cool cheek and tipped his imaginary hat.

"I'll do that. Real soon. There's something I'm absolutely dying to tell you, but not here."

"I can hardly wait."

"Thanks for coming by."

Peyton was nearly to his truck when Elise called to him and rushed across the yard. "Oh, Peyton, I have something to show you! I have proof."

"Proof?"

"Yes," she laughed, "proof." She reached in her pocket for the envelope but couldn't find it. She searched all her pockets, patting the sides and back of her jeans. Peyton stood in the middle of the yard, staring at her.

"Oh never mind. I guess I left it in the house." She watched his truck until it drove out of sight. Deep in thought, she walked back to the house wondering what she could have done with the envelope. When she reached the top step of the porch, Edwin came to the door.

"Was somebody here?"

"Yes."

"May I ask who?"

"It wasn't Lawrence Myers, if that's what concerns you."

"Elise, I'm getting awfully tired of your sarcasm. I'll never forgive myself for hitting you, but you can't go on blaming me for your problems. Get on with your life and stop sitting out here feeling sorry for yourself."

When Elise didn't answer he said, "I'm going to the shop to help your mother."

As soon as he left the house, Elise started down the steps. It took all her strength to make the hurried walk to Peyton's, but she couldn't keep the secret of the painting another minute. When she walked in the store, Peyton paled. "Are you okay? I'd of given you a ride if I'd known you meant to visit today."

"I didn't know it myself, but I couldn't wait. There's something I have to tell you."

"Let's go in my office. It's all yours, Bobby," he called as they walked to the back of the store. Peyton closed the door. "When you said we'd talk soon, I didn't realize it'd be within the hour. This must be good."

"It is. I found the painting."

"Good God!" Peyton stood up so fast he turned his chair over. "You found it?"

"It came to me in a dream. You're the only one who knows. I'm not telling my parents."

"You gonna tell me where it is?"

"Promise you'll never tell?"

"Promise."

"There's a secret compartment behind the cheval in the master bedroom. A small wooden clasp releases the panel. It lifts off, and there it is. Peyton, it's so incredible, it nearly took my breath away. It wouldn't be out of place in a museum. She was so beautiful."

Peyton gave a low whistle. "Well, I'll be damned. Sarah would have a fit if she knew that. In that cheval, huh?"

"I think that's why it stayed with the house all this time. Annelise wanted it to stay there. It's her proof that it was Coulton she loved. You can tell by the way she's looking at him in the painting."

"Coulton's in the painting too?"

Elise nodded. "It has to be his likeness in the mirror."

"Legend has it she was painted wearing the ball gown she had on the first time Coulton laid eyes on her. They were at the opera."

"Opera?" Elise interrupted. "I'd forgotten that. Here though?"

"Right here. At one time there was plenty of money for an opera house. Men like Annelise's dad made fortunes shipping cotton. All these newcomers . . ." Peyton hesitated, not wanting to lump Elise in the statement. "Well, this isn't the first time Apalach has risen from the ashes. That's why the lovely Annelise was able to wear a fine ball gown to the opera and turn the head of a handsome stranger."

Elise decided to help him out. "What you're trying to tell me is that Apalach is no stranger to progress."

"That's right. Not a stranger, but not always a willing participant either."

Elise gazed at Peyton and her eyes glistened with tears. She spoke softly. "You missed your calling selling shoes. You should have been a psychologist. I always feel better after I talk to you. It's funny that you and my mother don't get along and yet we're such good friends."

"Yeah . . . that's real funny."

"Peyton, could you give me a ride home? Edwin's in the shop with Mom, and I don't want him to know I left the house. And," she smiled sheepishly, "this hurried trip kinda tired me out."

She was still talking when he jumped up and ushered her outside to his truck. He pulled up in front of the house and ran around to open her door, just like Ty. He walked her to the rocker and turned to leave when she said, "Peyton?"

"Yes?"

"It didn't look like a ball gown."

"Huh?"

"Annelise's dress. It looked like an old-fashioned wedding dress."

"Well, I'll be damned. So much for legend, huh?"

She laughed and waved him goodbye. Soon the air was chilled and fog began rolling in, but she was on the porch when she heard Edwin's car pull up at the back of the house and still later when he drove to the shop and brought Margaret home from work.

"Elise! You shouldn't be out here in this damp air. Edwin," she called, "why didn't you have Elise come inside?"

He walked to the door. "You must be joking. If I suggested she come inside, she'd probably have her bed moved out here."

"Oh, Elise, I was waiting for you to get stronger, but I think we'd better talk now. Tonight."

After waiting so long, Elise was suddenly afraid of what her mother might say. "NO! I don't want to talk. My head hurts."

After dinner Margaret followed Elise to her room. "Sure you don't want to talk?"

"I'm sure."

"It's always so cold in here. Would you like to move to another room?"

Elise shook her head. "Thanks, but it wouldn't matter."

"Well, it might. You could try another room."

"Believe me. It wouldn't matter."

ELISE WAS SITTING BY HER bedside table, trying to think what to do about the painting, when she heard sirens. A short time later the sirens faded to music. She looked out her window and saw Ty's truck. Before she realized what an unlikely action it was, she rushed to the bathroom where she looked in the mirror and began applying lipstick. She froze with the tube to her lips. She was looking at her reflection, not her parents' or Annelise's. Elise Foster stared back at her. She looked at the lipstick in her hand, surprised by the gesture, surprised that it mattered. She fluffed her hair and started downstairs.

Ty gave her a big smile. "How 'bout going for a ride? Think your folks would care if I promise not to let you trip over the carriage stone?"

"I'd love to get out of here. Mom's in the back. Let me tell her I'm leaving. I'll only be a minute."

When they were in the truck, Ty eased onto the road and then floored the accelerator.

"Ty?"

"I'm sorry, Elise. There's something I want to show you,

and we need to get there before dark. Actually, I don't want to show you, but you'll find out soon enough, and I want to be with you when you do." He headed out of town and turned right at the fruit stand.

"Ty?"

"Yeah. That's where we're going."

Elise's heart began beating with joy, and she said, "Oh, Ty, you are the dearest friend."

"We aren't there yet."

A fire truck passed them going toward town and she gave an anguished cry. Her mouth went dry and she whispered, "Edwin."

It was dusk when they pulled up to the gate. The living room and most of the kitchen were little more than a pile of ashes. The rest of the house was black and charred.

"How could Edwin hate me so?"

"Why would you think your dad did this?"

"He threatened to have the home condemned. Maybe that didn't work out."

"Could be coincidence. A lightning strike maybe. It's a miracle any of it is left standing. This place was built of chestnut hauled down from the mountains before the blight. I doubt anything but a lightning strike could have burned it."

"Oh, sure, after all these years, the house is suddenly struck by lightning. Are the Myers okay?"

"Oh, Elise. The place was empty. You know that."

"It is now, isn't it?" She opened the door of the truck, and when Ty started to follow, she put her hand on his arm. "Wait here. Please?"

"You know what happened the last time I did that."

"I'll be careful. I promise." The gate hung open and she picked her way among the debris. The steps and part of the porch were intact. *Oh, Lawrence, I did destroy what you had. Oh, my love, I'm so sorry.* She started up the steps, coming instantly under the spell of the house when Ty called to her.

"Elise! You promised. You can't go in there. It's dangerous."

Something released her, broke the connection, and she turned and went back to the truck. She laid her head on Ty's shoulder and cried great racking sobs. "How could he do this? Oh, Ty." She looked up at him then with such pleading that he pressed his lips to hers, softly, tenderly, and she gave herself to him for just a moment before she stiffened and pushed him away.

"I'm sorry, Elise. I'm not trying to take advantage of a situation."

She didn't say anything, and he drove her home in silence. He walked her to her door and apologized again.

She pressed her fingers to his mouth. "I'm grateful you came for me. I think you understand more than anyone."

"Maybe I should come in."

She looked toward the door. "No, better not. This is my battle."

19

*M*argaret and Edwin were in his study. Elise stood in the door and spit words sharp as darts. "Are you proud of yourself, Edwin?"

Margaret stood up. "Elise, whatever has gotten into you?"

"Why don't you ask your husband? Ask him who burned the Myers' house?"

"What! Edwin?"

Elise sobbed, "And I obeyed you. I didn't go there. But you did, you and a box of matches."

"Elise! How dare you talk to your father that way?"

"He isn't my father. He never has been. He's the scoundrel. Deny that you're responsible. Deny it!"

"I don't have to deny anything. How can you believe I'd do something like that?"

"One way or the other, you got the place condemned."

"In the heat of an argument we all make threats, Elise."

"But you followed through. I stayed away! I STAYED AWAY!"

She pressed her hands against her temples. "You've destroyed everything I've ever loved, starting when I was three years old!"

"Shut up! Both of you!" Margaret raked her fingers through her hair. "This has gone on long enough. I haven't been the best mother in the world, Elise, but God, how I've tried, and I'm sick of you accusing Edwin of all that's wrong in your life. We're settling old scores here and now. I won't have you blaming him for things he's too much of a gentleman to tell you himself."

She turned and faced Elise and said in her coldest voice, "Edwin did not kill Gene. Gene killed himself. Yes, Gene and Edwin played golf every Saturday afternoon. At least that's what I thought. I saw no reason to question it until one Saturday Edwin returned to the house alone. At first I thought something had happened, that there'd been an accident." Margaret looked at Edwin, and his face crumpled.

"That long-ago Saturday, darling. You were frantic," he said, his eyes never leaving her face. "You came to the door and kept looking around the yard, looking for Gene. 'Where's Gene? Is he okay? Has there been an accident?' Once there, facing you, my resolve nearly vanished." He walked to the window and looked out, his hands in his pockets. "I had trouble saying what I'd come to tell you." His voice trailed off, and he swallowed hard. "All these years, and I still . . ."

Margaret sighed and took up the thread of the story. "You see, Elise, they hadn't been playing golf after all. Every Saturday Edwin drove Gene to another woman's house. Edwin went to the golf course alone. Gene had been having an affair for nearly a year."

Edwin stared at the window, seeing his own reflection, and went on, "God, I hated myself for being party to that, but I didn't hate myself enough not to do it. Gene and I had been friends since we were kids. We were like brothers. I felt like I owed him my life. That's no lie. In many ways I did owe him my life.

"I practically lived at his house when we were growing up. My dad was the town drunk, and my mother worked in the lunchroom at school. She always smelled like cafeteria slop. I didn't blame her. It's just the way things were. I thought Gene had the ideal life with his fancy house and rich parents. I wanted to be Gene. I never understood what he saw in me though." He hesitated a moment. "It must have been my loyalty. That was something he thought he could count on. I didn't know how much that meant to him until I wanted to go to law school and couldn't afford it.

"Mr. Compton, his dad, had bought stock in Gene's name, and without a second thought, Gene cashed it in and gave me the money. I didn't want to take it, but he said the damage was done once he sold the stock. He insisted I use it so we could stay together through law school. His dad was ready to kill us both, but it was too late to do anything about it. No matter how bad I felt about Margaret, I owed Gene. I owed him more than I could ever repay."

"You see, Elise . . ."

"No, Margaret, let me tell it my way. Gene knew he'd bought and paid for me years before. I wasn't supposed to question what he did. I begged him not to ruin his marriage, but I couldn't reach him." He closed his eyes and shook his head. "We'd lost something along the way. Finally I couldn't stand it. I let him out of the car one Saturday and drove back to the house. I told your mother where he was."

Margaret turned to Elise. "Edwin expected me to have hysterics and confront Gene and his mistress. I admit that was my first impulse, but the anger was so great, the emotion so overwhelming that it seemed too easy a way out for him." With the retelling, Margaret grew cold and hard, her words clipped like shards of ice. "Edwin tried to comfort me, and then we comforted each other in the way Gene had taught us."

"I loved your mother, Elise. I suppose on some level I'd always loved her, but afterwards I was sick with guilt. I knew I couldn't see her again. I loved Gene too. The following Saturday, after I left Gene, I drove to the golf course, but I never got out of the car. I had to be with Margaret again. I couldn't help myself. I simply couldn't help myself," he said, his voice choked with emotion.

Margaret interrupted, "Edwin, would you bring me a glass of wine, please?"

When he was out of the room, Margaret spoke softly to Elise. "I never wanted to hurt you with something so sordid, Elise, but you have to understand why you saw what you did that day. I knew it was wrong despite what Gene was doing. But I'd never known such pain. I didn't think I could stand it. And then Edwin was at the door again. I'll always believe it was pain, not desire. This was a way of settling the score with a man I thought loved me."

Edwin returned with the wine. "And wouldn't you know, that was the day Gene took sick and came home in a taxi."

"And found me crying," Elise offered. "All these years, I've thought I was responsible for his death, that I was the reason he found you."

"No, he knew when he saw Edwin's car in the drive. It was all over in that minute. Oh, Elise, this is so humiliating. Edwin and I aren't proud of any of it. We were all betrayed. We betrayed each other. But I did love Gene. At first I blamed myself for not being a better wife, but then my love grew bitter, and I hated him as much as I had loved him. I could never talk to you about him because," Margaret paused, realizing how much it still hurt, and said quietly, "because I've spent the rest of my life trying to forget."

"I don't think, Elise, it had anything to do with your mother. Some people can never have enough love, and Gene was one of them. It wasn't his fault. His parents were two of the coldest goddamned people I ever knew. They weren't young when he came along, and they never found a place for him in their lives. He told me that. His mother was indifferent and distant. She left a frost in him no woman could melt."

"It doesn't excuse us, Elise. But that's why you saw what you did." Margaret's voice broke. "I didn't know . . . I never guessed . . . Edwin and I married and tried to erase the past. But the past became a shadow that never went away."

Elise could hardly comprehend what she'd been told, and then she began crying for Margaret and Gene, crying for the Myers and what they'd lost. Edwin took Margaret's hand and kissed it and then left them alone. Margaret kneeled in front of Elise's chair. "Oh, baby, I'm so sorry."

"But you married him. You married Edwin."

She lowered her voice. "It wasn't a big romance, Elise." She closed her eyes. "I had to legitimize what we'd done. I felt, we felt, I guess, that we didn't have any choice. Whatever responsibility we felt toward Gene or each other, we didn't have any choice. We had a need, and we called it love. Maybe it was. Is. Over time love's edges are blurred and soften into something comfortable and secure. I can't tell you the difference between love and the fulfillment of a need. Who knows? Maybe I have both."

The longest walk Elise had ever made was to her room that night. And she'd never known her head to hurt so fiercely. She reached for the prescription painkiller the doctor had given her and poured several more than the prescribed dosage of tablets in her hand before pulling her beautiful gown over her head. No pearls this time though. Her last thought was *if I should die before I wake* . . . and she fell into a deep, drugged sleep.

Edwin was in his study swirling bourbon in a crystal glass when Margaret found him.

"Did you do it?" she asked.

"Do what?"

"Edwin, don't make this any harder. You know what I mean."

He drained the glass and turned to her. "Yes. But it was an accident. Oh, I went there with every intention of doing something to destroy that house, but it was weird. It was almost like a force field or a wall held me back. I took the box of matches from my pocket, but I couldn't do it. Then I saw the stub of an old candle on the piano. God, how that bunch of sticks was still standing." He shook his head. "There were so many trees they made it dark in there so I went to light the candle when a rat or something ran out of the piano. I swear to God it jumped at me. I dropped the candle and jumped back. I tried to stomp the fire out but it got ahead of me. I dropped the box of matches and left."

"Oh, Edwin."

"I tell you, it was an accident. That house wasn't worth burning anyway. It was a wreck."

"But, Edwin, it had been somebody's home."

"Don't go sounding like Elise now. Nobody lived there. It was a place for derelicts and tramps."

"And Elise."

"That's nothing for you to be proud of, Margaret."

"I'm not proud, Edwin. I'm sad."

"And I'm sorry. What do you want me to do, tell Elise?"

"No! Let's forget it and try to move on. Again. With time maybe Elise will feel better and forget all this nonsense."

THANKS TO THE MEDICINE, ELISE slept soundly for several hours but then woke suddenly in the middle of the night. She recalled accounts of people who had near-death experiences and wondered if she was near death as she watched herself get out of bed and leave the house. She couldn't recall the long walk, but she realized she was at the Myers'. Despite the destruction, she walked up the steps and across the porch. The screen door was gone but she walked through the hall and up the stairs to Lawrence's room. She inhaled the scent of his body as she pulled the sheet back and lay down beside him, curving her body to his back.

"What!" He turned toward her. "Elise?"

"Yes. Were you expecting someone else?"

"How . . ."

She placed her finger to his lips. "No questions, please. I've missed you so. I was afraid I'd never see you again. And then the fire tonight . . ."

"Elise, you don't belong here. I've tried to tell you . . ." He stopped talking then, his hands cupping her breasts, his mouth devouring her.

Later he held her in his arms, stroking her hair. She spoke against the warmth of his chest. "I could live the rest of my life on tonight."

"You may have to. For so long I wondered if you'd ever come back to me, and when you did, I knew that no matter how much we wanted it, it couldn't be. I tried to tell you, to warn you."

"Then why am I here?"

"Don't you know who you were? Who I am? For you to forget, I couldn't bear it."

"I . . . you're frightening me. I'm afraid to think . . ."

"Oh, my God, I have to tell you. Annelise, my love."

"Annelise?"

"Don't you know? We're old souls. Annelise and Seth. We've always been, will always be old souls. That will never go away, but you must. This isn't the first time we've said goodbye, darling."

"Oh, I can't leave you. I simply can't."

"If you won't, then I will. For you. Goodbye, my love."

Elise felt as though she was carried on a current of air, confident it was the medication and not death that called to her. She heard a voice from a great distance calling something. It was so faint she could hardly make it out, but borne on a breath of frigid air it seemed to call, "Seth?" Could that be? Not her voice though, surely not hers. Annelise calling Seth.

Without opening her eyes, she patted the bed with her hand, searching for Lawrence. Her hand sank into the mattress and she opened her eyes and screamed. She was in Lawrence's bedroom, but it was a room filled with moonlight and decay. The mattress was little more than gossamer and dust. The floor was wet and slimy, and his books were green with mold and years of neglect. She stepped into her shoes and made her way to the hall. A full moon provided light, and she looked down to see the shell of a piano in what was left of the living room. She walked down the stairs to the remains of the kitchen. The only thing left of that bright, warm room was Mrs. Myers' cast-iron cook stove, covered with ashes and decades of rust.

"Mrs. Myers? Mrs. Myers?" She knew no one would answer, but she had to say his name. "Lawrence? Oh, Lawrence." And then more quietly, "Seth?" Her voice broke then, and she couldn't bear to stay there any longer. She picked her way through the ashes and made the long walk home. The sun hadn't come up when she let herself in the house and tiptoed up the stairs. She went to bed then and slept without dreaming.

Margaret came to her room before leaving for work. She stared at the floor. "Elise, what happened to your bedroom slippers? They're black! That's what's on the stairs. It's from your slippers! What have you done?"

Elise rubbed her eyes and sat up in bed.

"And your gown! Look at your beautiful gown!"

Elise looked down at the moldering decay her mother saw. "It's death, Mom. That's what you see on my gown. Death."

"Don't be ridiculous, Elise. You went to that house, didn't you? You went back to the Myers'."

Elise stared straight ahead, not answering.

"I hoped we could come to some kind of understanding, Elise, but I don't know how to reach you anymore."

As Margaret turned to leave the room, Elise said softly, "You never did."

20

There was a ringing in Elise's head that wouldn't go away, and for several days she sat on the porch and stared into space. Ty and Peyton came by to see if she was okay, but she found it difficult to talk.

"I knew it would be hard on you, hon." Peyton had been sitting with Elise for nearly an hour. "You've had a lot to bear and then with the fire and all, well . . ." He stood up. "When you feel like talking, let me know. I always have time for you, you know that."

Elise looked at him then. She said only one word. "Karma." Peyton felt the hair prickle on the back of his neck. He kissed her cheek. "It'll work out, darlin'. You'll see."

Thanksgiving came and went in a blur. It was nearly Christmas, and Elise hadn't even looked at their tree. She wrapped an afghan around her and sat on the porch, defiant of the weather, but she smiled when she saw Ty's truck. He came walking up the steps carrying a box with a big green bow on it. He laid it at Elise's feet and lifted the lid. Inside was a small red puppy.

"Oh!" Tears slid down Elise's face as she took the puppy in her arms and pressed him to her heart. "He's so dear, Ty."

"Well, I knew you'd prefer a hound, but this was the best I could do on short notice. His mama's a cairn terrier named Toto, and his papa's a traveling salesman from a good neighborhood."

Elise couldn't stop crying, but she refused to let go of the puppy. Ty ran out to his truck and came back with a box of tissues. "Here, baby, let it all out. Get it out of your system once and for all."

"Ty, you always seem to know what to do."

"It comes naturally when you love somebody."

Elise stared into his eyes a moment and then looked away. "I suppose Mom will let me keep the puppy."

"If she won't, I'll keep it 'til you have a place of your own."

"You'd do that for me?"

"You know I would."

"Does he have a name?"

"No more than my company does. That's your department, remember?"

"I've never named a dog before."

"You've never named a company either. There's always a first time."

She shrugged her shoulders. "He looks like a Rusty to me."

"And my company?"

"That seems so important. So permanent. I can never think of anything that's just right."

"We'll let that one go for now then. Can you and Rusty get along without me? I've got some Puppy Chow in the truck, but that's it. He'll keep you busy, you know."

"We'll be fine, won't we, Rusty?" She kissed the puppy's nose and then stood up and kissed Ty on the cheek. He turned slowly until his lips were on hers, and she didn't pull away. He could feel his heartbeat in his ears as he stumbled down the steps and walked to his truck.

Margaret wasn't happy about Rusty, but she could see the difference he made in Elise. She'd take peace at any price, even a puppy.

ELISE AND RUSTY BECAME A frequent sight around town. Until he was old enough to be leash-trained, Elise carried him with her in a small basket. Miss Nadine was the one who surprised Elise the most, though. She adored Rusty. "I always wanted a boy to give me a dog. Nobody ever gave me one, though, and I guess I'm too old now."

"Why, Miss Nadine, no one is ever too old to have something to love. I'll ask Ty if there are any puppies left from the litter."

Nadine stood up and faced the screen door. "I'd like it, but no, I don't think so. I better not have a dog in the house."

"But there's no one but you . . ."

"No! I can't have a dog in the house."

"Well, if you change your mind, let me know."

Elise and Rusty left Nadine's and walked to town where Ty was remodeling one of the stores. "Could you take a minute for a break?"

Ty looked absolutely stunned to see Elise and stared at her a few moments before he climbed down off the ladder. "Well, isn't this something? Don't often get callers on the job." They started out the door and the guys working with him started calling, "Hey, Ty, you been holding out on us, buddy. Introduce us, okay?"

Ty gave a dismissive wave of his hand and followed Elise.

"Ty?"

"Yeah?"

"You remember that day you said you'd take me any place I wanted to go—Tallahassee, or any place but the Myers'?"

"Yeah, I remember."

"Will you take me to Tallahassee?"

"Sure, I will. But why?"

"I've applied to Florida State, and I want to see about getting a scholarship or work. I don't want to take any money from my parents."

"When you want to go? I couldn't be gone more than a day 'cause I've got a deadline on this job."

"It'll just be a day trip, and we can leave early. Day after tomorrow? I have an appointment."

Ty whistled, but then he gave her his famous smile. "I can do that. Pick you up about seven?"

"Let's make it six, and meet me at the corner. I don't want my folks to know."

"Lord, Elise, you always have me on edge with your folks. You're determined they won't like me."

"I like you. Won't that do?"

"If that's the only four-letter 'l' word you'll give me, I'll take it."

Elise kissed him on the cheek. "Thanks, Ty. I really don't know what I'd do without you."

"You don't have to, you know."

Her eyes softened and she wanted to kiss him again. Not on the cheek. Instead she whispered, "I know. Listen, I'll leave a note for my folks. I just don't want to say anything to them until it's settled."

"Okay. You know I can't refuse you, don't you?"

Elise smiled and looked up at him.

"Don't look at me like that, woman. I have work to do."

"Day after tomorrow then," and she waved goodbye.

IT WAS A LITTLE AFTER five-thirty when Elise propped a note against the coffeepot and slipped out of the house. Ty was leaning against his truck, waiting at the corner. He opened the door for her and smiled. "Everything is always a conspiracy with you, isn't it?"

"For now. Things will begin leveling out once I'm in school. I'll be on my own, with my own money and out from under my parents' thumbs."

"I'll miss you, you know."

Elise leaned over and brushed a soft kiss across his lips. "I'll miss you too, but it's not like I'll be that far away."

"I thought you didn't want to go to college."

"I didn't. But remember how I wanted to reverse things for Annelise? You know where that got me. Then I started thinking of Miss Nadine and how she always wanted to teach school. I decided I'd teach school for her. I'll take school papers over and discuss things with her. I can't reverse things for her, but maybe I can give something back that she missed."

"You're a good person. You know that?"

"No, just good-intentioned."

It was a pleasant trip, Elise always aware of the comfort she felt being with Ty. They made a few stops and were in Tallahassee in plenty of time for her eleven o'clock appointment with the admissions counselor. Ty walked her to the office, and as soon as Elise spoke to the receptionist, he said, "I'll explore a little and come back for you by noon."

When Ty returned shortly before twelve, the receptionist said, "Oh, sir, we've looked for you everywhere. Miss Foster passed out, and they've taken her to Tallahassee Memorial." Ty froze, but only for a moment, and started running.

After talking to the doctors at the hospital, Ty called Margaret at the shop and explained the situation.

"We're leaving now, Ty. We'll be there as soon as we can."

When Margaret and Edwin walked into Elise's room, Ty sat

by her bed holding her hand. His eyes were red and swollen from crying.

"Oh, my baby," Margaret said, gently kissing Elise. "Has she been awake at all?"

Ty shook his head.

"I want her moved to Atlanta, Edwin. Tonight. She has to have the best of care. I want her moved to Emory tonight."

"Margaret," Edwin began, "that might not be possible."

"You're a lawyer, Edwin. She's my child, and I want her in Emory. Tonight."

She looked at Ty. "You know it's a brain tumor? She may have had it since birth."

Ty nodded. "I told them about the fall on the carriage stone, and there is a small blood clot, but the brain tumor is the real culprit."

"I know. I've spoken to them by phone and again since we arrived. Edwin, I've never even told you this, but my mother died of a brain tumor. It's something that's always terrified me. All my life I've been afraid to even speak of it, afraid of causing it to happen. And now it's happened anyway, but I won't lose Elise. I won't!"

Ty was unable to speak. All he could do was stare at the still form on the bed.

Edwin arranged to have Elise taken to Emory by ambulance early the following morning. Over the coming days and weeks, he saw a changed Margaret as all her latent maternal instincts came to the fore. She fought, argued, and pleaded with the doctors. She wanted her child back whole, but she'd take any part of her they could save.

They took turns at Elise's bedside. Ty returned to Apalach for a few hours and then drove back to Atlanta. Margaret arranged for Dallas to take care of the shop and Rusty until they returned.

Following surgery, Elise's head was bandaged, and she was connected to tubes from nearly every orifice of her body. Margaret and Edwin grew accustomed to having Ty in the room. He didn't know if they discussed things in front of him because they felt he wasn't there or because they'd come to accept him as belonging.

"If only her recovery is complete, Edwin. If they got it all. If there's no permanent damage . . ."

"Yes, if only . . ."

"At least it explains all that business with the Myers and Annelise. You know, it occurred to me last night that it explains her make-believe friend when she was little."

"It probably does. I still can't remember what she called that kid . . ."

"I do. His name was Lawrence."

"That's it! Lawrence!"

"Yes, it all fits. All the pieces of the puzzle."

It was more than a week before Elise opened her eyes. Her first words were, "Ty? Where's Ty?"

Margaret stood at the window but turned and ran to the bed, sobbing, "Oh, my poor baby."

Elise raised her hand to her face. "Was I in a fire? Where's Ty?"

"Fire? No, darling, of course not, and Ty is just down the hall. He'll be here shortly. You're going to be okay. Your nightmare is over."

⌒⌒

ELISE HAD BEGUN TO FEEL she'd spent most of her life convalescing. Plastic surgery erased the scar from her fall, but nothing could erase the memory of her slow, painful recovery from hav-

ing a brain tumor removed. The brain tumor explained everything to everyone but Elise. But she was tired, tired of trying to
explain. A brain tumor didn't require explaining.

Dear Ty didn't ask for explanations. He wanted her on any
terms. He made that plain. And she wanted him. He wasn't
Lawrence, but Ty didn't need to be. He was wonderful in his
own right, in his own way. He'd become an integral part of her
life.

Through the long, dark months she kept one goal in mind.
She still wanted to go to college. When Margaret found her
working on applications for scholarships, she made a truly surprising confession.

"You don't need to work or have a scholarship, Elise. I lied
when I asked you to postpone college. There was never any
question of money. Gene's parents left a trust fund for your education. I knew the money would come to you in a year, and
anyway, you would come to feel at home here in Apalach. A
year would make a lot of difference."

"I wouldn't have minded working, but I admit I'm glad I
won't have to. This way I can finish school much more quickly
and return here. Return home."

Elise was eager to get on with her life when it seemed so
much had been taken from her. But it wasn't something she
could rush, any more than she could ignore the void no one
could fill but Lawrence Myers. Elise's illness, in arousing Margaret's maternal instincts, made her more alert to Elise than before. She came in the kitchen early one morning and watched as
Elise stared out the window.

"Do you have a sore throat, darling?"

Elise shook her head.

"You keep swallowing. I've noticed you do that a lot."

"Oh, that. Anxiety, I guess."

"Would you like to talk to the doctor?"

"Please! I've seen enough doctors to last me a lifetime. I'll be okay. Thanks, though." *Did you ever try to swallow your sorrow, Mother? When your marriage fell apart, didn't you gulp it down, all the hurt and grief? I swallow the loss of Lawrence and the love that won't die.*

Peyton kept telling her she was young and had plenty of time, but she resented the loss of time, of youth, of hope. Another Christmas had come and gone before she was able to leave for school. Her face was unblemished, and her hair had grown back. From scarves, wigs, and stubble, at last she had long hair again. It was dark, though, and this troubled her despite Margaret's assurance that it was nothing abnormal. Margaret's father had been a brunette. Elise was normal again. Perhaps for the first time.

No longer exploring but on familiar ground, Elise said her farewells. Nadine cried and walked toward Elise with outstretched arms when she saw her coming up the steps. "I won't have anyone to look forward to now."

"I'm going straight through, summers and all. I'll be back before you know it. And remember, I'm counting on your help grading those papers." She reached in her pocket and brought out three red pencils. "We can shed lots of blood together. I'm not kidding. I'm counting on you."

Nadine looked around at the porch. "I guess we'll have to bring a table out here and spread the papers."

"Or we can sit at your dining room table."

"Not inside."

"Miss Nadine, do you know I've never been inside your house. Let's go inside right now."

"No! Please." She stood with her back to the door and made a whimpering noise.

It's Nick. She believes he's in there some place. And Elise knew that believing was almost as good as having. "It's okay, Miss Nadine, I understand."

She went to see Peyton last.

"Would you look at that, Bobby, here she is, the picture of health and pretty as ever. Guess that's how a future schoolteacher should look, don't you think, especially with a little red dog at her side. What you gone do about Rusty while you're away?"

"He's going with me. I'm getting an apartment so we can stay together."

"And Ty can visit."

Elise smiled. "Oh, yes, Ty can visit."

"What you got there, hon, a map of Tallahassee?"

Peyton nodded toward something she had rolled up under her arm.

"Maybe. Let's go to your office so we can plot it together." Peyton sat at his desk and Elise leaned over and unrolled the canvas. The picture of Annelise stretched the length of his desk and then some.

He whistled in appreciation. "My God. I never thought I'd live to see this." He looked from the painting to Elise but refrained from saying it could have been her own portrait.

"What?"

"Nothing. Just marveling."

"Isn't she beautiful? See the reflection in the mirror? That's the man she loved, Seth."

"Seth?"

"That's what she was trying to tell me—not Coulton, Seth. I only hope she was able to tell him. Here, this is yours too." She handed him a faded, yellowed envelope.

"Annelise did have a message. It's all in here. It was hidden behind her picture. That's why she wanted me to find the picture. It fell out when I removed the painting. Put it in the book

you'll write. She's gone to so much effort to bring it to light. You
. . . we must tell the true story. No more legend. The truth.
They're yours. The painting and the letter. Going-away gifts
from me. You're the only one who knows I found them. I want
them to be yours."

"You think I'm that hard up for a woman, huh?"

"You know better than that."

He came around the desk and kissed her. "I'll always treasure these because they're gifts from you. It isn't the picture that's
valuable. It's you and what you mean to me."

"And the letter. I'm counting on you to write that book. I
love you, Peyton. My own family, well, you know. I told you how
it is. We've had lots of problems, lots of heartache."

"I think that's common to most families. Sometimes we
spend our whole lives trying to understand our parents, chewing
on little bits of information. And then one day we realize we've
been chewing all the wrong things. By then, though, it's too late,
but we start over again. We have to leave them alone, let them
live with their own mistakes and not try to understand why they
made them. If we're honest, it really isn't any of our business."

"I guess you're right. You're always right, Peyton. In so many
ways I resent my mother. In other ways I feel sorry for her.
We're closer now than we've ever been. I'll never believe she's
happy with Edwin, but after all the mistakes they made, she isn't
willing to leave him."

"I'd say that's to her credit."

"Yes, it is. She needs something to her credit. All these years
I think she's banked on her good looks. I always envied her
beauty, but I realize now that looks aren't as lasting as love . . ."

"And she envies your youth."

"You think so?"

"I know so. It's your turn now, darlin'."

Someone tapped on the door, and Peyton slipped the crumbling envelope in his desk drawer and was quickly rolling the picture when Dallas stuck her head in the door.

"Hope I'm not interrupting anything private."

"No, Dallas, I was just leaving." Elise stood and turned toward the door. "Could I ask you a favor before I go?"

"Well, you know you can."

"Would you look in on Miss Nadine once in a while? I worry about her. She tries to convince herself Nick is inside the house, waiting for her. I know she does, but if she lets anyone inside and they see he isn't there, well . . . there goes everything she has to live for."

"Of course, I'll go see her. Should have done that long ago. You really understand her, don't you?"

"I think I do anyway. Those shock treatments her dad had her take did a number on her."

"Don't worry about her. That's one thing I can do for you while you're away at college. Darlin', do you suppose I'm too old to go to school? Maybe that would settle me down a bit."

"Of course you aren't too old."

"It doesn't matter. You're not going anywhere but to have a Coke and peanuts with me, Dallas." Peyton propped the rolled canvas in the corner and came around the desk.

"What is that, Peyton?" Dallas looked toward the picture.

Peyton looked over his shoulder. "I think it's a recipe for a love potion. I'm pretty sure that's what it is."

"You crazy old thing."

Elise laughed. "I'll miss you two."

"We'll miss you too, darlin', but whenever you're home, we expect a visit. Apalach is in your blood now. You won't be able to stay away."

"I think you're right. I don't want to stay away."

C✐

WHEN ELISE WAS READY TO leave for Florida State, Margaret
wouldn't admit to being hurt that Elise wanted Ty to drive her
there. "He isn't what I'd wanted for you, Elise, but I have to admit
he's a fine young man. He's been very good to you, to all of us."

"Yes, he has—to all of us."

"There's only one thing I want you to do for me. Please take
the Jaguar. Don't drive up there in his truck."

"That'll be up to Ty. I'll ask him."

It was almost as though Edwin no longer existed. He re-
ceded more and more into the background where Elise was concerned. When she left for school, he stood just outside the front
door and waved.

Elise saw him and told Ty she'd be right back. "I'm sorry
for everything, Edwin. Sorry things can't be different between
us." She gave him a hurried kiss on the cheek and left just as
Margaret was handing Ty the keys to the Jaguar.

"You don't mind me leaving my truck here?"

"Not at all. Who knows. Maybe we'll have a gun rack in-
stalled before you get back."

Edwin came down the steps and put his arm around Margaret's shoulders. "I'll try to restrain her, Ty."

"You do that, sir. Wouldn't want you to go to unnecessary
expense on my account."

Elise sat in the front seat with Rusty on her lap and was
surprised by the pain she felt at leaving. With Ty beside her,
though, her calm assurance returned.

Ty drove through town, tapped the horn twice when they
passed Peyton's Shoe Store, and then made a left turn onto
Highway 98. "Your mom made a big mistake letting me drive
their car. I could get to like this."

Elise laughed. "I'm sure you could."

The Jaguar glided down the highway, sleek and easy as the animal whose name it bore. It was sunrise, and the morning light skipped over the bay, highlighting the simplicity of a quiet town. Elise turned and looked back as Apalach faded from sight. She swallowed hard, but refused to let go of the tears welling in her eyes.

By the time they arrived in Tallahassee, her furniture had been delivered and the power turned on. When they unlocked the door to her apartment, Ty asked, "Want me to carry you over the threshold?"

She gave him a look of pure fear and he laughed. "I was only joking."

"It isn't that. I was thinking of the first time I walked into the riverboat house and how I felt like a bride. Lord, that was so long ago."

When the car was unloaded and things were fairly settled, Ty said, "Now, I'm taking you to dinner at the Silver Slipper—if it's still there—so we can celebrate. And I have news, something to tell you."

"That's so sweet, Ty, but would you mind if we had something delivered and ate here? I'd like to share my first meal in my own place with you."

He put his hands on her shoulders and smiled. "How could I turn down an offer like that? Sure we can eat here, if that's what you want. I'll have to get on the road before it gets too late though. Better get this car back before they start looking for me."

"Don't forget they have your truck. They might have a couple of hounds by now, but I know you're tired and it's getting late."

When the pizza was delivered, and they were settled at the table, Elise said, "Now what's this news you want to tell me?"

Ty put a piece of pizza on his plate and wiped his hands

before answering. "I guess there's no way to do this but just say it. I don't want to bring up bad memories for you or anything, but I bought the Myers' place."

She swallowed hard. "You what!"

"Yep. I have the deed and everything. I'm doing some work for the county in exchange. I want to restore it. I know you loved that house and that somehow the Myers seemed like family to you. You were happy there. I want you to tell me everything about it, and I'll restore the house any way you want it."

"You'd do that for me?" Tears slid down her cheeks.

"That's what I didn't want to do. I didn't want to make you sad."

"Oh, Ty, I'm not sad. I'm overcome."

"There's more."

"More?"

"I want it to be our home. I want to marry you and take you there to live. If that's what you want." He pushed his chair back and dropped to one knee. "Like a true gentleman," he said. He took the diamond engagement ring from his pocket and held it poised to place on her finger.

"I don't know what to say."

"You're supposed to say yes."

"Oh, yes! Yes! Yes!" She dropped to her knees beside him and he took her in his arms. They fell over and started laughing until he began to kiss her.

Much later she walked him to the door. "You are a good person."

"Good-intentioned," he countered.

"You remembered I said that."

"I never forget anything you say."

"Then remember this. I have a four letter 'l' word for you, and it isn't like."

He kissed her again. "I thought so a long time ago, but I decided not to push my luck."

They were walking to the car when she stopped him. "Ty, that's it."

"What?"

"The name of your company. Wood Intentions."

"Wood Intentions? See, I knew you could do it. It's perfect. Like classical music. Wood Intentions."

PEYTON LOOKED UP FROM THE cash register and saw Dallas.

"I know Elise left this morning so I thought I'd come cheer you up."

"Where you taking me today, darlin'?"

"Our place."

"Gladys's?"

"Now aren't you the smartest thing? See how fast you catch on?"

When they passed A Touch of Class, Peyton said, "Wait here a minute. I want to yell at Margaret."

She was in the back room bringing out some new stationery. She looked startled but not unhappy to see him.

"Elise came by yesterday to say goodbye. I want to compliment you on raising a fine girl. She's always touched my heart but never so much as yesterday." He started out of the shop, and she called to him.

"Sorry, darlin', Dallas is waiting." And there she was, sweet and patient, just where he'd left her. "I wanted to tell Margaret what a fine girl she'd raised."

"You don't owe me any explanations, Peyton."

"Yes, I do."

There were several other couples in the coffee shop. "Gladys is building up her business," Dallas commented. She looked down at the blue checked tablecloths. "We're coming up in the world. Graduated from oilcloth to cotton. What next?"

Peyton blew on his coffee and looked at her over the rim of his cup. She rubbed her hand across the squares as though to remove a crumb.

"Penny for your thoughts."

"I was just thinking about the simplicity of this place," she said, "the comfort it brings me."

"You sure it's not just me."

"You?" she laughed.

"That brings you the comfort. After all, I'm keeping you in Coca-Cola and peanuts."

"You would think that. Just like a man. Seriously though, I am comfortable here with you, Peyton."

"Dallas, could I ask a favor of you, a big favor?"

"You can ask anything you like. I won't promise to deliver though."

"I know Margaret feels indebted to you for your leasing her that property and then all you've done to help out while Elise was sick. Ask her to sell you that cheval Sarah left. I'll give you whatever price she asks."

"Good lord, Peyton, why would I want it?"

"I don't know. Make up some story about longing for it since you were a little girl."

"You want it?"

"Yep, I sure do."

"Why?"

"Maybe I'll find me a pretty woman in that mirror."

"Be serious."

"Because it reminds me of Elise."

"Elise and not Sarah?"

"Elise. I hadn't even thought of Sarah."

"Peyton, I want to tell you here and now that I felt bad about Sarah. I never told you, but I thought she made a big mistake not marrying you."

He clasped Dallas's hand across the table. "I appreciate your saying that. Yeah, I was crazy about her all right. I'd be lying if I said I wouldn't always feel something for her, but it doesn't hurt any more. Hasn't in years."

"I'm glad to know that. Here I've been wasting all this sympathy on you thinking you were heartsick."

"Horny maybe. Not heartsick."

"Heartsick I can handle."

"You can handle . . ."

"Stop, Peyton. I don't want to hear it."

"Oh, Dallas, I'm just an old man trying to have some fun."

"You didn't act like an old man when you came to my house that morning and woke me up. Quite the opposite."

"I didn't think you noticed."

"Oh, I noticed. Have to admit I was a bit flattered." She laughed. "Why, Peyton Roberts, I do believe you're blushing."

"You're a wanton woman."

"You wish."

"Will you do it?"

It was Dallas's turn to blush. "Do it?"

Peyton gave her a wicked smile. "Get the cheval."

"Oh! The cheval. Yes, I'll try to get it for you."

"I didn't want to ask you until Elise left. I didn't want her to know."

"She'll find out sooner or later."

"Yeah, but later is always better. You know, for years she had a thing about mirrors. Could never look in one. She'd been frightened by something in a mirror when she was a child. That was the first thing I noticed about her. She came in the store one day to buy sunglasses and never even looked at herself in the mirror. I'd never seen a girl buy glasses and not look at herself. I like to think she looked at herself in that cheval once, that her image is there someplace."

"Why, Peyton. All these years I've been telling people what an educated, sensitive man you are, and now I guess I'll have to believe it myself."

Peyton held her gaze. "You're one sweet woman, you know that? Best day's work Tom Anderson ever did was the day he married you."

"As hard as my Tom worked, I'll take that as a real compliment, Peyton."

"Well, it's the God's truth. Did you ever know I was sweet on you at one time, Dallas?"

"Oh, go on. You weren't!"

"I sure as hell was. When you married Tom I realized what a fool I'd been to have ever wasted time on Sarah. And back then I'd never even seen you in that yellow robe."

She batted her eyes at him in a seductive manner. "I was desirable, you know."

"You still are, darlin', you still are."

ELISE'S THREE YEARS OF SCHOOLING passed quickly and slowly. Quickly, in terms of getting to know herself. She accepted her years of unhappiness as karma and knew these things could happen to old souls. Still, the time passed slowly until she could be with Ty.

Dear Ty, who always understood. He voiced no objections

when she asked that their wedding date be the same as Annelise's had been, the ceremony in the same church. "Still trying to make it up to her, huh?"

"Yes, in a way."

What worried Ty was Elise's insistence that Edwin not give her away in marriage. It wasn't a pleasant discussion, more on her mother's part than Edwin's, but Elise was adamant. She tried to be as kind as possible and made up something about her real father and so on, but she knew it'd always be a sore spot.

"I didn't ask Peyton to give me away because he's become the successful author, Ty. I did it because I love him."

"I know you do, and he loves you. I never knew Peyt wanted to write though. Never thought he could do it. All the times I went to his office and saw him working on that book, I didn't think he could pull it off. He said you were his inspiration, you and a letter. I thought I was the only man in your life, and there you were writing to Peyton."

"No. I gave him the letter before I left for school, and it wasn't from me. It was from Annelise."

"Now, Elise . . ."

"Peyton would tell you the same thing," she interrupted. "It was a love letter she had to share before she could go to her rest."

"If you say so."

"I say so."

21

My darling Annelise,

I write this letter in the bedroom that was to be your bridal chamber. I thought I would be coming for you tonight to take you away with me. Instead I can only write a letter to tell you what's in my heart, what I would have told you had you lived to be mine. I am a murderer but not for the crime of which I am accused. Coulton did that. That's why I had to get you away from him even before I had a chance to clear my name.

Coulton was clever, deceitful. He let me finish building this house before he told your father he just remembered where he'd known me. He said I was wanted for murder in Alabama, that I had killed a young woman there. I knew who he was the first time I saw him here. I'd have known that white suit anywhere. I kept my mouth shut because I didn't want to leave you. But murder? I didn't know what he was talking about.

When I left without a goodbye, it was to go back to Alabama and find out what he meant. That's where I first knew him, in Alabama where I had rented a small cottage from an elderly man, Mr. Morgan. He had a young invalid daughter I befriended. She was born with deformed legs and never walked. Carrie had a little pug dog she adored. I did a charcoal likeness of him for her. She was grateful, and we became friends.

Later, when Mr. Morgan fell ill, Carrie told me he had sent for their only relation, a distant cousin named Coulton. She'd only seen him once. She'd been a small child then. He was slick. I saw that right off. All soft voiced and manners. Never saw him in anything but a white suit.

I did odd jobs for the barrister Mr. Morgan hired to handle his estate. I was repairing a desk for him and saw the papers there in plain sight. In exchange for looking after Carrie, in case of Mr. Morgan's death, Mr. Morgan agreed to make Coulton beneficiary of half his estate. Carrie's condition shortened her lifespan. She wasn't expected to live past twenty-five. When she died, Coulton would inherit her half of the estate as well. It would be an impressive inheritance.

It wasn't long before I came home one night to find the house locked, my belongings in the yard, and Coulton sitting on the porch like he owned the place. He accused me of making improper advances on Carrie. Said she told him she was afraid of me. I knew it was all a lie and started to the big house to see what was going on. Coulton called after me, said he'd tell Mr. Morgan if I attempted to see Carrie, that no one would believe me. Mr. Morgan wouldn't take a stranger's word over a relative's. Mr. Morgan was a fine man, had been good to me, and he was sick.

I came back, tied my things in an old quilt and left. I didn't need that kind of grief. Neither did Mr. Morgan. I went to Louisiana for awhile and then here. And then Coulton shows up. I figured Mr. Morgan had regained his health. I never went back to find out. I was in love with you by then and had no interest in going back.

I avoided Coulton every way I could, but he had me again. Told your father he hadn't been able to place me though I'd looked familiar to him. Once I finished the house, his memory returned. He remembered me then. Said I was wanted in Alabama for murdering a young girl. I had no way of knowing Carrie had been murdered, that I was a hunted man. He killed her with my finishing knife. Buster too. Killed her little dog. The knife was a gift from Carrie after I did the likeness of Buster. My initials were carved on it so there was no mistaking it was mine. I thought I'd lost it when I moved. When Mr. Morgan heard Carrie was dead, he died of a heart attack and made Coulton a rich man.

I learned all this when I left here and went back to Alabama. I wanted to clear my name, but like I told you, when I found out you were marrying Coulton, I had to get back. I couldn't let him do to you what he'd done to Carrie.

I don't care what people think of me. I don't have any family. I don't have you. Nothing matters any more. I'll just keep moving, but Coulton won't hurt anyone else, not in this lifetime.

When the candle flame flickered in here I knew someone had opened the front door. I'd just finished putting your picture in the back of the cheval I'd built. I'd made a cover, planning to surprise you. Without the cover, you'd always be visible in the cheval, mirrored, or in the painting.

I got as far as the hall when Coulton was there at the top of the stairs. We fought. Not an even match. He was soft, and I knew I had him in muscle and anger. I told you I wasn't a murderer, but I am. I broke Coulton's neck. His body is at the top of the hidden stairway. It'll be a long time before they find him, and by then I'll be miles away. Anyhow, you and Coulton were the only ones who knew I'd come back. Without you, I'm not alive so I don't care what happens.

Well, my darling. I'm putting this letter behind your picture. It's the closest I can come to you. You never looked at the painting so you don't know that I'm there too. I painted my likeness in the mirror to show you were looking back at me, our eyes meeting for all eternity.

My own dear love. I miss you unbearably.
Seth

Peyton's book made him an instant celebrity. Even his former love, Sarah, came back to Apalach to watch him personally sign her copy. With a little encouragement, she would have stayed, but she didn't get it from Peyton.

Margaret Foster had the book prominently displayed in the front window of her shop. Peyton said he might not have the best-written book, but there wasn't another one that smelled better. He had a few copies by his cash register but refused to display it more than that. Bookstores on "the island" invited him for signings and were generous with window displays.

It was a beautiful book to display. The oval cheval on the cover with the faint reflection of a lovely girl. Ornate gold lettering showcased the title:

HOUSE ON THE FORGOTTEN COAST

The story of a young woman who returns from the grave to clear her lover's name

22

On a sunny afternoon in early May, Elise and Ty were married in the historic Trinity Episcopal Church. Her grandmother's pearls hung luminous against the ivory lace of her mother's wedding dress, a simple but elegant style more becoming to Elise than it had been to Margaret. The church was crowded, but Elise could pick out Miss Nadine sitting in one of the pews reserved for family. And near the front she saw some of the bridge club ladies, Francis, Sue, and Lucille. All these people were a part of her life now.

Before she marched down the aisle on Peyton's arm, she drew a deep breath and looked up at the stenciled ceiling, just as Annelise must have done.

Peyton patted her hand. "You okay, darlin'?"

"Never better."

"You got a mighty handsome groom waiting for you up there, not to mention your matron of honor."

"Dallas Roberts. Has a nice ring to it, doesn't it, Peyton?"

"Sure does, hon. Roberts is the name of the game here today."

Music from the antique organ flooded the room, Elise knew, just as it had for Annelise. She swallowed hard, lifted her veil, and kissed Peyton. "I'm so glad we'll soon be relatives." He patted her hand, and they began their march down the aisle.

❧

WHEN THEY RETURNED FROM THEIR honeymoon, they decided to let Rusty stay awhile longer with Payton and Dallas until they were settled. The restored house was to be a surprise for Elise. There was a picket fence in front now, and the house had been painted a pale cream color with cobalt blue shutters. It didn't look like a black and white painting any more.

Elise gasped with delight, and Ty didn't ask permission to carry her over the threshold. He held her close and she buried her face against his neck as he pushed the door open with his foot. "You're my warm blanket against a cold day," she murmured and felt safe, happy, loved. Dreamily she imagined that his arms were a double helix, the entwined DNA of Lawrence and Ty, separate but never separated, so that she could love unconditionally. She snuggled closer, inhaled deeply, and touched her tongue to Ty's neck.

"Oh, your pheromones," she murmured.

"My what?"

"Never mind. It's a compliment."

When he put her down, she turned round and round, looking at everything. "I simply can't believe what you've done here. It couldn't be more perfect. *You* couldn't be more perfect." She put her arms around his neck. "Oh, Ty, I do love you so."

Ty flashed his most charming smile. "And I love you, Mrs. Roberts, but it still seems like a miracle to me. The two of us together, here together. For a long time it seemed so impossible. It has to be a miracle."

"But don't you think that in a way love is always a miracle? I mean, it's such an incredible thing that two people can feel the same way about each other."

"That's exactly what I mean. Don't forget, though, I loved you first."

"I'll never forget that, Ty. Never. And I love you all the

more for it." She tilted her head to the side and looked up at him. "I do believe I've embarrassed you. You're blushing."

"No, just glowing with happiness." He lowered his head and looked at the floor. "Well, what'd ya know! Our first visitor."

Elise looked down, a memory beating in her heart as she knelt to pet the orange tabby cat with a star on its forehead. Ty dropped to his knees beside her and began massaging the cat's neck. He looked thoughtful as his fingers explored beneath the thick fur.

"What?" Elise asked. "Is something wrong?"

"Here, check this out. There's a small chain around his neck. It's dirty, but I'd swear it's gold."

"It probably is, Ty. He's an old cat for sure. Nothing but gold would be good enough." Elise smiled and kissed the star on Flynnie's forehead.

ABOUT THE AUTHOR

photo credit: Deanne Dunlop

RUTH COE CHAMBERS takes pride in her Florida panhandle roots, and her hometown of Port St. Joe has inspired much of her writing. She attended Florida State University, the University of South Florida and graduated Summa Cum Laude from California State University, Fresno. It was through creative writing classes at the University of South Florida that she found her "voice" and began writing literary fiction. Listed in *Who's Who of American Women*, she does freelance writing, has recently republished one novel, has self-published its sequel, and has written two award-winning plays. She is currently working on the third novel in her Bay Harbor Trilogy. She has two daughters and lives with her husband and one very spoiled Cairn terrier in Neptune Beach, Florida.

SELECTED TITLES FROM SHE WRITES PRESS

She Writes Press is an independent publishing company
founded to serve women writers everywhere.
Visit us at www.shewritespress.com.

The Lucidity Project by Abbey Campbell Cook. $16.95, 978-1-
63152-032-7. After suffering from depression all her life, twenty-
five-year-old Max Dorigan joins a mysterious research project
on a Caribbean island, where she's introduced to the magical
and healing world of lucid dreaming.

The Wiregrass by Pam Webber. $16.95, 978-1-63152-943-6. A
story about a summer of discontent, change, and dangerous
mysteries in a small Southern Wiregrass town.

After Midnight by Diane Shute-Sepahpour. $16.95, 978-1-63152-
913-9. When horse breeder Alix is forced to temporarily swap
places with her estranged twin sister—the wife of an English
lord—her forgotten past begins to resurface.

Water on the Moon by Jean P. Moore. $16.95, 978-1-938314-61-2.
When her home is destroyed in a freak accident, Lidia Raven, a
divorced mother of two, is plunged into a mystery that involves
her entire family.

Glass Shatters by Michelle Meyers. $16.95, 978-1-63152-018-1.
Following the mysterious disappearance of his wife and daughter, scientist Charles Lang goes to desperate lengths to escape his
past and reinvent himself.

Conjuring Casanova by Melissa Rea. $16.95, 978-1-63152-056-3.
Headstrong ER physician Elizabeth Hillman is a career woman
who has sworn off men and believes the idea of love in the
twenty-first century is a fairy-tale—but when Giacomo Casanova steps into her life on a rooftop in Italy, her reality and con-
cept of love are forever changed.